Of Love and Gravity

Of Love and Gravity

G J MARTIN

Colley Books

First published 2018
Colley Books Ltd
All rights reserved
© G J Martin 2018
The right of G J Martin to be identified as author of this work has been asserted in accordance with Section 77 of the Copyright, Designs and Patents Act 1988
ISBN 978-0-9955320-4-5
British Library Cataloguing in Publication Data.
A catalogue record for this book is available from the British Library.
Printed in Garamond 11/12
Colley Books Ltd
C/o Brown McLeod Ltd
51 Clarkegrove Road
Sheffield S10 2NH
www.colleybooks.com

Cover illustration, *Oronsay*, watercolour © Sue Lewis-Blake
Frontispiece, *Loch Fada*, etching © G J Martin

Of Love and Gravity is a work of fiction. The people, businesses, places, and events of the book are remembered, re-imagined and invented, and where real, are employed in a fictitious manner. In order to maintain anonymity some names have been changed.

This book is dedicated to Alasdair McMorrine

*O woman, you take the place of every solid thing. When you walk in the sky I
am steeped in shadow. Following you into the night, I passionately abandon all memory
of day. Bewitching substitute, you are the essence of the wonderful world, of the
natural world, and you are reborn whenever I close my eyes. You are the wall and its
foundations. You are horizon and being. The ladder and the iron bars. Total eclipse.*

Le Paysan de Paris by Louis Aragon

Acknowledgements

Chagall, Marc: *My Life*, Orion Press, New York, 1960.

Lorca, Federico Garcia: *Collected Poems of Lorca*, Pan Macmillan,
Rev. Ed. 2002.

Other poems are based on the writings of Janine Marshall and are
published with her kind permission.

Part One

A Private View

Madeline

I knew she'd be here. She would arrive late, and slip amongst the people unnoticed, then watch from a corner. I wonder if Laurie has noticed her yet. He's probably been looking out for her as much as I have. We'd both deny it. How old is she now? Twenty-three. It's six years almost exactly since I first saw her. She was then at the end of the first year of Sixth Form. She was seventeen.

Walking up to her I say, "Hello again."

"Again?"

She's puzzled. I reassure her. "You look really well."

She doesn't but she looks interesting. It's hard to describe her effect. She isn't tall but seems it. She isn't pretty but you feel she must be because she is so attractive. There is a beauty about her, but nothing that is traditional. She is oddly old-fashioned, someone from the Thirties. She is skinny and her facial bones are angular. Her brown eyes shine but their surrounds are grey, perhaps from little sleep. Her hair is a fashionable mess, long and untrammelled. She has a habit of redirecting it around her head as if it were liquid, adjusting its flow with a comb of fingers. The act takes effort, as if the hair was leaden. She is wearing an ankle-length overcoat. It is expensive camel hair so hangs elegantly. She wears it like an evening dress. So far, she hasn't taken her hands out of her pockets. She looks annoyed, bunching her coat into a pile as she joins her pocketed hands across her stomach.

"Do I know you?"

"We have met but you've clearly forgotten. We were formally introduced."

"We were?"

She's not really concentrating on this conversation or me. She wasn't invited here to see me. But she is polite and ready to introduce her hovering companion.

"This is my friend, Peter. He drove me here. His girlfriend works at the school. That's why I could come to Laurie's show. I had this lift, you see."

She points to Peter who looks delightfully shy. He nods with great gusto and offers me his outstretched hand.

"Hello," I say.

He doesn't reply, just nods a lot more and backs away into the crowd.

"I'm Iain Stewart. Ian with an 'i', Iain."

"Does it show?"

"What?"

"The 'i'. Does it show when you say it?"

"No."

She shrugs her opinion.

I imagine my parents were hoping to turn a very ordinary name into something marginally more distinguished. I'm beginning to feel a little foolish. She comes to my rescue.

"But you know it's there," she says gently, accentuating the 'you'.

"Yes. Just a small eccentricity."

Maybe I needed it. I'd flown from the bank's London office to the private view, so I was still in a suit. Pinstriped and anonymous but my inside pocket said Paul Smith so my lining knew I was fashionable. We'd sponsored this for Laurie, so I suppose in some respects it was as much my show as his. No doubt the bank would buy, through me, at least one of the fifty pictures on display. We'd see.

"Hey." She's looking at me with the beginnings of recognition and wagging her finger in my face as though I've done something wrong. "You came to my school. You're a friend of Laurie's. You buy his pictures for your bank. I've been to your boardroom. I remember. I'm sorry I didn't recognise you. It's a long time ago."

"Six years."

"That long? I'm a little dazed. I've just returned from South Africa. There's no jet lag but Great Britain is still something of a shock." So is her voice. It's really husky, quite hard to follow, young Lauren Bacallish.

I'd first met Laurie at his art college in Glasgow. I bought a painting from his degree show to go into the bank's Scottish collection. In effect, it was my collection. I'd wandered from finance to fine art and managed to persuade the bank to follow. It was more than an amateur whim. I did pursue several courses of study so my judgements weren't entirely untutored and, with accidental shifts in taste, markets and the dangerous misbehaviour of money, it was suddenly fashionable and prudent to collect art. I've bought regularly since and the bank has sponsored a number of Laurie's shows, including this one tonight. I act as his agent but we are friends, I hope, despite the difference in age, perhaps because of it.

For most of the intervening years Laurie has been teaching in a small private school in Scotland. I visited, six years ago, to present the end of year prizes. The winning student is standing next to me now.

"I still remember your painting," I tell her. "It was a fine landscape, dark and brooding. It reminded me of the work of . . ."

2

"Laurie McPhee?" She interrupts me and smiles wryly.

"No. Perhaps both pupil and teacher were equally inspired by D Y Cameron."

"How amazing. You even remember my project."

"It was memorable."

It was. I wasn't flattering her. She is called Madeline. Her name was one thing I had forgotten, until this moment. Laurie was an evangelical teacher. He loved landscapes and the people who belonged in them. There had been the odd exotic venture, private wanderings in India and Morocco, school trips to Tuscany and the Hebrides. He was ambitious for his young artists and campaigned for good working spaces, the best equipment and proper status within the value systems of the school.

The empty space he began with he transformed, adding a mezzanine floor, spiral staircase and a well-lit studio. When I was invited, he made the event into a social evening with live music from a gifted jazz piano player, a less accomplished string quartet and a huge drama teacher who sang Mahler lieder for half an hour. We sipped wine and exchanged platitudes as everyone who thought they ought to be there was seen to be. Laurie nimbly attributed all his cleverness in the design to earlier suggestions by the headmaster, who accepted the gift readily and embellished it with further borrowings of his own. We all admired 'his' new studios and 'his' unfailing eye for detail as we were carefully guided around what the headmaster had made.

Laurie's praise of his students was genuine. He was a generous teacher, offered what he knew and acknowledged every sign of promise or achievement in the work of others. His reward was admiration and a palpable affection. He'd managed to engage the minds of both sexes. The young men thought him funny, randy and always drunk: the young women believed him gifted, tantalizing and available. I've never seen such adoration from a class.

Whilst Laurie pointed to different areas of canvas, in praise of Madeline's emergent skill as a painter, she set her gaze on him and never removed it. It was a visual umbilicus, linking master to slave. She wasn't the only one. There was a languid blond who specialized in flower painting and a violet-eyed Polish girl with film-star looks, wavy hair and wavier contours who seemed to need to stand close when talking. How did he concentrate? Was he ever tempted, I wondered?

"No. We know too much for them, Iain, far too much. They're just fledglings," he explained.

It was nice to be included in the fantasy. It wasn't entirely the doe-eyed looks that were memorable. I understand there are standard procedures for dealing with teenage crushes of either sex. Why 'crush', I wonder?

It's not a pleasant word for such a pure and hopeless longing. What troubled me was their complete trust. Laurie seemed to accommodate this deification with ease. It had to be exaggerated, surely, and must disappoint them one day. Did he ever warn them, assure them of his fallibility and the truth of his being only a little out of the ordinary? Did he advise them that much of what they adored was his adulthood? That what he knew and had done they all might do in the course of time, to be similarly admired by the inexperienced and less skilful young.

Madeline's painting was good. Laurie had encouraged each student to adopt a painting mentor. The Glasgow Boys, the Scottish Colourists: Peploe, Cadell, Fergusson and Hunter had all been chosen. Her idol was D Y Cameron. The influence showed but she was no copyist. What pleased me was the size of the canvas, a metre and a half by a metre I'd guess, the boldness and confidence of the brush strokes, the drama and energy of the scene. What startled me at that time, as I glanced from Madeline's elegant frame, back arched, legs stepping, arm stretching as she spanned the curve of the spiral staircase above my right shoulder, was the maleness of the technique. You wouldn't believe this frail girl had made it. Or, if she had, then to reveal such dark intensity must have involved tapping into secret angers, untold dislikes, some power that her serenity belied. Or perhaps, that's how she achieved her calmness. As I gave her the envelope containing tokens for books, an entry ticket for an exhibition in Glasgow, and free access to the public and private collections of the bank, she held my hand and gazed at me nervelessly. She'd said thank you but didn't appear to need this recognition. There was no teenage disaffection nor planned indifference. She wasn't being 'cool'; she was cold. She spoke properly, thanked nicely and smiled sweetly with a hint of a blush. All well and good and normal. But, it was dispassionate. She was looking beyond this moment for significance. This had no value for her. The prize didn't count.

It was puzzling. I looked to Laurie, shrugged and clapped happily. Madeline's had been the last prize I was to present. We were applauding the end of the seriousness. Then, standing side by side and looking back together towards the winner, surrounded by her congratulating friends as they shared the contents of her untidily torn open envelope, she looked our way. She stared for several seconds, offered us neither recognition nor respite, and then rejoined the chatter of her friends.

Laurie simply said, "Doesn't she."

Any introductory sentence of mine was not needed. Madeline had won her prize because she looked exactly as Valerie Kinsell had looked at a similar age, some twenty years ago. Valerie was Laurie's first wife, and my second.

Claudette

Solex

I was seventeen when I first met Claudette but by then I had already fallen in love with France itself. I had been placed in a French family for half of the summer break as part of my 'A' level course. My hosts were the Pasquiers. They had three sons, the eldest of whom was my official correspondent. The first of many invaluable gifts was the right of access to the family Solex. This clumsy hybrid of bicycle and moped gave me the freedom to roam.

I found busy cafés beside dirt roads, alerted to their presence by huge advertisements for popular aperitifs written in faded letters on the sides of barns: *Byrrh, Picon* and *Suze*. A splendid old crone, with a twinkle in her eyes, taught me swearwords in the local patois and tortured mispronunciations to overlay my classroom French. The family would laugh when the sun shone and I would declare, '*Il fait beeyoh*'.

I learnt to delight in things black: pepper, coffee and tobacco trapped in *Gauloises* that would sizzle and fizz when being smoked.

I ran to a nearby farm to fetch unpasteurised milk, bought butter unwrapped, ate tomatoes stuffed with fish, a duck from a jar and a vegetable called salsify that I've never seen since.

Sundays were best. We dressed for church but in truth for the café, for after the incense and seriousness we were licensed to play. All the young came together to sip aperitifs before family feasts that simply wouldn't end. Happy aunts kept arriving with magnificent tarts, precise arrays of transparently thin apple or multicoloured collages of soft fruits.

Life was to be celebrated. Even the sun seemed bigger there, the giant disc fully apparent above vast horizons left clear at the edge of hedgeless fields. And beyond all that, one morning there was Claudette.

I was walking down an unremarkable road between rows of modest houses and there, on the opposite pavement, she stood. She had long, dark brown hair parted to the side and swept in a shiny swathe across her forehead. She had brown eyes, a delicate nose and regular, pretty features. She was wearing a black T-shirt and white jeans. She was trim and neat. I just stood and stared. My gaze turned her head and, unperturbed; she smiled full into my face. What had seemed pleasing before was suddenly radiant. That smile, not quite symmetrical as she bit into a corner of her bottom lip, animated her being. She seemed lit up, perfected.

Then the smile went. Her face looked perplexed and she walked away. The road wasn't long. Just before the corner she turned and looked back.

It wasn't a glimpse or a coy peak over the shoulder; she had stopped, turned fully and looked back at me carefully. Then she was gone.

I didn't know who she was but the rhythm of her walk, the elegance of her bearing, the neatness of her appearance and the completeness of her smile appeared to me as the essence of Frenchness.

I tormented my hosts with endless enquiries. I described her, could have drawn her if asked, but no one could give her a name. The young people of the town tended to go away to school. It was only in the summer that acquaintances were renewed. The family tended to subsume within itself everything and everyone. There were few strays and limited opportunities to meet. The café on Sunday was my best chance, but she never appeared there. I left France without discovering her name.

She had caught sight of me on the ferry returning to England. Later she claimed she had immediately turned to a friend and said: "I don't know why, I find that boy very pleasing. I seem to know him. Do you think it is an act of fate? 'Once upon a time . . . the end.' We don't know the rest, for the moment, but we hope it won't be too tragic."

We met on a train. I was negotiating a crowded corridor looking for a seat. The door to a carriage half-opened and I heard laughter and the voice of a friend speaking execrable French. *'Mon père travail dans un . . . office'*, was the last offering, and then I saw her.

She looked up at me and calmly whispered in English, "It's you." I was the awkward one. I played the clown and pretended, anything to mask the overwhelming sense of excitement and apprehension. Finally serious, I wriggled along and sat opposite her, touching knees. I leaned forward and asked her name.

"Claudette. My name is Claudette and you are Iain with an 'i'. I have already found it out."

We exchanged kisses on that train, formal cheek to cheek and one very special, deliberate moment of lips to lips that signalled our involvement for that summer of exchange parties and outings and trips. We were both seventeen. She was a little older, by a few important months. She was a wonderful mixture of seriousness, laughter and dance. We were quickly close and seemed happy to all who saw us together. My parents liked her, even my sister said hello. Her exchange partner, Anne Bailey, was someone I knew through school. She made our meetings easy and we behaved as honourably as curious teenagers could. We were sexually competent and naughty enough. We kissed, rummaged and on two precious occasions, found ourselves naked in a bed. I thought we'd had intercourse but apparently hadn't, at least that's what we decided the following day. I was fastidious about such things, with a Ruskin-like aversion to the messiness of the act. We stained the second bed with a pallid mixture of blood and semen that seemed a distasteful marker of success. I'd had to own up that the dribbles were ours and offered to wash and change the sheets.

But there remained a profound innocence in all that we did. In my second marriage with Valerie it was the experience that went awfully deep. Claudette and I had fun. We were light-hearted. I was happy.

A Private View

Touching the surface

Madeline and I are talking in a splendid area. We are beneath the apex of the atrium that forms the entrance to the new painting schools, built at an unmentionable cost above one of the courtyards in Scotland's most expensive private school. It is so prestigious it describes itself as a 'public' school, in the English manner. Certainly the setting is quite magnificent. Vast panes of glass have been angled into spires to form a spectacular roof that spills a constant light throughout the building. The entrance lobby has been designed as a permanent exhibition area. Clever wires can suspend works in space, adding interest to the traditional lining of walls. Beyond are several studios with desks, donkeys, and angled drawing boards permanently in place beneath all the windows with views. There is a printing press and acid-resistant sinks, turntables and kilns. It is a very privileged space.

One or two sixth formers, young men of eighteen in neat uniform, wearing fine smiles, wander amongst we guests offering canapés and wine. I envy them their confidence and social grace. I can do it now but I couldn't then. Such panache. Even Madeline has opened her coat to them, flapping its edges like giant wings, revealing baggy white trousers, and a neat linen waistcoat over a grey silk blouse. I hesitated about the word 'blouse'. I was going to say 'shirt', largely because that's what it is. It is a shirt. There is a hint of androgyny here. Or is it my desire to diminish her female sexuality? That is unlikely. Fundamentally, I need her to be all that femininity dares to muster; after all, she is the perfect replica, albeit in the next generation, of the object of our love.

"Have you seen Laurie yet? Does he know you're here?" I ask her.

"Yes. He knows. He asked me to wait and see him afterwards. He's very busy."

"Yes, isn't he? All I've received so far is the odd regal wave. Oh! And there's another one." I mouth 'Hello' to him across the crowd. He grins and mock mops his brow. It's busy work pleasing so many people. "He's so good at being the centre of attention."

"He isn't." Madeline is quickly defensive.

"I'm sorry. I didn't realize I'd said that out loud. I hadn't meant to be disloyal."

"You weren't, just wrong. He always told us that he liked to blend into the background. He always said, 'Never volunteer, ever, for anything at all.' We always thought he was really good at avoiding things. He said it was a natural skill. He was born to mislead. That was one of his sayings. He was a natural delegator. He said that allowing others to do the messy work was the height of selflessness. He was always asking for volunteers and everybody stepped forward and he stepped aside. It amused him, I think."

It doesn't always amuse me, nevertheless; I've always thought Laurie handled these situations with immense skill. He was charm itself. With guiding hands and subtle self-praise, he deflected compliments but never contradicted; he rarely discussed prices but knew every one. The smaller prints always came in pairs, and the missing scene was sure to be on his easel at home. He was a brilliant salesman, reassuring and deft. Everybody smiled as they signed the cheque, myself included.

"Are you still painting?" I ask Madeline.

She's drifted over to the work. I've just followed and peered over her shoulder at some lithographs that were in the last exhibition. Most of the new paintings are dangling on mysterious wires. It works well. There are four huge drawings of water falling over rocks in blue, red, black and sepia; a limited palette of coloured pastel and crayon relying entirely on the energy and certainty of line for their effect. All are happily enhanced by hanging in space.

"No. No, I'm not." She doesn't turn round, just peers closely at a small painting in oils. It's charming. I follow her nose to the surface, not quite as closely. I think she might be short-sighted. "I never did, you know, not after school." She's turned to me now. I can't interpret her expression. I'm not sure if it's disappointed or triumphant. The sudden smile confuses me further.

"I thought you went to art colleges. London foundation, Glasgow to finish? Laurie was very proud, often bragging. I'm sure he ..."

She stops me with a twitch of the finger, obviously certain of her own life. "I did. I just didn't paint. Well, certainly not landscapes in the rain. I designed. For textiles. I only painted big for Laurie. I think pretty small when left to my own devices. And smallness didn't lead anywhere."

"What do you do now?"

"To earn money? You won't guess."

"No, I won't."

"I am a writer, a journalist, a freelance." She's suddenly brightened. She animates well.

"How splendid."

"If only you knew how bad I was at English at school. Or maybe you did. My teacher was kind enough to choose one sentence to praise. He would rescue it from the mess before making me read out loud the other nonsense. He was always right. It couldn't be spoken or thought."

"And still you make a living?"

"Yes. I seem to. I'm not in the black any more. Or is it the red? Whichever means I have no debts. That's enough isn't it?"

"Yes, it is. It is enough." I've just warmed to her. I'm not sure why. She suddenly seems vulnerable.

"Are you based in London?" I ask her.

"I thought I'd said. I work in East Africa. Nairobi and Mombasa on the coast. Occasionally Zimbabwe. But I have a little toehold rather than a whole foot in Wimbledon. It's an address and a place to unpack."

"Why Africa?"

"I grew up there."

"I didn't realize."

"Why should you have known?"

Why indeed.

"My father worked there. Works. Still does, occasionally, for a huge tobacco company. He manages 'risk', whatever that means. I work for a couple of newspapers and syndicate anything that might interest the world." She pauses and smiles. "That makes it sound grander than it is. I'm yet to syndicate. Most of what I do is only of local interest. But, I'm learning. That's all right, isn't it?"

"Yes. It is all right. Do you do this intrepid reporting on your own?"

"Yes." She seems puzzled.

"There's no boyfriend?"

"No."

"No?" I interrupt the pause I've caused. She seems capable of intense privacy. It's difficult to guess what crosses her mind.

"There's no time, really. I never settle long enough to attract attention."

"But you keep in touch with Laurie."

"No."

So much for my suspicions. She's telling the truth, I'm certain. That was a very matter of fact 'no'.

"I thought . . ."

"The invitation came out of the blue. It was sent on from my old home address. The chances of it ever reaching me were tiny. It was pure chance that I was even in England. It was lucky for me."

"And for Laurie."

"Why?"

I suppose I'd hoped to discover tales of inappropriate and unprofessional behaviour by the iniquitous Laurie McPhee. Hear tell of secret trysts in the Moroccan desert or some such fantasy, fulfilling a life none of us lead and few would dare to, yet still allowing me to feel morally superior to my wife's former husband and lover. But it seems there are no secrets.

10

"Do you think he'll mind?" Madeline suddenly asks.

"Mind what?"

She moves closer and lowers her voice, as if speaking of something shameful, "That I'm not a painter. That I didn't become one."

"Can he mind if it's not what you are?" I ask.

"I thought I might disappoint him."

That's a different idea. I don't know what to say to that. Does Laurie McPhee have expectations of you? Yes, of course he does. He always did and he always will but it has got nothing to do with you, cub reporter out of white East Africa. He had high hopes of Valerie, the earlier version of you he married, and he'll probably find a later model to replace you. You can do what you like, Madeline, but you'll be what he decides.

"I don't think you could. And anyway, are you sure he had plans for you?"

"No. You're probably right. Even I don't have plans for me."

I don't think she does and that's a pity. I suddenly feel full of advice. She has no direction. She did once, but that was his, not hers. He gave her his passions. Was that an obvious generosity? He filled her and those others with the charge of his creative energy. He was the charismatic teacher, the defining influence on these young, impressionable minds. What lucky souls. Not always. Not Madeline. Denied his influence, no longer in his flow, she flounders, her talents hidden, passive, waiting for someone else to make her come alive.

She's just reached out to experience the surface of the painting that appears on the catalogue cover. It's on all the invitation cards too. It was chosen against my advice. I don't think it's the strongest of the new work and I wasn't convinced it had been reproduced to best advantage. The colours seemed too vibrant, a little unsubtle. I know he liked it because it was different, a Tuscan roofscape full of tiles, reds and lush oranges, a gaudy respite from the green and grey subtleties of Scotland. There is a lot of paint and Madeline is sensing the textures with the tips of her fingers, reading the surface.

"You let me do this once. Do you remember?" She hasn't turned round. She knows I'm watching.

"When?"

"You let me touch the pictures in your office."

"Yes, I remember now." I'm not being obtuse. All her class were there. It wasn't a private moment and it wasn't my office but the company boardroom.

"They're normally across a barrier, aren't they? Out of reach." She's looking at me now, as if this denial of access really mattered to her. " 'Don't touch!' and all that hidden wiring. Everything alarmed. And the guards, if you reach out, instantly they're there. 'Please, Miss. Don't touch

11

the paintings.' And you said the opposite."

"I did?"

"Yes. I was looking, not just at the D Y Camerons—you had mostly framed prints and I needed his oils—but they were all there, Fergussons and Cadells, so tiny and homely, pictures I'd only seen in books or across those gallery barriers. It was the Peploe, the beach scene, in beautiful blues and mauves, a whole picture made out of two dozen strokes of the brush. I had this yearning to follow his route, to trace the image and guess the order of each placing. But I heard the voice saying 'Please don't touch, Miss!' when I started to reach out towards it and suddenly you said, 'Take it off the wall if you want to look closely.' And I daren't. I just stood there, overwhelmed. It wasn't the thousands and thousands of pounds, it was the intimacy. And you saw I was stuck and you just reached up and plucked it free. I sat down and you put it in my lap. One of the most famous paintings in the country and I was nursing it. I thought the room would explode with alarm bells, but it didn't—just paint." She touches my arm as gently as the picture's surface and says, "Thank you for being kind."

I just breathe in a scent of intense loneliness and something else. As she rearranges her hair a cling of cigarette smoke that lingers there wafts upwards. She's leaving. I think the intimacy is a parting gift. Why am I suddenly so anxious?

"Madeline." I call after her. I recognise a face from a television soap opera. I can only remember her character name, Mavis, Mavis someone. "Madeline." There's such a buzz of chatter and the awkwardness of elegantly dressed people forced to become clumsy as they juggle catalogue, wineglass and plate. I can get no nearer so shout my message across a few heads.

"You have to give up smoking!"

She looks puzzled, a little embarrassed, "What?"

"You absolutely must. No more cigarettes."

She hasn't heard. It suddenly seems to matter. I'll know why soon, but at this precise moment I wish I'd kept my advice to myself. I wave.

She's still frowning. That's my last look. She's gone.

Claudette

Literary loving

One autumn evening I received a letter from France. It was from Claudette.

'I have been back at school for one whole day and already it's sad here. You see; I haven't forgotten you. I have kept in mind a perfect memory of our meetings and my dearest wish would be to see you again next year.'

She talked of family and mutual friends, described the rigours of her school day. There were several such letters and then one that announced she was leaving school.

'It's rather unpleasant but the doctors have told me I'm overtired and that I must leave for health reasons.'

She had some kind of problem with her lungs. It wasn't as Keatsian as tuberculosis but it was sufficiently serious to rob her, eventually, of two years of normal life. It still might kill her. She was moved to an isolation hospital, her 'establishment' as she called it, some distance from her home.

'I am now a little ill. Above all don't tell anyone. I am telling you because I trust you.'

I tried to honour that trust and did my best to encourage her and never lapsed in writing my letters. I confess to a sense of romance in all this. I secretly enjoyed the danger of it and its extremity.

'Here I am always sad. I have to stay in bed for months and months. My veins are punctured and I am very frightened. I am so unlucky. I am condemned to spend my birthday here. Please write to me. I am not contagious.'

There were times when she seemed near to defeat.

'I've really got the blues. I want to cry, shout, to do anything, it's so sad here. I want to gnaw the curtains, clang the iron bed, hurt myself. Any sensation, even of physical pain is better than the still, quiet, dreary emptiness of this place. I am caged. This is so cruel. I have such a longing to live. In the last analysis it doesn't matter. I've become brave because I must.

'I don't know what it is I fear. My confidence has all seeped away. I don't know if I dare leave here yet. I've hated and loathed being condemned to this bed. I've picked and torn at the red blanket until all the softness has gone from it. I've clutched the iron bed-head so often and so tightly that the cream paint has peeled away and the shiny metal has rusted from my sweating hands. I've paced up and down our tiny ward and stared longingly at the trees and grass outside in the park. I longed for visitors then hated the fact they could leave and I couldn't. Can you imagine what it feels like to reach out to your mother, father, sister and see them shrink from contact, nervously looking at the nurse to see if they can touch me in safety? I'm not a leper. I'm only poisonous to myself. I long to be touched. I'm afraid of never seeing you again.

'In my room is a new girl. She's nearly twenty years of age. She's actually engaged and she's crying after him. I hate her tears. I don't understand her. It's only two paltry weeks since she last saw her husband to be. What does she know about waiting and about longing? Her tears should be for herself. We know from her treatment that she will die; so all the rest is futile. I grow bitter. That's why you must write to me. When I receive your letter I am always happy and cheerful for the whole day because you know how to give me the strength, courage and confidence I lack. Only you can produce this effect in me. Do you understand? The one thing I have to tell you is that I love you more than anything else and that I have never experienced such a powerful feeling for anyone other than you.'

I would be at a loss what to say to her now; how on earth did I reply then? How could I enter such a troubled world and appear wise in my advice? Did I lie to her? Yes, I think I probably did. I talked of futures that I only imagined. I made plans in my mind or on the page, never in reality. When I began to write I became someone else, the romantic, loyal man of loving words who would solve all her troubles and my own. It must have been an elaborate game, a literary loving. And I must have believed in it myself to be so convincing.

She gave me every option and always invited the truth.

'I know perfectly well that for us it is very difficult, practically impossible. A YEAR! It's a long time. But, as for me, I am perfectly happy to remain friends in this way with you and when I return to England, certainly in two years, I should be your girlfriend again. If you wish. I am content. But, if I am wise, it's because I am ill and will be locked up far from other people. But if you want to go out, especially this Christmas, to parties among friends, I will not be annoyed or jealous. One of us must live.

'If you really want me to wait for you I should do it. I only ask one thing of you that is to be very frank with me. I have changed character a lot. I still laugh but I reason things out as well. I am very romantic and above all, very sensitive. Then again, don't be afraid to tell me the truth, even if I am ill.'

I don't think it was ever as simple as deceits or untruths. In the context of the letters what I said was sincere. I must have been consistent to a fantasy that was shared. She was as romantic as me and we lived in our dreams.

'I always think of us as having a huge love affair in the Grand Style,' she wrote in one letter. And I thought I was having that same affair. I was just as loyal to the idea but, whereas Claudette could say: 'I've seen no one but you since I've known you.' I could not. There were few girls in my life, but there were some. Even if I was alone I had the distinction of loving a dying girl in France.

But then she was getting better.

'My friends come into my bedroom to dance and even smoke. In nine days time we're going to meet here for my birthday. We're going to buy biscuits and chocolate. The doctor has given us permission to dance after supper until ten o' clock.'

There were lapses.

'I'm always having nervous outbursts. This morning I made the cleaning orderly leave my room. She was moving things and banging doors. I want to throw one of my shoes in her face. I am becoming dangerous, don't you think?'

And unjustified praise.

'I was afraid you would abandon me because I was ill. But, on the contrary, you have helped me. You have given me courage to get well and that is why you will always rest in my heart.'

At least the progress to health was constant. With X-rays clear, the injections could stop and capsules could take their place. Even this happy chance, with the promise of returning home, was fraught with difficulties. The timing had to be apt. If she had continued the original treatment, taking the medicines without being ill, they were sufficiently strong to kill her.

'I never want to take the capsules. They are huge and come in thirty-a-day mouthfuls. They require an acrobatic throat not to catch them sideways. I always make a terrible scene. My father saw this today. He was upset. He made me give him one. He's swallowed it and said it was good. My mother has just come back. He's told her it was horrible and that he felt for me. I am laughing.'

Throughout her time in hospital, Claudette had a friend called Francine. She used her as confidante and shared all her hopes and misgivings; even read her parts of my letters and her replies to me.

Then: 'Francine had been very ill and she talked for an hour and a half in her dream. She was speaking to an imaginary friend. She spoke clearly, with a hint of anger.

"But you know, oh, you understand everything I say and everything I feel. You know me better than I know myself. No one should have that much knowledge."

'I thought she was talking to me at first, but her voice was deep and gruff, not like normal. I tried not to listen. I thought it was too private and overhearing her was impertinent. Then I heard my name spoken.

"Claudette? You ask about Claudette? She's nice enough. She's not very old. Oh yes, she's engaged. I see she is. He's called Iain. She loves him very much. Theirs is a beautiful story."

'I wanted to laugh. But then she became very serious and talked about dying.

"Death doesn't frighten me. It's the emptiness of my life now, that's what frightens me. Sitting on the edge of the dark. How can you know? Please, don't chide me out of my mood. I've got to be angry. I've got to fight the emptiness. If I'm calm, then I'll die. That's what tires me, the need to demand pain. That's the only way I know I'm alive. To relax is to be finished."

'She frightened me. When she woke up she let out a horrible scream and she called me. I won't tell her what she said last night.'

A few days after the incident, Francine died.

'I have terrible news. News I have feared coming. And the radio plays on, in my room, talking of love and life. The voice of the speaker chatters and Francine is dead. She is dead. I cannot compete with the noise of radio happiness. Please let it stop.

'You see, I don't ask why. I am strong. I am well prepared. I know about this kind of death. If I cry, then I cry for me. When Francine died, so did all my secrets in her. All the hours of trust, all the hopes and fears, confided, she's taken those and I can't ever get them back. She's taken you with her too. Can you see that? You and I came to life in Francine. Your letters, my hopes, us, she made them real. She believed in them, wanted them too. She was the only person in the world that gave them truth and she's gone. Francine is dead and she loved us. Tell me what to do.'

Only my teenage self would have had the nerve to dare to comment on such sorrow.

'Again, you have helped me. I have re-read all your letters, from A to Z. It's only now I realise that it's here that I have discovered all my love for you. You were right; I wasn't strong enough to cope with any more sadness. Now I am. I've seen her buried. That finality had given me strength. I'll not think or talk about it. I'll learn to live again. Help me, won't you?'

A Private View

A tower

I must visit Laurie with the dot count of 'solds' and 'reserveds'. Sixteen red, four green and several dozen others scattered like unexplained rashes in the corners of the prints. It always seems like cheating, this right of the artist to reproduce an image, albeit in limited numbers. It is certainly good business. If one or two of the really large pieces go tonight then the sales from this private view alone could keep him for most of the year. I've no idea what the residual sales will be here. It's a new hanging space. I'm not sure who knows of it yet and even when known if many serious buyers will seek it out. He has a following, a very loyal one. But, I do find the teachers here somewhat difficult. I can't be entirely dismissive because I do a little teaching myself, but that's to college-age students, in the evenings, on specialist subjects, and they ask questions, answer back, buy you drinks, and occasionally provide you with a wife. But, trusting young souls, trapped in the traditions of disciplined belief, unable to challenge and not even wanting to rebel, 'It's such a privilege to be here, Sir' tattooed on their breast pockets, will accept without challenge or ridicule this bogus pomposity. Their masters glide around in patterned tweed, solid bellies testing the buttons of their matching waistcoats. Old Boys to a man, perhaps, or hoping to be thought so, speaking in English voices that taunt their guests in the very place that taught them to forget their Scottishness, whilst claiming to be her finest sons.

Laurie never tried to lose his Hebridean voice, but then, he loathes the Scots with a passion. Here he comes. It's the first time I've seen him close to. He looks dreadful.

"What has happened to you? Are you ill?"

I hear these words echo in my head and remember with a shudder the time they were first spoken. It was fourteen years ago. Valerie and I had been together for two years. When she left Laurie she'd come to me for help with her thesis. She was doing a Master's degree on Chagall. I'd given a course of lectures on the painter. I'd bought Chagall pieces as private investments for a number of the bank's clients. Chagall is mysterious. A lot of pictures went missing from the early years. I'd found pieces in the oddest of places and bought well. I was earning my spurs, so came to share Valerie's studies with the added kudos of a man of affairs.

She'd concentrated on the works inspired by Bella, Chagall's wife and lifelong sweetheart from Vitebsk. She came to me to remake it all. Valerie was talented, could draw, sometimes would paint, but she studied art

17

history. Laurie never seemed to understand that. She was an academic, with a little flair. She never was an artist.

She'd lost confidence in both herself and the project. She came to me because I knew Laurie. His success was important for my career. The show we sponsored for the Island paintings was one of the largest I had mounted. To be able to sell every large work, to empty the walls of a substantial gallery in central Glasgow and leave a few tiny prints unspotted, was as much a triumph in my life as his. I was yet to take control of the bank's Scottish collection but I'm sure Laurie's success helped me. I'd found him in his final year at college, bought cheaply on his future promise and my eye for new talent. To confirm that choice, we had a sell-out of his postgraduate show.

But it had been far from easy after the marriage break-up. Laurie had followed Valerie to the mainland. On every visit he brought completed canvasses. His output during that year on the island had been astonishing. Not so much the number (well over fifty substantial pieces with preparatory sketches, watercolours, plates for etchings, drawings for lithographs) but the quality he sustained was stunning. He had found his way as an artist: Valerie had lost her way as a person.

I went between them trying to explain the one to the other for several months until one day Laurie disappeared, with enough money to keep him for two or three years and for a long time we heard nothing. After the necessary two years, the divorce began, and in helping them I'd helped myself, because by then Valerie wanted to be with me.

We found him. There was contact and conflict over a tiny cottage. It was worth precious little and was to be sold but he wouldn't agree and couldn't afford to buy the extra half, so everything was put on hold. There were reasons for urgency but that wasn't the cause of the worry. Valerie feared for Laurie's state of mind.

He was clearly depressed and his obsessive personality lent itself to a variety of excesses. He began making late-night calls from remote phone boxes, would run out of change and yell out a number that didn't accept incoming calls. Valerie would become increasingly distressed as Laurie became increasingly drunk as he wandered from pub to pub and telephone to telephone, stretching a few words of information across three or four infuriating hours.

It seemed to me an elaborate and cruel game. I thought him selfish and immature, Valerie thought his suffering was genuine and that he might harm himself. Would I visit him? I was reassured that I had some kind of authority over him, that Valerie's presence would only hinder our plans. I was reluctant to do this but was persuaded. There was a lot at stake, for all of us. Despite feeling manipulated and even used by the feuding pair, I agreed to intercede only if I could resolve the situation on what I considered reasonable terms.

Laurie was living in the Central Highlands, within sight of the contested cottage. I didn't want to think Valerie was being petty laying claim to a property she had no right to and little interest in keeping. The local laird had gifted the cottage to Laurie. It was to be a place of refuge in a much-loved landscape. She knew it meant a lot to him. Was this the point? Did she want to hurt him as he had hurt her? I hoped not.

With an address and a map I ventured north.

He was living in an abandoned tower that once served as the lodge to the estate across the loch. From the roadside the building seemed grand, perhaps romantic. But it quickly revealed itself as a narrow façade, slashed with tiny windows and dominated by a stone stair. The door was open; its base was swollen with rainwater so it never could shut. Laurie was on the first landing.

"Hello, Iain," he shouted. "Good of you to come. Why have you come? Remind me."

I began to climb the stairs. He backed into the small living room that admitted a little light through its long narrow windows. As he stepped into view a shaft of sunlight lit his face. I was shocked.

"What has happened to you? Are you ill?"

I hear those echoing words. Then, they received no answer. Near to the top of the stairs I stumbled and placed the flat of my hand onto the wall to steady my step. It was wet through. I looked where I had touched and saw, not a patch of damp or lichen or even slime, but a steady runnel of water. This building had gone beyond notions of damp.

The living area was haunted by an acrid, nose-pinching smell. There was a stove that gave off a clammy heat. Laurie looked wretched. Cowed, emaciated, he crouched around his own middle, arms folded defensively and when he finally looked at me his eyes were yellowed and red-rimmed. His complexion was grey and his hair dulled with grime. Suddenly he smiled and leaned towards me as if he might shake my hand.

"Do sit down, Iain. You look so awkward standing there and so annoyingly superior."

He waved me seated. I had thought he might be a little calmer than this. How long can a man contain an anger that is tainting his life? A matter of years, clearly. When does it stop?

Laurie suddenly asked, "Will you marry her?"

"Yes, I will marry her."

He raised a finger in warning. I didn't let him speak. I didn't want to entertain any illusions of power he might have or invite any misgivings into my mind. I wanted this settled.

"She's not yours to give, Laurie, nor mine to take. She will be free. You can't stop this happening but you could continue to be a nuisance and to hinder us. No, don't speak. You cut a pretty pathetic figure at the moment. I prefer you arrogant and self-confident. This implosion is unpleasant for both of us. What is it you want to settle matters? I will agree to any reasonable requests. I will not play your games."

"If this is a game, I'm not having any fun. Look, I do accept that she is yours now. Will you share this moment with me, Iain?"

"What moment?"

"An expiation. A purge." Laurie stretched to reach a worn leather pouch with a carrying handle and a brass buckle strap that folded and collapsed under its own emptiness. Before peering inside he clicked open the door to the stove and let the light of its flames flicker into the room.

"I want you to be my witness. This was a bag of trophies. It is nearly empty now, as you can see."

He tipped the open top towards me in confirmation.

"This ..." He produced a postcard from within like a rabbit from a hat and grinned. The speed of his act had startled me.

"... is no longer valid. It was once a surety, a guarantee. I won't embarrass you, or me, by reading it out. It says, 'Expiry date: Never'. Now is never." With a deft flick he spun the card into the fire.

"Now this." He ferreted deep into the bag.

"Stop this, Laurie, please."

"Shush. This is quality." He began to unravel a single sheet of heavily folded notepaper. "It's a poem of Lorca's. Let me say it, it's only short.

¡Ay qué trabajo me cuesta
quererte como te quiero!

Por tu amor me duele el aire,
el corazón
y el sombero.'

It translates into a list of hurts that the labour of loving involves. The funny bit is that even his hat hurts. That was shorthand we both used to understate the pain we were in. It was oddly powerful. No histrionics, no shouting, just a quiet and dignified, 'Valerie', or 'Laurie, my hat hurts'." He dangled the paper in the stove and didn't let go until it was in flames. He clutched the bag to his stomach as if the burning touched him. Without looking, he dragged a supermarket plastic bag across the sofa to his side and, jiggling, spilled its contents onto his lap. There were seven or eight sketchbooks, a couple of card-covered notebooks, a spiral journalist's pad.

"These are my commonplace books. They are full of drawings, watercolour sketches, notes and writings. Their contents are mainly mine; some are borrowed. I'd like you to see them. They're not to be destroyed because these do have a future value. They're about the time on the island. There's only this", he picked up the journalist's pad, "that contains something of now. The sketchbooks are work, valid work. The words are to explain and describe; they underpin the work. And you've had all the paintings. And they've all gone, but they had a lot to say, there was no other way. You take them, they'll be damaged here."

I took them from him.

"It did change us, you know, our year on that island. It made something new. It was a special place, even for her, at first. Then she came to hate it. I know that. I lost my wife to a landscape. And, in losing her, I lost all means of belonging. You know, 'In love' is a place. 'In hate' is a place. The desperate search for a lost woman is its own landscape. It is an eliminating space. It closes out, or traps in, I'm not sure. The effect is the same. It prevents relatedness. It has denied me the world, both people and place. It has meant I cannot work and that means I cannot be." He paused, dropped the empty leather bag over his shoulder, beyond the settee and clasped his hands together in his lap. He leaned forward.

"Let's get out of here. Was there anything else, to do with business, I mean? Anything that can't wait?"

"Yes. There is one thing."

"What's that?"

"Valerie is pregnant."

Claudette

The age of reflection

At three o' clock on the afternoon of Sunday, the tenth of July, Claudette was released from her 'establishment' and sent home. She left hospital clutching many presents: books, records, an opaline vase, but instantly found the relative pleasures of home and hospital ambiguous and confusing.

'I feel so alone and everyone gets on my nerves. I find it difficult to agree with my mother. You see, at the establishment I learnt how to be independent and now it's not the same. I must do as my parents tell me. I must obey.'

She had become, temporarily at least, an outsider, matured and distinguished by her illness. Oddly, the hospital became associated with freedom, home with oppression.

'I am alone in the midst of these happy, reasonable voices. All these characters spend their time explaining themselves and happily recognising that they hold the same opinions. I seem to have forgotten how to live. I don't know how to talk to normal people anymore.'

Then she feared she might lose me, or already had, the necessary bond of illness lost.

'When I turned my back on that death-filled place, I suddenly realised that in a way I was turning my back on you. Yes. You, Francine, iron beds, red blankets, pain were all closely linked together in that one place. Your letters, thoughts and dreams of you seemed to go hand in hand with all the rest. Would I leave you behind, locked in there, a necessary part of the whole memory, to be lost, forgotten? No. As always, life has much subtler ways to be cruel. I didn't leave you behind alone, I left myself trapped in there, with you.'

What gave her hope was the arrival of the exchange students from England.

'The square was alive with laughter and talk. The excessive laughter of the ones who had been before, and the nervous talking of the embarrassed first timers, just a little bit afraid to be suddenly alone within a strange family.'

She knew I wouldn't be amongst them but sought my face there, nevertheless. All our letters for weeks past had been dominated by the difficulties of meeting. My correspondent had failed his examinations so was no longer a student of English. I wasn't really eligible to repeat an exchange but I'd tried for a private arrangement with Monsieur Pasquier.

Claudette's father was anxious for her health and my parent's offer to have her stay with us proved too advanced a notion. It wasn't dismissed out of hand, just displaced for a year or so.

The father had said to Claudette: 'I don't know what keeps you close to this boy. Later, if you are still corresponding, we will see, because you will be much nearer the age of reflection.'

In the end she was allowed to make a private visit to Anne Bailey, for just two weeks, at the end of the summer. Obliged to holiday with her correspondent's family, we met only a handful of times. It was tantalising enough, yet I have few memories of those meetings. I know we were close, spent little time alone and then life began in the letters once more.

Claudette returned to school, a year of her studies lost.

'Winter approaches. This morning I realised all the trees in the boarders' courtyard are naked. The yard is covered in their leaves. It's strange. It's sad. It's monotonous. Outside I seem very cold, but deep down I nourish myself essentially on dreams and hope.'

Our intimacy was verbal, our only reality the power of the words we shared. The interminable waiting began again and the undefeatable hope.

'In the establishment, as you said, I couldn't think clearly about things because I was ill and your letters were my only consolation. Now I'm returned to normal life and amuse myself from time to time, I recognise I need to see you and to wait for you. You represent for me the ideal and I love you. So why did I tell you this, huh? It is because I am very much afraid of being let down. We've been writing for a year. That's good, isn't it? I hope the next passes quickly.'

The letters became more erotic as we practised for the times we would meet. But life in her boarding school was demanding. Even I couldn't fulfil her assignments in English. Life was utterly regimented.

'On Thursday afternoons, to keep our healthy looks, we go for a walk. All in line, in uniform, beret on head, two hundred unhappy boarders march through the town before the curious admiration of the passers-by. Every time our giant crocodile causes huge bottlenecks of traffic. It's absurd. All the girls in the class are tired. We work, even on Saints' days. I can do no more. Too many are b⟨...⟩ ⟨...⟩ill from over-tiredness. I have lost five kilos in the last three ⟨...⟩ Now I am completely cured, two capsules a day ⟨...⟩ is only a memory. I recognise that a friend like ⟨...⟩ again because our friendship was born out of ⟨...⟩ that isn't so easily forgotten, is it? At the mom⟨...⟩ crisis of complete disinterestedness. One of m⟨...⟩ establishment. She has Francine's illness. She i⟨...⟩

and doesn't want to go. She feels ashamed, can you believe, ashamed? I'm OK anywhere, but she's nothing like me. She likes to be at home. I wonder what she's going to do? A sad sense of destiny has descended on the class because every year there are the poor victims.'

And still she counted the months until we could meet again.

'I love adventure. I am very sentimental deep down and, above all, very pessimistic even though I always appear gay. I've already been so disappointed in life that I am ceaselessly afraid of spoiling everything. This summer I will give myself to you. I trust you. I desire you. I know you will be prudent and in truth, I am not afraid. I wait with impatience. I send you all the most beautiful words of love which can exist.'

A silence that lasted for half a year was explained, finally.

'I have just been through the most painful moments of my life. I have not done well enough in my exams to carry on at school. I have had to engage in a struggle at home. Now my father has decided that I will go to work. I will join the Civil Service and begin my adult life. For these passing months I have thought a great deal about you and I have been obliged to see things in their true light, in reality, not in my imagination, like I have always done before. I asked myself if I truly loved you and if I was capable of waiting like this for years at a time. The discovery was very painful for me. I now feel myself incapable of being alone. I have resisted the temptation of going out with others but now my whole being revolts. Too many things separate us. Can you tell me that you have never touched another girl since we last met?

'It is now impossible for me to still dream. I have to live, feet on the ground. Perhaps now you are going to hate me and write to me no longer. That would be the worst of things for me and without doubt, my greatest punishment. But I can no longer live life in the past or in a future always deferred. I will live now. If you would write from time to time, I will always reply and with great pleasure because, in my heart, in the very depths of my being, you are always my boyfriend.'

There was a Christmas card and two notes talking of her life at work. She began as a receptionist in the Tax Office over the bicycle shop. She swapped the long summer breaks for just two weeks leave and the rigours of school for the routines of an office. She was by far the youngest there, but thought the company of adults would help develop her character.

She learnt how to conduct herself as a 'grand personage' while I went to university instead. We didn't write for all those three years and shared nothing of our lives in-between. I carefully trapped a whole teenage affair in a shoebox full of letters, sealed with transparent tape. In moments of sadness I lifted the lid and let free the genie trapped inside.

A Private View

A child

"What has happened to you? Are you ill?"

"Not any longer. I did look much worse. This . . ." Laurie is drawing attention to his own torso with an elegant swirl of hands, his fingers flared. He is on tiptoe, taking an imaginary bow, like a neat bullfighter anticipating the award of an ear, " . . . is better. Although I wasn't actually cured."

"Of what?" I ask him.

"Mrs Peterson." A devotee is separating us. A tiny matron with cruelly pinioned hair has taken Laurie's arm with the confidential assurance of a purchaser.

"Thank you so much." Laurie accepts her gratitude with an unforced smile.

"A virus," he continues, not deflected by praise, "for which my doctor informed me, with obvious glee, there is neither medicine nor cure. He left me to be ravaged."

It has been a long while since I've actually seen Laurie. We often speak on the phone and exchange annual cards. It's probably two years. He was never overweight, but, avoiding any form of organised exercise, there was always a tiny cornice of flesh overhanging his trousers. Tonight his belt is drawn so tight it nearly cuts him in two.

"Just how much weight have you lost?"

"Masses." He instinctively holds in what is no longer there.

"But, it's arrested?"

Laurie smiles at this ponderous word. "Yes. It's arrested. But with no obvious suspect, to extend your metaphor. They've no idea what it was. I think my innards have suffered a one-man outbreak of cholera. Before this, I didn't understand the level of anxiety involved with incontinence. Even breathing had its dangers. It was no fun. Hello, Mrs Cameron. So good of you to come."

"Sorry to interrupt, but, I just wanted to say, I've done it again." Mrs Cameron giggled, girlishly.

"Really?" Laurie is waiting with ever widening eyes. She's giving no clues. It seems we'll never know. She's walking away.

"What has she done again?" I whisper.

"Haven't a clue."

"Madeline's here."

25

"Really?" He's still concentrating on the retreating Mrs Cameron. "I'd just better catch up with her."

"I thought you'd spoken to her."

I catch his arm.

"She didn't say anything. You were standing next to me."

We are at cross purposes.

"I'm talking about Madeline. You're meeting her afterwards, it seems."

"What a good idea."

He's obviously distracted. I send him away.

"Go find out what's been repeated."

"I'll be straight back."

I see one of the *Waterfall* pieces has gone. Judging by the possessive loitering, it's been bought by one of Laurie's colleagues. I'm surprised he can afford it. It will cost him his month's salary. Or perhaps that's the point, material bravado.

Laurie is returning.

"Indecision," is his word of explanation.

"Mrs Cameron tipped the balance in our favour. She couldn't make up her mind between two very different paintings. She couldn't last time."

"How did she solve her dilemma?"

"Then?"

"Yes."

"She bought both."

"And now?"

"The same. That's more than half sold. Solvency beckons."

Laurie has an annoying habit of understating his return from a show like this. He'll make a handsome sum in two successful weeks but still insists on undermining his and my pleasure with an endless list of framing costs, gallery fees, commissions, wine bills—the expensive inconvenience of it all.

"McPhee. That's my dot on *Waterfall 1*, if you were wondering."

"That's marvellous. So nice to know where it's going. Reassuring. I'm delighted. Thank you."

After a self-conscious handshake, I ask Laurie, "And where exactly is it going?"

"I've no idea. I'm not even sure of his name."

Laurie is still looking around nervously. There's a fizzy disquiet about him. It's annoying me.

"Will you relax? Everything is going splendidly. It'll be another sell out, you'll see."

"Do you think?"

"Why not? I wasn't sure of the venue but then, I didn't expect quite so many tonight. And they're still coming." I glimpse Madeline in a far corner. She is studying a picture with over-deliberate care. I imagine she's bored.

"So what did Madeline have to say to you?" I ask Laurie.

"Nothing. I told you, or you told me, that I'd see her later."

"She's working in Africa. Did you know?"

"Is she?" He's smiling. "That's great. I hope she's happy."

"She's not painting."

"Oh?"

"Does that disappoint you?"

"Yes." On reflection he adds, "Perhaps not. I felt I'd made things difficult for her, at one time. I had too much influence in her life and she was too loyal."

"What happened?"

"When?"

"With Madeline?"

"Iain, there is no scandal to report. No 'Prime of Miss Jean Brodie' misbehaviour, despite the apt setting. We just liked the look of each other. I saw a resemblance, a manner. You see it too."

"Valerie."

"Yes, Valerie. I was over-protective. Perhaps I imagined her to be the child I never had."

"Child?" This was a surprise. Was Laurie taunting me in some way?

"Yes. Valerie's child. She reminded me of what I didn't have. A child of hers. So I probably favoured Madeline. I don't think I was ever actually unprofessional but I would acknowledge a bias, too much enthusiasm for her work. It was noticed. Not by anyone important, just an envious colleague who took a perverse delight in misleading her, deflecting her from her strengths, loosely painted large landscapes, to focussed work, small and detailed, so she might learn how to fail. I ensured she did well but I feared her confidence had been undermined. I had no right to influence her work or her career, especially as I doubted my own motives. If she is happy now, then I didn't damage her, did I? Perhaps she never was a painter."

A Child

There was no easy way to tell Laurie of the child. Pregnancy is obvious and inexorable in its progress and Valerie was determined to produce a legitimate child.

"Just explain the situation, Iain. He'll understand the urgency." She was anxious and cajoling.

"Is it urgent? There are still five months to go." I was prevaricating. She knew.

"If he agrees to a divorce settlement today and raises not even the tiniest objection, then it will be six weeks to absolute freedom, even if we can get the court to start the clock ticking instantly. If anyone so much as hiccups, add a fortnight. If there's anything minor to dispute, add a month, anything major, forget it. It can't be done. He'll understand. He won't stop this. Not now."

"How can you be so certain?"

"He won't want to hurt me."

"He has in the past."

"Don't you see I wasn't having a child before? That will mean a lot to him."

"But, it's not his."

"No. But it is mine."

This was the conversation I parted with on the day I went to Laurie's tower.

We were living in my flat in central London at that time and I was flying to Glasgow to stay in one of the bank's apartments, before hiring a car and driving further north. It was very quick and unusually convenient. The London flat I had owned for a while. It was the ground floor of a Georgian terrace with a surprisingly large garden, high ceilings, lots of character and no parking. Valerie loved where we lived, just off the Bayswater Road, a stroll from Westbourne Grove with its many restaurants in a row. We enjoyed the quirkiness of a neighbourhood surrounded by the muted roar of a major city's traffic.

Her first visits to me were made to one of the Glasgow flats. I worked there all week and returned home when convenient. I was required in London at least once a fortnight and often had to go to Europe. But, when she needed to talk or sought advice on Chagall, we met in Glasgow.

That was city enough at first, but the light in her eyes when she first came to stay in London imaged the need to be at the vital centre. The gaudy neon of Piccadilly, flickering above its shuffling crowds, the tasteless beckoning and tarty display of its shop fronts and signs, the shoddy wares and shoddier wearers, the dangerous loos and overt sleaze, filled her with delight. She would stand outside a theatre and gape at the display of people and place, energised and delighted and just a little bit afraid.

We indulged her need for a year. Every weekend, sometimes in the week, we sought out London's special offerings. We were 'Friends' of every inviting institution: The Royal Society, The Royal Shakespeare, all the Tates and the National Trust. We listened to harpsichords in Hampstead, opera in Hyde Park, Promenade Concerts, first and last days in the Albert Hall. We saw all kinds of theatre from the West End to 'Pub'. We watched films in many languages, delighting in the quirky discoveries of a members-only cinema in the Portobello Road. We jumped when Jean Cocteau's painting bit him; I sought to leave when Jimmy Anger tried to rape the lens. We both cried at little-known French films, *Le Grand Meaulnes* the remembered name of one. They always seemed to capture the ineffable sadness of ordinary life.

But ours was an extraordinary life. The centrepiece to our searching was the galleries. We saw them all. An absurd claim, but true. If it was listed we peeped at it. If it was interesting, we stayed; if not, we ticked our list. Valerie used our time in London to satisfy a lifetime of greed. I had the means and, at last, the partner to see all that I valued and had rarely been able to share.

I'm not reluctant to describe her. By implication, you've seen something of her shape in Madeline. But, during our cultural courtship, Valerie kept changing. Her slimness made her seem tall. Her poise made her interesting. Her body was neat and convenient to fashion. She always stood straight, back gently arched, like a mannequin poised to walk on stage. She appeared confident, but wasn't entirely. It took some reassurance before she would parade. Once exposed, to the light of a party, a private view, or something we were doing at home, she was quickly at ease. She chose a stance and a vantage point, the arm of a chair to ledge on, a mantle shelf to lean to; a table corner to crowd around, then, she would stay still and let others come to her. She attracted a private attention.

There was a mystery around and a secret within her that drew others close. I was proud she was with me and confident she would stay because I valued her freedom as much as she did. She wasn't pretty; there were no soft lines to her face. Her nose was sharp, her cheekbones clear, her chin ended square not in a point. Her eyebrows were heavy and so, when still, her face always frowned.

There was a look of seriousness that implied the challenge you would always find in her talk. She made young men nervous; me, she thrilled. I could never presume to speak on her behalf. She wasn't inconsistent but could be persuaded by argument to change. She said she was learning, was too young to be wise, so held firm to no position or point of view.

"That was yesterday. I've learnt something new in-between," she once declared.

She was young and impressionable and impressive. Two things that enthralled me, now as then, were her eyes and the fluency of her voice. There was something crystalline in the iris that flickered from violet to blue. It was like looking into a kaleidoscope. She held your gaze but you couldn't guess her focus; the eyes seemed to melt and rearrange as you looked. Then, they'd be just blue and would pierce with an intelligent glare, made brighter by the frowning brows and crown of dark hair. But at night, the looking could become still and a violet glow tempered the blue with a gentle haze.

The voice was deep, modulated and slow. It's so rare to see a face and set of clothes that imply a being that ought to sound as it appears. The advertisers have delighted in accentuating the gap between the way 'she' looks and speaks. Valerie sounded herself. There was a thoughtful musicality, a precision and a resonance in the words she let go slowly that seduced me on the instant. I would swear that I could see her voice.

"I'm dizzy. There's no more room. I'm joyed out."

It took a year and a half to satisfy her. It's more exhausting when it's new. I'd been taking her along roads I'd travelled. The familiar lets you rest. I fed on her joy. They were her explorations; I merely provided the map. My pleasure was watching her journey, responding to the places we found.

We were never normal; aren't now. When she asked for a child I expressed no surprise. I didn't offer any hint for her to change her mind. I made it seem natural, something to fit in, when secretly, I couldn't believe what I'd heard. There was so much I didn't think I would ever have. I rationalised the loss of them all. I'd a life full of compensations offered in exchange for what normal people were given and kept.

My signet ring bore the inverse imprint of a swift. Their legs cannot stand; only cling to a nest or a mate when the occasion is right. It is born to fly, spends its life on the wing, its first flight might last half of its life. It takes its food from the air and when the night comes, it floats on the thermals that lift it into space where the cold numbs its mind to a coma. It trusts to the atmosphere that supports its weight, buoyed above the earth, out of our sight. The dawn thaws it through. The swift drifts back to the earth that it never needs to touch, except in death. It served me as an image of trust, of endless travel, of finding nowhere to belong, simply claiming a right to the ether. 'On the move'. 'In motion'. 'Always nearer by not keeping still'.

But I kept very still for Valerie in case I frightened her away. A child, from her, for me. If I were honest, I never thought she'd stay. If I were honest, I wouldn't and couldn't have minded. All that I'd had I'd loved; if there was more I would accept it. If it were to end, I would accept that too and thank God for the time I had been given. The eternal gratitude of the older man flattered by the care of the young girl. I gave her what I knew and was content with the giving. I wanted nothing from her. I don't now; that lightness of touch lets her stay. The freedom I grant is unbearable at times, but, if I grasp to possess her, all will crumble to dust.

A child meant she would stay in my life. A child meant I'd stay in the world. I wished the thermals farewell, tumbled to earth and learnt to walk.

She was right about Laurie. When I told him of the child he accepted everything. He was clearly stunned by the news and folded into himself as if winded by my words. He began the negotiation, not me.

"She'll want it ended now. There's no need to speak."

It was true. I wouldn't have known what to say. I couldn't feel guilty; my own happiness crowded it out. I was thirty-nine years of age. I was fit, slim, not bad looking, in a post-war sort of way, but certainly right at the back of the parenting shelf. All I might have shared with an athletic boy-child was nearly over now, let alone in a decade when I might be called to sporting arms. I'd be retired before university was out. If I didn't start now, I never would, or could. The habits of selfishness are hard to kick. I thought I understood the disruption this would bring. I, like every parent before me, geriatric or not, underestimates the changes hopelessly. It would devastate my life. But, it would give it a dimension and a meaning I had never suspected.

Laurie had just begun. I saw his youth as full of possibility. So few doors had closed on him. Except the one to Valerie. Soon she would be doubly beyond reach, remarried and a mother.

"I'll move to somewhere civilised, with a phone. She'll want this quickly. The child will need to be legal. It will matter to her. Look. How to put it? This child, it's yours, yes? Yes, of course. Please, I knew. I didn't mean anything. You will marry and you will keep them both? That is the plot? I've not misunderstood?"

"No."

"Good. Good. And, you've money, work and a future and a past. Affordable, all of this is affordable by you. Yes?"

"Yes. All of it."

"There's nothing from me. There's no request?"

"For money? No. None at all. Of course not. You are in no way obliged, not in any of this."

"And there are no things?"

"Things?"

"Well, we didn't really have a house, did we? There's no washing machine needing a good home. We don't have to divide the silver."

"I understand. No. There's nothing to divide. Except—"

"Ah!" He pointed at me, smiling, rocking on the sofa. "Ah! Now we come to it. Go on. Say it."

I didn't really understand this reaction, but I assumed he meant his cottage. At this stage it was all there was to contend. It was the only card he held and the law had ripped that in half.

"You mean your cottage."

"Yes, my cottage. Thank you for calling it 'my' cottage."

"Laurie, I'm here to speak on Valerie's behalf. I wish you no harm. I pray you'll believe I intend you none. I can't apologise for loving Valerie, or for giving her this child. I'm not here in triumph. Quite the opposite; I'm humbled by this gift. But, there remains you and me. Independently of all this. We were friends in the beginning. We've done business together. We've been good to and for each other. There was your wonderful show and the praise I received for spotting your gifts. I respect and envy your talent. I have hated to know of your sadness and your despair. Let me help as a friend. I've seen the price of the cottage; it's in the paperwork back at the flat. It's precious little money for something so clearly valued. I don't know why Valerie covets it so much. It must have meaning for you as a couple and I don't need to know and I don't want to. Buy it from her. I'll give you the money you need, if you will let me. Pay me when you can. It's not a loan. If the money's never spare, I don't mind. It's an advance on work in progress. With a proper roof and drier walls . . ."

"They're eight feet thick at the loch end, eight feet." He tried to span the width, watching closely as I produced a chequebook from my inside pocket. He let me write. I folded the completed cheque over to conceal the amount, my nervousness, and his potential embarrassment. He placed the tiny square on the cushion by his side. He prodded it with his first finger and laughed.

"That's all it takes to set me free. That tiny bit of paper. Is it really mine? Can I go now? Or will the paperwork throw me out?"

"No it won't. I'll see to that. I'll take you myself. I've a car outside. We can put your few things on the seats. How do you get about? Everything's too far apart to walk, isn't it?"

"I've a little bike, a moped thing with shin guards. It's ridiculous but it goes and it doesn't mind if I'm drunk. I can fetch it. Come to think of it, I don't think it's here. It's at a friend's."

I left him at his cottage. He was so excited. I think he wanted me gone so he could sigh with relief. He'd asked me a few questions about where

I'd raise the child. I told him about our garden. He said nothing. His cottage was basic but dry, and black plastic bags had saved all the rottable contents. It took a couple of journeys to empty the tower. How he'd survived for so long there beggars belief. I drove him to Fort William so he could deposit my cheque and arrange to draw another of equal value of his own. The bank agreed to broker not just this but all our dealings and Laurie could ring the manager there to arrange any meetings at the seldom-open branch office nine miles from where he now would live. We thanked each other on parting for the gifts that set us free. So much of the pain had gone from his face but he still looked ill. I suggested a doctor but he had a cure of his own. He waved at the hills across the loch, the trees and the mountains beyond. "I'll paint myself into perfect health."

And in time, he did.

I returned to London with the Island books. Laurie had insisted that I keep them despite his new dryness. I put them on the bookshelf in my study. They were an obvious addition, clearly in view, but in the turmoil of the divorce, marriage and birth they were overlooked.

I remember those months as oddly furtive. They shouldn't have been. Even Valerie's pregnancy was discreet. She just grew a child, not an ounce of unnecessary or misplaced fat. Half a stone of baby and significant liquids stuck to her belly in a specific hemisphere. The child was tacked on to the perfectly preserved body of the mother. It was a self-contained, non-invasive growing; the foetus seemed too polite to incommode. It meant the mother never bloomed. She always looked tense, oddly embarrassed, not really involved.

We were married in time. Her desire to be socially correct was satisfied comfortably. Clever clothes and a select, knowing few, meant the civil ceremony looked like any other childless event. A stranger couldn't have guessed. But then, I didn't see the difficulty. Does anybody watch, or care? Do eyes still rove for wedding rings? Do busy fingers count the months?

The families were invited but stayed away. Fear of central London was a convenient excuse for mine: the huge distances to travel equally powerful for hers. We didn't need them to come but I felt oddly shamed when they didn't. We'd each had a proper marriage; maybe we were only entitled to one. The language of the ceremony makes this assumption, and vows for life can ring oddly hollow when the living rather than the dead did the parting. If only there were new words for the ones trying again, that accepted relationships in series, recognising each succeeding attempt as approximate, rather than this pretence of a single perfection that must overlay the one before; and where words like 'everlasting' echo as unhappy reminders of failures in the past.

Claudette

The compulsion of sad loving

When I graduated from London University with a goodish degree in law, I was, for a while, very sad. I was certain of only one thing; I didn't want to pursue a career in the law. I deferred a postgraduate place and suddenly gained a year I hadn't planned. With no future in place I looked to the past and reinvented my love for Claudette.

I wrote to her family to find her latest address and renewed my acquaintance with the Pasquiers. I tried to be controlled and suggested a meeting on some ground neutral to us both. I booked into a hotel overlooking the great square in Arras.

I wouldn't swap the moment of our meeting for any later wisdom or the demands of common sense. It was on the platform of a station without any convenient clock. I really was the last one left and, with no one there to meet me, I walked into the main hall where you could buy tickets and trinkets and a meal. The place bustled with noise and people knowing which way to go. I felt oddly buffeted, in everyone's way, wondering where to look. Was I early, or more likely, late? Was this the only possible place I could be?

In my confusion and anxiety I never noticed how close she was to me. Without seeing her come, she was in front of my face, saying, "Hello" with a beaming smile. I scooped her up, impulsive and daft, and danced with her round and round. Everyone looked, nobody disapproved, one charming old lady even clapped. I wanted to share this moment of joy with everyone I could see. We kissed and laughed and danced again and drifted a hallway away from my bags. It was only then I said, "Hello".

Self-conscious at last, I ran to reclaim my things. I was so excited and elated; I just wanted to stare at Claudette and grin. We stopped for a drink that developed into a meal; we were so reluctant to defocus our eyes. I have no memory of words or plans or information exchanged, we just sat and took each other in.

We were used to waiting but the delight this time was intensified by having come of age. We needed no one's permission to be. We stayed in Arras and only slowly made plans, greedy for each moment alone. Claudette had a job in the *Gare Maritime* in Boulogne-by-the-Sea. I would find work there, see the Pasquier family, her father and family and friends, from school and from work and, and, and . . .

Mistakes are best made in a hurry. We registered and married with unthinkable haste, careful not to involve the Church in the act. That was a kindness that would protect her family and any future proper marriage Claudette might make. We had no thought for the future, just for something concrete and precise that we both could parade. A sliver of diamond and a curtain-thin ring were badges enough to prove we were valid and grown-up.

We didn't stop to think. Consequences were none of our concern. It was crazy and heady and the fun disappeared with depressing speed.

We rented a flat on the fourth floor of a huge grey block in sight of where Claudette worked. It was in the area of the docks and whilst never threatening or grim, it was not the bohemian world I thought I'd grasped. There were no shutters with peeling paint, no wrought iron balconies, the sound of typewriters or café chatter. This was no artistic quarter and day-to-day life was drab.

The romance had gone in a month. An awareness of error began the very first day we lived an ordinary life. Claudette was everything she had ever claimed to be. She was lovely, truly pretty, attractive, brave and sweet. She was practical and sensible and shopped with skill and care. She could cook, make beds and make love. But she made no plans for me because, in reality, there was nothing there. We could only love in absence, through words on a page. Face to face we liked each other but had very little to say. She was already quite senior in the world of her work and I felt immature and untried by her side. I trailed behind. With calm and precision, she cut me free.

Wisely, she knew that the only thing that truly separated us was being together. I would have tried for longer, pretended there was more than there was. She knew the error of our ways was best resolved by ending us as quickly as we had begun. She did so with great subtlety and blamed herself for letting us down. She never let me feel badly and I parted with as little as I came. But, whenever I read those letters, the genie is set free just the same, tantalising and beckoning with a dreamed-of loving that can never really be.

She was good enough to write three, no four times, there are four letters, barely notes, in the shoe box. The first came four years after our last meeting.

'You will be surprised to hear from me. I think of you very often and should be pleased to know what you are doing now. I have been married for a year and I've got a son. He looks like his father, just a little like me. How are you? Have you married again? I haven't heard from you for such a long time and that saddens me. Perhaps you will answer my letter. If you come to France, I shall be very pleased to receive you at home, and my husband too.'

I must have responded because there is letter, dated a few months later, giving directions to where they lived.

I didn't go.

I was invited the following year.

I didn't go.

Nearly seven years after our last meeting she wrote.

'How are you? I hope, one day, you will write because I would love to know what has become of you. My son is growing up. He is very naughty. My family is well. I hope your family is well. If you send a recent photograph of you, I shall be very happy and I'll send you one of me and my family. I don't know what else to say.

I kiss you,

Claudette,

Her husband, her son.'

There is still an ache when I hear her voice talking in the letters. Such sad loving is compulsive. Where is she now, I wonder?

A Private View

Sarah

I don't know what I expected, being married again. There was so much love for Valerie and a pinch-myself-disbelief that she could be saying yes to me. There was the thrill of the child and the heel-kicking joy that my mind imagined, even if my legs didn't carry it through. There was the less pleasing male pride that a child proved me virile and I could wear its beautiful young mother as a trophy on my sleeve. But there was little time to gloat and even less to reflect.

The flat didn't work. It always seemed large when we came and went but, as Valerie realised, we'd never stayed in. It was a really great flat to avoid. We hung up clothes, made tea and toast, rang for tickets and tables. Valerie had been doing freelance research for T V, radio and me. The bank was thriving, its profits were obscene and my bonuses inexcusably large. I used to giggle when I knew what I earned. I didn't trust it, so asked my own people for investment advice. Of course, it was excellent, and what I saved also bloated in worth.

Nevertheless, a proper house in the city centre was beyond our means. So, we left. I did mind. I can say that now. At the time, I wanted to please. We moved to the outskirts of High Wycombe, within Sunday morning walk of Chequers and not far from Roald Dahl's writing shed and the oldest pub in the world. It was nice. It was decent. With any tweed jacket I'd belong. My only rebellion was tiny. I bought blue 'Hunter' wellingtons instead of green.

The child was a girl and we called her Laura.

"How is Laura? Is she with you?" I'm joining in the looking even though I know she isn't here.

The person who has asked this question is called Sarah.

"Hello, Sarah."

She is hard to describe, not in and of herself, that's straight forward enough. She is just over forty, widowed, with two young sons. Sarah is short, precisely fringed with a gentle smile and a loving nature. It's her relationship to Laurie I find hard to define. They're certainly not married and they're barely partners, but in a part-time, very responsible way, Laurie and they form a family. He doesn't live with them but he's always there. They holiday together and he takes an active fatherly role in the life of the boys. They're companions, a group that interdepends and basically, it works. She's a lovely lady, really, really kind. It's often the case with people who have suffered. Sarah's life has been tinged with tragedy. I only know a few main events and she is so modest, other hurts have probably remained unsaid and so, are unknown to me.

Her father died of unspecified wounds in an unmentioned war in some unspeakable place beyond China. He was barely fifty and left an intrepid widow who raised Sarah and her two brothers in randomly chosen living quarters in the Far East. She then married a military man herself, gave him two fine sons, and he wandered into a booby-trapped jungle and only bits of him ever came back. His death was controversial and, so it never need be explained, the Government funded housing and education through the benign offices of a regiment that really did care for its own. Sarah's mother hankered after her roots and exchanged the exotic Far East for grey bricks and mortar on the edge of Inverness. Sarah joined her and set up home nearby. She does her mother's shopping but they keep their houses to themselves. I'm assured it works well. She enrolled both boys in Laurie's school and that's where they met. She was a good parent and he a keen teacher so they 'associated' over time.

She's homely and private, the exact opposite of Valerie.

"I am well looked after," is the response that Laurie always offers if asked why he spends time with Sarah.

"And I will teach the boys how to paint the island. And soon, before I forget, or there's nothing left to share."

Sarah has made Laurie calm. He feels necessary to other lives. Fathering suits him. It exhausts me. Where is Laura? I don't know.

"She's with friends, Sarah. Staying with friends."

"I see." Sarah would go nowhere without her sons. The sense of disapproval isn't hers but mine.

"I did ask her to come with me. I thought this exhibition might interest her. It's a long time since she's been in Scotland. I thought it might serve as an antidote to her urbanity. She is becoming a real city slicker, Sarah."

"Is she?"

Her boys love the hills. I know Laurie takes them up high and teaches them to name all the peaks. It's his gift of place. All London and the South East seems to have achieved for my child is the complete destruction of the letter 't'. It is absent from Laura's words and that of her friends. I believe it's called 'estuary' English, an unholy blend of east London, Dick Van Dyke cockney and suburban Australian. It's sloppy and it's ugly and it's everywhere. It's not the English that her parents speak and that seems to please her. It defines her tribe and excludes me. Valerie seems less concerned.

"How old is your girl now, Iain?"

"Sixteen."

"No!"

"Yes. And no longer a girl, I'm afraid. Very much a young woman now."

"Why afraid?"

She's a canny woman, Sarah. She knows that I'm anxious.

"I fear what she's turning into. It seems out of my control. I only have words and they don't appear to work."

"Would you want it any other way?"

"No. I wouldn't hurt her, ever. But it's so difficult to watch her stray. To know she's doing damage, building regret and she's deaf to all that's said."

"What's this about, a boyfriend?"

"Yes and no. Of course, there is a lad. That's not the difficulty. It's the group. It's the attitudes and the inertia. You've lost a lot of people in your life, Sarah. I'm sure we've both learnt the wisdom of letting go. I have let Laura go. I influence her life but I don't try and run it for her, as she claims. But I think I've lost her friendship and that really hurts. She won't confide in me and she doesn't seem to trust my judgement."

"I'm sure she does. I remember her as a delightful lass, just like her father in looks and good manners."

"She's not like that now. These new friends seem to drain her, rob her of her liveliness. She was so excited by every new thing. She used to shudder with anticipation, the very image of joy. Now she sits around, negative and drab. Her hair is full of their cigarette smoke and her mind absorbs their apathetic notions. She'd dropped out of my world."

"She'll come back. She'll take her time and you must let her. She has to find her way. It might not be yours."

"I can only offer her what I know. I just beckon and drop markers on the way. It's not her, you see, Sarah. What she seems to have become is not authentic. She contains all the things I once recognised in her. She is still full of the qualities you once saw. She is living a lie."

"What does . . . Valerie say?"

Sarah always pauses before speaking Valerie's name. She senses a danger, the means of a future fracture between us all. My answer is prefaced by a disloyal sigh.

"Valerie is a lot tougher than me. She's less taken-in, perhaps. But then she's not as involved. She's been travelling a lot, you know. Her work is going well. She's doing another degree and . . . Then, there's a sudden coming together and she and Laura huddle in a way that only they can. Their shared confidences seem more profound than mine."

Sarah reaches out and in touching my arm seems to earth my sadness through her own being.

"It will change. You'll never lose her love."

By simply looking round, Sarah changes our subject from my private worry to the public view.

"It's going well, isn't it? All these people."

"Yes, it is going well. Sales are excellent. Laurie will need to start painting again."

"Yes."

Having scanned the room, Sarah turns to me.

"What do you think of his latest scheme?"

"What scheme is that?"

I'm still smiling encouragement to any eye that I can catch.

"Hasn't he said?"

"Well . . ." I give her my attention. "We've been totally consumed by this. It was a rush in the end. We didn't really have enough work. I didn't realise how much space there would be and this free-hanging idea suddenly emptied huge areas of wall. I'm surprised he's been planning beyond now. Some of this work here has been shown two, even three times. What's he thinking of?"

"He hasn't discussed it with you, then?"

"No, why?"

"If he'd told you it would be more likely to take place."

"What's he been saying?"

"A move. He's planning a move."

"Well, we're used to that, aren't we? What's this, his five-year itch? Is there another long service tie due at his school that's caused this panic? He's a pretty rooted man, our Laurie. It would take a lot to get him to move school."

"It's not to teach. It's just to paint. He thinks he could afford to, if he lived there."

"Where? Not on the island?"

"Yes. So he has said."

"Not Seal Cottage? He's not thinking of going back there, surely?"

"No. More civilised. He's thought it out, so he says. He'd rent for a summer. There's a plot, in front of the hotel. You can build locally. He'd live there, sell up here. It used to be a fishing village. Fallen down, now, it seems."

"Yes, it's all cleared. There are three new houses already built."

"You've been?"

This has surprised her. I hadn't meant to say. Sarah does that. Her honesty invites yours.

"Yes, I've been."

"When?"

"Recently, very recently. I thought it was about time I did."

"Could you live there?"

"Me? Why me? I'm not planning . . ."

"I know. I'd just like your opinion. Just an impression. That would do."

"No. Absolutely no possibility. Four days is plenty. And only that many if I can be in the hotel. Does that help?"

"Some."

I don't like to see her troubled.

"Have you been asked to go?"

"No. Well, I didn't give him the chance. I couldn't, you see. Not with the boys at school and Mother's shopping. Yes, they could board, but we weren't discussed. I was thinking about him, what it would do to him to go back there. That's what I was thinking."

"You'd miss him, if he went."

"I thought you said he wouldn't."

"Did I? It sounds like an idea he's floating to see the possible effect. It's like a Government leak. He'll probably deny any intent if you're critical."

"Will you ask him? Is that rude?"

"No, Sarah. It's not rude. Of course I will."

"Why did you go?"

"Pardon?"

"After all these years, why did you go to the island, Iain?"

Valerie found the Island books almost a year after they were given to me. They had been forgotten, ignored. Pregnancy, birth, and the reality of Laura had consumed all my attention in the first year of marriage. Nor was there any sense of priority on my part to look at what they contained. I had seen myself only as their guardian. I had no compulsion to peer inside. Valerie had.

"Were you meant to give these to me?"

"No. Not at all." I rather resented her hint of suspicion. It was the middle of the night but the only one asleep was Laura, who relapsed from screaming alarm to calm content within moments of being fed. Thoroughly disturbed and entirely awake, we had gone downstairs and were sitting in my study. It was warm. I had a stove in there. We were drinking chamomile tea.

"Why would he give them to you?" Valerie asked.

"I don't know. I remember some comment about a future value. I assumed he meant that the sketches in them might be used for establishing provenance for the later paintings which had been based on them."

"Did you think there were just drawings?"

"No. Not entirely. There were writings. Journals. There were proper pads, you know, shorthand books, flip over things. He kept those."

"Do you know what this is?" 'This' had become a neat array of sketchbooks and hardcover notebooks fanned across and almost covering my desk. There were a dozen volumes. The notebooks were red, the sketchbooks brown and green and blue.

"Well . . ." I got up to touch them but Valerie waved me away.

"No."

"What do you mean, no?"

"I've started to read them. You shouldn't. It will be embarrassing for you, and very embarrassing for me."

"Why?"

"These are his diaries, our diaries. Some of these I put words in. Not many and not often but I did contribute. It is a description of our year of marriage. It is about the island and his pictures, obviously. That was the best thing to come out of it, wasn't it? But it's also very frank. It describes us, in detail, everything we did."

"Valerie, this took place before us. You were free. Whatever you did . . ." I didn't feel as liberal as I sounded. My head was pounding and I felt a little afraid. Although nothing written could possibly relate to me, Valerie didn't wish to be revealed in an unpleasant or unfavourable light. That much was understandable. Nevertheless, what had she, or they done, that I would find unacceptable?

"There's nothing horrible. God, we didn't perform unnatural acts. Well, not often." She laughed, unconvincingly. "But I was his model as well as his wife and we lived an unsupervised life. There's always the possibility of Sodom and Gomorrah without a god or neighbours watching."

"If you'd sooner I didn't read them, I won't."

"That's not really fair. It's just that, even in the bits I've read, it's only his version. It isn't complete, not without my point of view. He must have sensed this. That was why he asked for my written comments on some of the difficult days. I'd no idea he'd written so much. But then, he was often alone."

During the silence that followed, Valerie arranged the books into their order of writing and, holding the first volume, came to sit, uncomfortably, on the arm of my chair.

"Can we read it together, then at least I can explain or excuse."

"You don't have to, you know."

"Yes I do. This is Laurie's test. He's daring you to love me after all that this shows."

"Will I be able to?"

"I don't know. I'm not ashamed of what we did. Some of it was beautiful. But, in the end, I had to leave and in leaving, I found you."

She opened the front cover to show the drawing of a tiny cottage immersed in hills of sand.

"That's Seal Cottage. That's where we lived for a year."

I eased the covers to, in the full grip of my hand and placed the book beside us on the floor.

"Not now. Let's wait until daylight."

Laurie would describe The Island, when in reality there were many. The sketchbooks weren't bound to the particular places of Oronsay. Images intruded from scenes further north on Skye, the Summer Isles and attached land. His typical route began at Oban and the ferry crossing to Scalasaig. His ancestors came from Colonsay where an aunt and uncle still lived. Jura to the south, Islay further west, the chunk of Mull blocking the north; this was the Inner Hebridean cluster that had captured his young mind. The tiny spur of Oronsay, the part-time island to Colonsay's south, was to be the base of his adventure and the one thousand year-old home of the family to which he felt he belonged.

In truth, it had been a place to holiday. He never fully lived there, even as a child. He had been educated on the nearby mainland, then moved further north to study, and in the end made the outskirts of Glasgow his actual home. But, his spirit lived on these islands; reinforced by the carefree summers he spent there throughout his youth. He could name each rock on Oronsay, knew the story of every inlet and the secret history of each discovered relic. But such knowledge can appear in a guidebook. The Ordnance Survey can put every name in its place. Laurie intended to capture in paint the spirit of this place that always lived in his mind's eye.

He'd graduated well from the College of Art. His traditional skills pleased me. Even his earliest work found its way into distinguished collections, especially in the north. Artistic London was almost wholly conceptual. It meant that amongst painters Laurie had no peers. He sought a voluntary exile. He could see no easy place to belong. Valerie might dream of bohemia and still warmed to the idea of smoke-filled cafés on Paris's Left Bank. Laurie could readily abandon the city for his silent island, with no noise of people to distract his hand. He'd described it as a paradise, a place of wonder to wander in. But his Eden lacked an Eve and he'd sooner not go alone. He offered this to Valerie with such enticing words that he overwhelmed her misgivings.

Suddenly they married.

There was a free cottage that he'd played in when he was a boy. Such little need of money, for there was nothing for sale. The earnings from his paintings and a retaining advance from my bank, arranged as a loan through me, gave them enough independence to live out this crazy dream for six months to a year.

And so they went.

Part Two

The Island

1

There were many lists: candles, Calor gas, sacks of solid fuel and firelighters. Flagons of drinking water, water purifiers and buckets confirmed the absence of electricity, plumbing and trees. Neither Laurie nor Valerie wanted to own a car. They'd persuaded a friend who'd admired them both, the one for his talent the other for her face, to drive a college van from Glasgow to Oban. They'd packed a trunk with clothes and bedding. Each had a removals box with cord handles. She packed books for her thesis; he packed paints, paper and the makings for canvasses. He bought a few ready made to carry under both arms.

They stopped at a supermarket in Oban, filling another two boxes with tins and imperishables: pasta, rice, beans, desiccated soups and sauces. Nothing grew on their island.

It took several trips to board the ferry. The gangway stairs were steep and narrow. The flimsy iron steps, chained loosely to the ship, wobbled unnervingly as the weighty packets zigzagged aboard. Their belongings half-filled the area set aside for stowage but no one seemed to mind. There were already a number of mysterious boxes there. At least one contained something alive as, on occasion, through the dark letter box slit in its side, eyes glinted.

There was hardly anyone on board and no one waved goodbye. Assured that they could cope, the college friend had shrugged his farewell and was well on his way home before the ferry left the harbour. Laurie sketched the disappearing town, his attention drawn to a pattern of light on the western face of the mountain that towered above the neat row of houses fringing the shoreline. The white rock looked like snow, but it was late July and the high temperature and low peak warned of the illusion that a passing cloud confirmed. Returned to dullness, he looked away to acknowledge the many greetings. Everyone half-knew everyone else. Partial recognition was made easy with so few island people to remember. Laurie's childhood visits, the odd scandalous excursion during his college years and his spectacular arrivals by private plane to the tiny airstrip beyond the golf course, had fixed his face in most minds.

He was a mother's son, an uncle's nephew, a cousin's cousin, an island lover and a returnee who might decide to belong. Laurie was happy to divulge his plans. They seemed less absurd discussed here with these people. In various degrees of discomfort, they were doing the same. Nevertheless, no one underestimated the potential uneasiness of his choice.

As Mull receded to their right, an alarmed Australian couple knew for certain that they were on the wrong ship. No, they weren't going to Tobermoray, clearly, because that was already out of sight beyond the edge of Mull's brown and infertile land. Assured of their certain and only destination, a pretty Rebecca with soap opera looks and the casual innocence only an Australian abroad can manage, asked of her small but concerned audience, "What happens on Colonsay?"

Disapproving wives of a certain age would like to have said, 'Bra's happen on Colonsay'. More helpful husbands, entranced by the wind's skill in revealing nipples through cotton, closed in to confide for the few moments they were allowed.

The island arrived slowly. A thin cliff of dark land grew to fill the horizon. It was hard to tell where Colonsay ended and Oronsay began and whether the farthest seen edge was of either place but rather the western reaches of Islay, beyond Loch Gruinart. Eventually, the jetty was visible and beyond it, the messy clutter of Scalasaig.

The arrival of the ferry mattered. It was an important event of the day. For less than an hour, disused buildings and chained-off areas suddenly admitted entry. People bustled, a crowd formed. The islanders wore hats and coats of office, momentarily important, as they played their temporary roles. Ropes were caught and skilfully fastened; stairways rattled into view. Everyone looked nervous, a little out of place, as a bookseller became a harbour-master, a fisherman, a guard and everyone on board, it seemed, were willing porters for Laurie. He didn't even carry the stretched canvasses and they had no weight at all. By the time Valerie emerged, waving a friendly farewell to the Australian pair who never finally set foot on land, she discovered all they had brought resting in a neat pile on the quayside, not a parcel amiss, only Laurie, who was already exchanging handshakes and the occasional hug with a new group of willing helpers at the harbour end of the jetty.

Before the ferry could blast its signal for leaving, a tractor and trailer had appeared alongside. A lad in the back and the driver, most probably his father, quickly loaded the trunk and boxes and offered Valerie a place beside them that she refused, happy to walk the long jetty and take in her first view of the place.

Everyone had gone. They couldn't all have taken the boat. At the top of a long hill, a bus without a side door slowed to offer a lift, but again she refused, content to walk. She could see the long white side of the hotel. Way up high to her left, she glimpsed the tip of a beacon, a monument for something or someone? To her left and below her gaze was the fishing harbour. Nets and floats and wicker creels littered the roadside.

"We have a lift. Robert will take us across. He'll come back for us later. Do you need anything from the boxes? He'll leave the trailer by the hotel. We'll meet him at five."

He'd shouted all this, as if briefing Robert, not really addressing Valerie at all. Only when finally alone, did he stretch out his hand and remember the newness of all this for his wife. He'd introduced her to no one.

"Come, we'll visit the shop. It's right here."

Valerie walked behind him, reluctant to move her gaze from the harbour and the hills beyond.

"Are there any messages?" he asked, as they walked inside.

"There's a letter from your Uncle Stuart. He's left it here because he guessed you'd need to come. He's out. He apologises. A family loss on her side, sudden but important. He'll be in the Borders for the week. Seal Cottage is open. He's put you some wood. I've arranged some coals. Here's a key to the farmhouse if you need more comfort. Mind you, that's only marginal. Choose what you need. Shall I open an account? That's the best idea."

A huge hand from a giant of a man stretched across the shop counter and gave Laurie the letter. Valerie had never met anyone so unmistakably Scottish. When he emerged to help pack their bag of chosen groceries she was disappointed he wasn't wearing a kilt to match his beard, moustaches, mass of hair and lilting voice. Laurie explained that the shop was the Post Office, its keeper the postman, its cluttered aisles, the centre for gossip and concern.

The fresh produce wasn't. There'd been no time to replenish from today's ferry. The wooden trays displayed limp and depleted wares. The bread was cellophane-wrapped and the milk long-life. But, there was a lot of news and welcome reassurances and a promise of better foodstuffs to come.

They walked the slow incline to the hotel, added this new box to their pile in the discarded trailer and sat in the front lounge to drink tea and eat shortbread biscuits. There was no one about. The cleaner had made their tea. The hotel contained the only bar on the island and it didn't open for over an hour. By then they'd been towed to the top of a steep hill that suddenly offered a glimpse of The Strand, the wet sand causeway to the island that was to be their home.

At the edge of the land was a waiting area. There was parking for four or five cars. That evening there was only one. Opposite the surfaced area a lorry waited. A young official-looking man waved a menacing clipboard in front of the face of an obvious local. The closed windows and glass screen muffled their words but the reprimand was failing as the censured driver looked over to the tractor and winked at Robert as he passed.

"Can we stop?" asked Valerie.

She walked onto the sand that was solid to her tread. As far as she could see, in front and to her right, a wide, flat space of water-filmed sand glittered in the evening sun. It was dazzling and hurt her eyes. Tyres marked the direction across; some thick treaded, others thin, made by bikes. Vast islands stood above the sea that had shrunk to a few centimetres in most parts. A square kilometre of sand must be revealed every day by each tide. She'd not expected such a spectacular gap. The word 'strand' sounded thin; you ought to be able to hop across. If not that, then an elegantly narrow walkway, best approached on foot, in the evening, well-dressed before dinner. But this was grand, magnificent, something of a threat. The island opposite, its steep edges wholly reflected in the water still there, protected itself well. She wouldn't have liked to walk across, not yet.

"Is it safe?" she'd asked Laurie, who was clearly surprised by her fears.

"Yes. It's sound underfoot. There's nothing hidden. The sand doesn't give way. We're heading for there." He pointed diagonally across to where water still lingered: "There's a track. We can go across soon. We can walk the first part, if you like?"

"No, I'll go with Robert today."

"What do you think?" Laurie wasn't looking at her but gazing at the shimmering expanse beyond.

"Stunning. I never thought it would be this vast."

He didn't react. It was familiar to him; he'd absorbed its scale. It was the changing light and the individuality of each day that thrilled him. No one, even those who crossed daily, ever knew it the same. The patterns of light, the shifting cloud, the wind, the calm and the rain repainted The Strand's surface hour by hour with a subtle palette of tones. It was a giant kaleidoscope made of sky mirrored by sea shifting ceaselessly across the sand.

"Is it time?" she kept asking of the absent-minded men. Laurie seemed bemused by this place, glaring across at Oronsay, suddenly changing focus as his head twitched with the staccato shifts of a marionette. Robert seemed impassive. His only movement was to scratch the tufts of sandy-coloured hair that stuck out of his cap. As his forefinger twitched, the cap would dislodge and slip to a jaunty angle that failed to change the seriousness of his broad-cheeked face. He nodded 'No' glumly four times, then without being asked, answered 'Yes' and strode to the tractor. Laurie was still climbing in as they jolted away. Robert's eyes were fixed firmly ahead. As soon as the tractor moved, they could feel the wind that the nearside land kept at bay. Valerie knelt high, clutching the wriggling boxes to her chest. She looked back and around, feeling exposed in-between the lands. It seemed impertinent to be driving on the sea, and thought, absurdly, that it might mind.

"How did they know?" she shouted to Laurie.

"How did they know what?"

"That this would work."

"I'm not following."

There were shallow basins on The Strand that still ran with water half a metre deep. The insistent speed of the tractor ploughed easily through, but the water sluiced past the tyres with a hiss that drowned both question and reply.

"I said, how did they know they could cross?"

"Always. It was always known. They built the priory on the tiny island, not back there." Laurie turned and waved towards Colonsay as Valerie shook her head and mumbled, "Monks?"

The last few metres were difficult. The path up the hillside was clear but it began amongst seaweed and rocks. Robert, knowing the terrain, drove into deeper water still, before the land flattened out and, with an unseemly trundle, the trailer was pulled onto the shore. Robert was untroubled and Laurie simply grinned, eager to point out to Valerie the only tree that had ever managed to grow on the island. All that was visible were a few twisted twigs that poked from a crevice above their heads.

They climbed a steep hill, bounced down the lee side, forked left at the bottom and drove through an open gate along a path flanked by giant tyre tracks that ended in a field. They bobbled across the grass, now facing the sea, when above the next rise a roof appeared.

"That's it. That's Seal Cottage," Laurie cried.

2

Valerie could see the blue-tiled roof and grey stone gable end of the cottage but it was the horizon beyond the chimneys that distracted her.

"Where's that?" she asked, pointing to a spectacular pair of mountains divided by a parabolic valley that dominated the seascape beyond the cottage.

"They're the paps of Jura," explained Robert, in a whisper.

"Paps?" Valerie thought 'fathers'. Laurie explained, "Breasts, you know." He cupped his hands to contain the curves of the distance. "A pair of breasts."

Valerie repeated, "Paps," thinking it too small a word for such grandeur. "Paps of Jura I'm delighted to meet you."

The trailer stopped outside a gabled porch and before entering, Laurie and Robert began to lift down the boxes. Valerie sat on one of the three sea mines that, unexploded and red with rust, cluttered the paving stones by the porch like giant marbles.

"I take it they're safe?"

Valerie's comment seemed to surprise Laurie who had clearly never before wondered. Even Robert shrugged his ignorance.

"Bound to be. Yes. Of course they are. Thank you, Robert. You've been a great help. We'll come over one Saturday. Let me buy the drinks. Will that be sound?"

"One Saturday," agreed Robert and left.

"Isn't he? Shouldn't we?" Valerie was surprised at so abrupt a leaving.

"He's a few things to do at the farm before evening and he needs to catch the tide. We can manage. Come."

He stretched out a hand and led Valerie, not inside, but beyond the cottage to the beach. There was a front terrace a metre wide, a small wall, but effectively, the cottage garden was the sand and the sea. It was thirty metres, no more, to the crescent of gently lapping water. In the near distance was an island Laurie named *Caolas Mor*, and beyond that rose Jura, the paps at that moment were half-hidden in cloud.

With backs to the sea, they turned to look inland. Full in view was the cottage end, stubbornly built out of multi-coloured rocks locked together by thick seams of cement. But the toughness was made lyrical by the giant arched bite of a beautiful window. From floor to above head height, and four metres across, latticed into half-metre, glass-filled squares, the window filled the wall. It was cathedral-like, massive, and would bring the outside in.

As the door was opened, the whiff of chemical toilet came from the cramped little khazi in the porch. There were pegs for hanging jackets and just inside the main space was an unlidded bucket. There were shelves that could serve as a pantry, and a few simple tools hung on nails in the wall. There were only two rooms. The one with the bed was to the right. The giant window lit the living space. The ceiling was waxed wood and the walls showed the inner surfaces of the stones of outside, but that was two feet away and thick enough to keep inside dry.

There was no upstairs but a small, square window above the arch implied a bedroom. The floors were pine, except for the hearth and hall that were protected by stone flags. At a glance, all the furnishings were basic. There was a kind of window seat in green painted wood that flanked the two-foot wide, stone sill. The table and chairs were worm-eaten and bleached, the seats string-latticed and new. There was a basket of logs, a wardrobe/cupboard that balanced a creel, a high shelf guarded by a ram's skull. The fire surround was metal, the 'place' filled with a tubular stove. A wood surround supported the stovepipe and kept the rain and flue gases out. In the far corner was a Sixties' chair, a flimsy affair in wicker, with a coracle-shaped back to recede into. The only decorative things were high up. There was a grand chandelier, a farrier's creation of six candleholders spaced around a circle of metal a metre across. Four sturdy chains supported this. Thoroughly rusted, the base made a red halo around the dark green baubles suspended in string nets in the space at the centre. They'd once been floats and markers for the lobsterpots dropped offshore.

Above the fireplace was a mirror elaborately ornamented with shells. The tall sides were edged with scallops, each successive fan hiding a tail. The centre of the top was a magnificent affair. Two dozen or more of the greyish pink shells had been layered to form a giant rosette, mimicked in miniature at the base. The effect was splendid. It was Louis Quatorze and pompadour hairstyles, a remarkable badge of dizzyingly high office.

Laurie explained he'd made it one summer when the rain left little to do. "It's wonderful," declared Valerie. "It's so . . ."

"Isn't it," agreed Laurie, equally at a loss for the word.

"I'll call it your *folie*, with an 'ie'. These things sound so much better in French."

The sill of the side window was trophied with bones, the grim collections of Laurie's teenage years. There was the single vertebra of something huge, half a metre by itself and a part of something vast. There was a delicate circle of rodent skulls, one larger that might be a fox. There was the lower jaw of something with incisors that must be prehistoric. An upper thigh like a fan cooled a skull with fangs by a bowl full of scallop shells that hadn't made it to the mirror.

The bedroom contained a bed and not much else. In the far, right hand corner was a hipbath, its enamel stained and blemished with metallic bruises. There was a minute chest of drawers and another basket full of wood. A ladder led to a mezzanine shelf that was cluttered with several oars, a bundle of gardening canes and two saucepans with smaller pans inside. Everything there was skilfully netted with spiders' webs.

As the boxes came in it was clear they would have to double as both carrier and container. The trunk of clothes would serve as their wardrobe; her box of books, upended, would become the 'case'; his painting kit was instantly scattered but she would always return it to the original carrying place.

The stone shelf in the entrance hall was effectively the kitchen. There was a double gas burner there already and they added another. They'd bought a number of canisters and Laurie's uncle had made sure the domestically large one, hidden behind a shabby, dangling curtain, was full.

The tins and packets she scattered everywhere; the clothes she left alone. It was important to make up the bed but Laurie had already gone. She lifted her eye from his box of materials, ransacked then scattered in the living room, and glimpsed him outside, by the edge of the sea, with a sketchbook in his hand.

"Good God!" Valerie said this, not him. The low, evening sunlight was playing on Jura and had turned the whole island salmon pink.

"It's ridiculous," she added.

"I just had to get the colour. What do you think?" His sketchbook was covered in swatches, each moving towards the level of gaudy before their eyes.

"It's so extreme. It's tasteless. No one will believe the colour." Valerie grinned with delight.

"Despite the pink, almost pure pink and despite the orange … it really is an orange." Laurie was furiously overlaying one oil pastel over another, there'd been no time for paints, brushes, easels. He'd no idea how long this effect would last. It would be the best part of an hour but it could easily have gone in a minute. It just needed one uncooperative cloud.

"But it's muted. See. I need a gentling tone."

It wasn't the Mediterranean intensity she'd first thought. Valerie offered, "Greek", and pre-empted his denial with "Bleached by the wind".

"Yes. Yes, that's near. But I don't think it's lost anything." His voice was breathless as he greedily rushed to capture the colour of this light.

"Bleached means robbed, less than. I don't think this is inferior."

"Nor I. What then?"

"The light is so low and it's coming from the ocean. Oceanic light."

He smiled and stopped rushing; wrote his phrase in red pastel on the page. "Greek light falls on your head. It comes from above, over you, and casts shadows, magnificent shadows that leave the colour pure. I can take the blue and the turquoise straight from the tube. I can't here. And the light colours a sea, not an ocean. Jura is being lit from the ground up. You know, in Wales, you get beams of light. Remember, what was the name of that painter? We were there, one Easter?" Valerie smiled her encouragement, hoping for clues, not wanting to divert his excitement.

"David someone, massive canvasses. Lived in a stupidly exposed cottage in Snowdonia. The name doesn't matter."

"No. It doesn't. Go on."

"He painted shafts of light that", he paused and attacked the page, "knifed through the gloom and lit something precise: a rock, a petal, a half-rainbow over splashed spring water. The Mediterranean light is bigger than David somebody's spotlight. It's bright, footlights, front lit. Dazzling. Beautiful, as spot-lit rocks are beautiful. But this. Oh look at this." He waved at the glowing warmth of the radiant pink and orange light on the mountains of the island. "This is inside the rock. The light enters at ankle height and seeps upwards. The mountains are suffused. That's the word, isn't it? Entirely filled with this colour." He showed Valerie his final mix. She nodded. The sun dimmed and he started a new page.

Then it stopped. The light died from the peaks first and within seconds, at striding pace, the grey rocks returned, in readiness for night. Valerie stayed looking at artist and place, already a little in awe of both.

"Now we must rush and use the last of the light. When it's dark it's dark."

3

Laurie helped with the bed, lit the chandelier candles but no fire, and put everything to hand for the night. There was a torch in each room, boxes of matches, tapers, candles and gaslights. In the porch there were storm lamps and Laurie checked these for fuel. They ate a supper of pasta topped with sauce from a jar. There was some cottage crockery in an enamel bowl but they'd thought to bring their own. They picked a few pieces from a stylish set amongst their wedding gifts and a few glasses. The linen and duvets were of use but so many of their presents plugged in.

The candles cast a gentle light but it wasn't enough to read by. They would need to rise with the day and intrude less into the hours after dark. Tonight was so strange, and although tired, neither could sleep quickly. They fondled each other hopefully. Neither was really in the mood. There was too much to take in, especially for Valerie, and they'd been so randy the night before both felt sated and sore.

When Laurie snuffed out the last candle, on the floor at his side of the bed, the darkness was absolute. There were no curtains at any of the windows, no moon, and low cloud masked off the stars. There was no other light on the island, no streets to be lit, no cars. At some point of danger on Jura, a lighthouse swept its occasional warning across the bay, but in-between it was black.

And the other new thing was the silence, the sort that echoes and keeps you on edge. If there was any sound it was a stranger; any footfall or cry, it couldn't be right. They'd just moved from central Glasgow where people exchange shouts all night and buses change gear and stereos play and planes fly over and trains rumble by. It was only lulls in the noise that disturbed you. The quiet seemed out of place. Soon the rustle of the sea on the beach and the swish of wind through the grass of the dunes would impel a sleep. But meanwhile, Valerie heard a spider step or something bigger scurry down the roof. And what was that creeping from the sea half-lit by the beam of the lighthouse?

He perched on the edge of the bed and sketched her sleeping face. She was turned away from him and partly hidden by the sheet. They slept under a duvet but added top and bottom sheets for a little extra warmth and to extend the clean-life of the cover, laundering now would be far from easy. Valerie was between hairstyles. The grey light beyond the window was enough to define the edges of her spikey fringe. Not long before, she had had it cut short to hug the neat roundness of her skull.

The effect was too severe or so Laurie thought, in the first seeing, the night it was done. She'd added grey streaks to her brown and the mixture aged her, added a torment to her narrow face and meagre form. She looked emaciated and the clearly exposed skull protruded her ears and made her eyes stare. She couldn't be made ugly, her features were too well organised for that. But the look was startling, 'raw' and 'exposed' were the words Laurie had offered when forced to define his response.

"What is it you don't like?"

"I do like it."

"No, you don't."

"I do, really. But for the wrong reasons."

"Which are?"

He thought out the reply.

"It doesn't suit my idea of you. It's too severe. But it makes you more interesting to draw."

That was not a good reason and jangled a nerve. Laurie painted landscapes outside, to be finished in a studio and still-lifes inside, of anything found. But he did draw the faces of characters local to a pub, city or island. He was skilled at catching a likeness and his juvenile sketchbooks were full of such work. He enjoyed going to life class where he'd made countless images of the nude figure. He liked to work fast, in different media, linocuts were a favourite as they offered easy potential for stylisation. But he'd never drawn Valerie, at least, not when she was aware. He said she'd never asked. She didn't feel she needed to but when she chanced upon sketches made in the past, when he was seeing someone else, it annoyed her the more.

"You'd better draw me now then, if I'm finally interesting. I wasn't ever going to ask, you know," she added.

"No. I realise you can be hurt." He avoided saying 'stubborn'. He'd not drawn her before because ... in truth, it was never clear to him. It was something to do with distancing, turning her into the object of his gaze instead of the subject of his care. An inarticulate part of his brain, that couldn't form words of advice, nevertheless stayed his hand, hinting at dangers in the act.

They were dismissed. He drew and drew. Valerie enjoyed his intense looking. She was a good model, skilled at sitting still. Her mind was always active so she'd plenty of places to go. Laurie always left her nowhere. In prints, she was a collection of significant white spaces on black. He never painted her but when drawing there were always double, even triple profiles—part faces, sometimes just an eye—in space. He didn't give her a context.

That first morning on the island he did. He drew the edge of the bed, the line of the window, the wall of sand outside. He gave her head something to lie on, a place and a narrative in which to belong.

Out of sight, under the cotton (he'd inched forward and pried, had begun to loosen the longer hair laying there) but thought better of it and left her as found. Now the nape of her neck was hidden the added grey had inched to the edge. Her face was softening as the returning curves and flounce of hair balanced the angularity of her looks.

But in the drawing the face itself looked rounded. He'd shown it sinking into a pillow, islanded in white, serene for the moment. The second she woke she would frown as her mind took its grip on the world. In this dawn silence he loved her and crept away unheard. He left his drawing on the table and added an inscription that made it a gift.

If you love me
Stay awhile
And I'll die
With you.

A few lines from *The Spanish Tragedy*, a play she'd read at school. The words appealed to them both as a sign of the long term, a vow that would last all the futures they could guess at, both difficult and glad. The sentiment seemed tougher than romantic so he was happy to use it too.

She was thrilled when she found the drawing and added other words of her own.

If I die
Nothing has mattered
But you.
Nothing at all.

And the surprise was, she meant it. The sudden certainty took her breath. She'd found it easier to write down than to say. She read her sayings with as much interest as a stranger. She learnt from them too, realised in an oblique way that her own words revealed as much as they expressed. Turning her feelings into words and finding definition of how she felt in the literature of others was a necessary hobby. Laurie knew she loved him, surely that much was clear, but other men had declared her enigmatic. It seemed she wasn't obvious in what she felt. Laurie made her make it clearer. He demanded she try.

At first she came to him at a tangent, offering poetic signposts as routes to how she felt.

"Listen to this, please, Laurie, listen. It's just two lines.

And we always castled opposite sides
So our pawns led brief but exciting lives."

She smiled as if she'd explained it all. He stood as baffled as before.
"Doesn't that help?"
"No. Is that one of yours?"
"Of course not. It's by . . ." She would need to check. "I didn't write it. It's too good for me."
"Good or not, I'm no judge, obviously, but it's not an answer to my question and it's just somewhere else to hide."
With a shocking simplicity, he'd asked her when together on that night in the past: "Are we a couple or just visitors to each other's lives?"
She'd liked the way he'd expressed it and was distracted by the sound so missed the content of his words. He would force her to an answer. He made no apology for his lack of tact.
"I don't know what I'm to allow myself to feel," he stated, slowly, accentuating each word. "I don't want to hurt."
"I know."
"I think you're being defensive and evasive and—look at me, please— look at me."
"I don't need to, Laurie. I know I am doing what you say, that's why . . ."
She tried to reintroduce the lines of poetry but he wanted to use words of his own.
"It's as if you are drifting, not in control. As if this isn't your decision, when it is."

Laurie left after breakfast with everything he needed for the day. All that he wore was traditional: wool, waxed cotton, canvas and leather. He did own a pair of Gortex boots, a three hundred tog fleece and more than one breathable Helly Hansen top. But when he worked he dressed old-fashioned. He looked like a casual Paul Cézanne with more than one mountain to climb.
Valerie had disliked her breakfast. It would take time to become accustomed to the chemical taste of long-life milk in her tea. She cleared the table, happy to make it her own, with a scattering of books from her cardboard case. But first, she would clean and improvise something protective for the bed. With no ceiling above, she stared into the gables and witnessed the teeming life that thrived there, until now unnoticed and unknown. What the spider didn't trap fell onto her pillow and although harmless and tiny, she didn't want such beings that close to her face.

She needed a canopy, the time-honoured solution to catch dizzy mice or clumsy rats. Her prey was less massive so a spare sheet would have the strength. It was getting it up above them and keeping it there that was the task.

She would use the oars. Tied to each bed leg, the four blades would ably keep the sheet aloft. When they did, it still looked improvised, until covered with the green netting she'd found tangled amongst the oars. She hooked four hoops over splinters in the rafters to give a grand sweep to the affair. It looked good and served a purpose, the ample net falling down the ends and sides, proof against any mosquito of Amazonian size.

She dragged the hipbath outside and gave it a good wash. Once dry she used its blemishes as the centres of flowers crudely painted with pots of acrylic from Laurie's supply. Yellow daisies and garish poppies entwined with inappropriate stems and leaves, quickly brightened the sad interior and changed the ugly bath to a pretty chair to sit in by the bed.

She swept and sprayed polish onto every wooden surface to trap the dust. She began, but didn't continue to clean the glass of the cathedral window in the living room. It really wasn't dirty. The air here was pristine. A dust of sand lingered on the edges of the frames. You could feel its presence everywhere even when too fine to see. But Valerie realised that the nature of sand is clean. It is only offensive in the mouth. The crystals of its makeup only melt under heat but when cold on clothes or skin it doesn't feel like dirt. Valerie felt untroubled by its constant presence, invisibly blown in by the outside winds.

The sea and the sight of Jura calmed her and content with her morning's efforts, she settled to her reading at the table.

4

Laurie was on the western edge of the island working on a painting of a rock. In the distance he could see the buildings of the farm with its huge barns and outbuildings and the walls and roof of the Priory at its side. The farm was leased to members of his family at a rent that was low even before the Great War. His uncle was the last in line and his retirement would coincide with the end of the lease and the eventual sale of the land. Oronsay was practically worthless. The buildings were unsound, the dilapidation thorough, the damp engrained, the roof beyond neglect. It would take a deep purse and an obsessive care to make this place grand again. Laurie was saddened by this gradual decay.

As he crossed the beach at the base of the point, he stared down the narrow channel of sea. It was called *Port na Luinge* but in Laurie's mind it was always the place of the whale. One summer, as a child, playing at the sea's edge, his eye had been drawn to the magnificent presence of a giant black creature that sighed its presence, and then spouted to confirm it was 'whale'.

"Whale! Whale! Whale!" he'd cried but there was no one else to hear. He couldn't contain his need to share. Who would believe him? Its size was probably exaggerated when seen with a child's eye, but he'd swear to this day that its back was as high as the land. The tail, when it rose, was oddly scarred where other creatures had taken out bites. What he remembered most had little to do with size; in fact its smallness was the greatest shock of all. As he'd run along *Rubha Breac*, the name of land to the north of the whale, he'd caught a glimpse of its eye. It was so small and much further back than he'd expected. It was looking and moved to focus. Laurie was certain he'd looked into that eye and had been seen. It was so sad looking. Such a small portal, lost in the huge body it owned.

As the great being edged closer to shore, Laurie realised the danger it was in. It was too big to turn round where it was; further inland was wider but dangerously shallow.

'Which way was the tide running?' he'd asked, out loud, praying it was coming in, not out. If rising, the whale might just survive, the water deep enough to edge itself round. He'd shouted instructions, told it what to do in a desperate attempt to save its life. Even now, he wondered if it was polite for such a small boy to speak so bossily to something that could swallow him whole. He'd waved his hands, pointed to the sea, clambered higher, beyond eyeshot to lead the way. When nothing changed, he regained the beach then ran into the water to splash and splash his warning of the lethal dangers ahead. He attended the hapless creature for more than an hour when, without warning, it sank from view. By the time he'd reached high ground the whale was nearly gone, swimming backwards with no apparent effort, much to Laurie's surprise.

"Can they do that, Uncle Stuart? Can they go backwards at any time?" he'd asked his bemused guardian, greedy for information to explain what his eyes had seen.

"I'm not sure, lad. It's certainly rare. They tend to push forwards onto the beach. Once there, they die. It's happened before, in that very place, but not in my time and there were lots of them, but tiny ones compared to yours. I'd say you saved it. I reckon your warnings were just in time. I bet it dozed off and didn't realise where it was. I'd guess your splashing woke it up and your pointing put it right. Well done, young Laurie. You did something special today. If I were you, I'd feel proud."

He did, whatever the truth of the outcome of his act. He always looked for whale whenever he crossed this bay.

The first sketches of the day had been to do with texture. It was the surface that intrigued him. He'd nosed up to the rocks and discovered a range of colours only such close looking could reveal. There were greens, pinks and a mauve, marble white, yellows and greys. Lined and patched, scarred like ancient handprints, this was nature's Jackson Pollock, only somehow more apt. The lichens and the mosses engraved in, and embossed on, the rock created the same exciting surfaces. Layer on layer, at times fibrous, sometimes sheer, as the light jumped across the textures, it surprised the eye as skilfully as those studio-created drippings but this was less immense. The pleasure was in the privacy. The places of greatest variety were out of sight, on the hidden side, only offered for the most curious of eyes.

The subject of his major painting, already well advanced on that first day of work, started out as both seat and shelter, a hideout on the edge of the beach that excluded the powerful wind with its prickly content of sand. Once aware of its beauty, he shifted to a spot further back. He sat on the sand and this looking up added grandeur to his prize. The rock was ancient and layered. It had once lain as strata, neatly banded, a hundred slices thick, and comfortably horizontal. But now, it pushed through the sand, the lines of its formation at a forty-five degree angle to the earth. The wind had blasted it smooth and apart from grainy blemishes sneaking into its flank, the rock was black with an ebony shine where wet. The angled sides fractured into crevices but the exposed top, two metres wide, presented the edges of the layers like thick pieces of stacked slate, resting upright, together, then pushed so that the parting layers looked like scales, or a thousand fins. It was the discarded tail of a rock dinosaur, bits of a Stegosaurus with no spikes. Laminates and plates, the ribbing of the sides, the shining blacks against the sand and the distant curve of *Ben Oronsay* mimicked the foreground shape and acted as a distant horizon for the piece. All these elements offered Laurie the perfect subject for a large-scale painting in oils.

He returned in the late evening, full of excitement for the work. He forewarned her of his arrival by shouting out 'Valerie' as he approached the cottage through the dunes.

"How did you get on?" she asked him politely.

He raised the canvas for scrutiny by way of reply.

"Yes," she nodded, whimsically, hardly focussing on the painting. He frowned his confusion and propped the canvas against the wall. She'd stepped outside to meet him, attracted by her shouted name. He took a few steps back and with a cooler look, wondered if he'd overestimated the value of his start.

"I'd thought . . ." He began rocking on his heels to vary his viewing of the scene.

"Will you do this every day?" she asked him, coldly.

"I don't suppose I'll always be so lucky. I literally sat on this. I'm sorry. I wasn't being deliberately obtuse. You didn't mean the painting. What's wrong?"

She wrapped her arms around herself thwarting his embrace. "You've been so long." She shivered despite his warmth.

"I wasn't following the time. I came back when the light weakened. I thought you'd find me, if you had a need."

"I didn't know where you were, Laurie."

"When the sea is running, I can never be more than a mile away, and that's at the very limits of the land. If you go outside and stand on the dune above the roof, you can see where I've been all day. If the wind is kind, you've only to shout out loud and I'd hear you on all the flat pieces of land. If I'm going to climb, then I'll be able to see you. I don't want you to be afraid here, and I don't want you to feel alone. When I'm out there, I . . . You come too. I don't have to work alone. I'll draw you in the landscape. I'll . . . I don't know what I'll do each day. It isn't something I've planned. Today was just a start."

Something she was whispering interrupted him.

"What did you say?"

Still she whispered, her face buried in his chest.

"It's good."

"What is?"

"The picture," She wriggled free and finally looked at him. "Your picture. It's going to be really good." Her burst of insecure laughter shuddered into tears.

"I've never found trusting easy, Laurie. It was your confidence in me—no, wrong word—certainty. There was a, I was going to say 'benign' but 'innocent'— and I don't mean that rudely—'innocent' is a better word. You tempted me to believe I was better than I was because of your innocent acceptance of me as reliable and predictable. No, that makes me seem boring, which I may become but I wasn't then."

"Or now," Laurie interrupted her, his mouth full of food, so his 'n' came out 'm'. "Sorry." He waved her to continue, and dunked his face into a bowl full of vegetables, a profligate ragout of all the fresh things in the pantry.

"You see, I always think that I've said things to you, but maybe I've only thought them. When you asked if we were a couple and you declared us one that night, forced a crisis, made me say it, I really thought I had, you know, I really did. And the reason I lived alone and never let you stay, not all night, not deliberately, was to practise, no, rehearse your leaving me, finally. Like the others did, always. I used to let them stay and they left. So, I thought, if I kept you out, you might linger. But you did stay."

"Why so surprised?" Laurie, his empty bowl placed silently on the floor, didn't turn around but looked through the window into the distance, its dark highlighted by the occasional glimmer of a fishing boat light.

"Nothing had happened to give me confidence. Whatever I appeared: self-contained, mature, together, 'cool', my own man/woman, whatever the titles and the assumptions, whether glib or knowing, I never was confident." She paused. "I bought this with me. In fact, I intended at some time to give it to you as a gift." She was referring to a notebook, a rather splendid affair, in hard covers adorned with a late eighteenth century block print full of long-legged birds and exotic flowers in gold, bleached reds and browns. The print carried to the inside covers, front and back, and the book contained some of Valerie's writings, neatly written out in long hand, and dated.

"They're sayings, thoughts, prose poems. It's not grand enough to be called poetry but it tells me what I am. What I was. You can know, no need to guess, what I was thinking when you came. And before."

The 'before' worried Laurie. He knew there'd been other men, a number. Not a lot. He was confident in his sexuality and with good cause. He'd attracted women with ease from the moment he understood what they were. He was allowed to be promiscuous. Casual and even dismissive, he attracted little but praise even when his actions might be thought cruel. Women forgave him. It was not ever his fault. Laurie thought it his destiny never to be brought to account. Affairs would overlap but the heroines never accidentally met. They could be from the same school, the same class, on one daring occasion, the same family, but the ways parted neatly, the farewells were kindly and former doors were always left ajar.

College was a continuation of the same. All these liaisons were entered on freely and when they ended, the participants knew they'd only themselves to blame. When he first met Valerie, Laurie had an eventful past but there was an air about her that made him feel sexually small. She was something of a mystery, hadn't dated any of the students he knew but still there were whispers of scandal. She'd been seen in the company of tutors; was clearly privileged in whom she got to meet. She sat on every key committee and was respected as a scholar. A doting friend of Laurie's observed, as Valerie walked past, "Not only is it beautiful, it's a smart arse as well."

"Here." Valerie offered the closed book but Laurie waved it back.

"Read something to me, from early on, before we met."

"They're not very good, you know."

"How would I know? I'm a painter but I know what I like." He smiled his encouragement, leant forward from the window seat, and stroked the fingers that held the book high above the table. He wondered what he'd hear. He was a little nervous.

She opened to the first page and a photograph fell out onto the table. She picked it up at the same time as him. She let Laurie take it.

"It's from when we first met and I had hair." He was staring happily at the photograph, remembering it all, the smells, sights and first touching of that challenging new being that stared out of the picture and looked, with equal fascination, across the few feet of space that separated them now.

"I don't know how to speak this. They're just slightly rearranged thoughts, written to me."

"Is that the end?"

"What?"

"Have you started?" His teasing distracted her. Then, smiling, she relaxed.

It is cold
And so I slide
Beneath the duvet
Where once, once
A man has kept me warm.
There are nights
Sometimes afternoons
When the light
Laces shadows through my window
And I,
Stretched upon my
Iron framed bed
Am so lonely
Thinking how
Nice
It would be
To have an old lover
In the warmth
Content
Beside me.
Yet,
I've thrown them all out.
Gently, though.
They understood, they said.
Except that half-year bastard.
And tell me
They respect my ambitions and
New needs
And offer sexless help
Now sex is
Impossible.
So, I laugh
And lower my eyes
At yet another man.
Relieved.
Then,
I remember
The agony
Of a blue toothbrush
In my bathroom
Still.

She looked down, embarrassed in the silence, oddly shy.

"Say something," she prompted.

"It was great. You've taken me by surprise. It's so sad. I didn't know you were so sad."

"You couldn't have known."

"Read another."

"Really?"

"Yes. It was nice. It sounded so like you but . . . not. I don't know. Read another."

"Okay." She turned a couple of pages. "This one's sort of funny. It's called *Don't Call Me*.

'I know I'm ambivalent about it
But I really don't want you to call.'
So he called me at college and
I said, 'Don't call me at college
I can't possibly talk to you there.'
So he called me after six and I said,
'I'm on my way out, please don't call me after six
My flat mates answer my 'phone calls
And I don't like it.
Besides, I may not be there so,
Please don't call me after six.'
So he called me in the morning before college began
And I said, 'Please don't call me in the morning,
I'm trying to get off to college and it's not
A good time to talk, so please, don't call me
In the morning.'

So I called to tell him not to call me at all,
That I really didn't want to talk to him any more.
But he was so happy that I called,
He spoke brightly and said he was so thankful that
At last I'd called him that I couldn't say
'Don't call me.'
And so he still does.

She looked up sheepishly to acknowledge Laurie's happy applause.

"That's great. More! More! My wife's a star."

The word shocked her. There was nothing and no one to ratify this change of status.

She'd actually forgotten they were married and that she was now someone's wife.

"You read them. I copied them out for you."

"One more. Please."

"A short one. It's called *Stupid Me.*

I don't fall for businessmen
With long neat fingers
White GTi's
A real heavy act
And a wife
I fall for foolhardy academics
With sensitive blue eyes
Greying hair
Golden thighs
And short, capable fingers.
Oh yes, and a wife.

His silence was longer. This one he didn't like. It was too recent and it shocked him. Her sexual knowledge of a married man threatened the achievement of his loving.

"Was that true?"

"Which part?"

"His being married."

"Yes. That part was true."

"Did it feel wrong?"

"No."

"Did you ever think of his wife?"

"Never."

"Honestly?"

"Honestly. I saw that as his problem."

"She might have looked on you as hers."

"Why the moral tone?"

"Isn't it an issue? Weren't you ever squeamish?"

She puzzled over his choice of words. "Squeamish. What an odd word. What do you mean?"

"I don't know. It just came out. It seemed to follow on the heels of 'moral'. It's clearly a problem of mine not yours."

"I never concerned myself with the rights and wrongs of it. If I'm to blame in that, then I'm sorry. But, he was over twice my age. If there were issues of morality to resolve, I figured he'd already done it and in taking responsibility for his actions, had somehow absolved me from needing to do the same. I didn't ask how he came to be free during the nights, the long weekends, even whole weeks to be alone with me in Italy and France. It was his business. He did all the arranging. I was available and complied. I trusted the wisdom that his age implied."

"Just how old was he?"

"You can answer that yourself. You know him. He thinks very highly of you. He says that you've 'polished' me. That when I left him, I was rough and opaque, a diamond but, with no shine. He says you've made me glitter, as only a young man can."

"Exactly who? No."

"If you ask, I'll answer. There's nothing secret from you, Laurie. I'll tell you everything you want to know, answer every question that you ask with complete honesty. That is the marriage. But I don't feel obliged to blurt out everything of my life. If it's now, then it matters: if then, who's to say? You can know all you want. I'll do the telling, but don't make me responsible for the effect of what's told. It's up to you how much truth you want and the level of detail. I'm a woman, I prefer to be kept guessing. That way I can make up all sorts of vile versions of your past. Or, believe the better of you, instead. Well, do you want to know his name or just whether he was better than you at sex?"

"No. Yes. Oh, I don't know. You decide."

"No. That won't do."

"In that case, don't tell me his name."

"Okay."

"But."

"Yes?"

"It's just . . ."

"Laurie, without going back on anything I have said, you need to know that there has been no one in my life who is as exciting to me sexually as you. You didn't so much polish me as polish me off. I still haven't got my breath back, and it's been over a year."

They'd always known that the other existed but occupied different parts of the college for most of this time. His work was entirely practical, with teaching credentials tacked on. Hers was only partly active, most of her course was theoretical, historical and, eventually, entirely academic. Their paths and social worlds hadn't connected. He'd noticed her, even managed the odd sketch at a shared life class. She wasn't the model intended.

One Monday she appeared in his studio making paintings as part of her course that included symbolism and naive art. She was particularly keen on Gustave Moreau. She'd been to his house/museum in Paris a few weeks before. She was yet to become distracted by the works of Marc Chagall. It is possible to hide technical inadequacy behind the assumptions of the naive but Valerie could draw and use paint with more confidence than a theoretician was allowed. The full-time artists felt obliged to be patronising about her skill. Laurie's 'That's far too good for an amateur' was the nearest to praise.

"I do it to learn how to appreciate their skill, not to display my own," she explained.

"Clearly," had been Laurie's comment. He provoked an undreamt of egotism in her.

Happy to be self-denigratory, she hadn't realised how much criticism could hurt. Or was it just his? He hoped to be encouraging, explaining later that he thought her more talented than a copyist, skilled enough to evolve something of her own rather than work in the style of others. But it wasn't important enough to matter, not finally. Her sense of value would lie elsewhere. But the need of his good opinion was a surprise.

They watched each other working, talking, just simply being there, drawing attention that was extraordinary to them both. The attraction that began intensely didn't grow, it simply asserted itself as a presence. So, long before any speaking, they felt familiar with each other, better known than any courting chatter could have achieved. There were no preliminaries. Their first conversations were overtly sexual, but dispassionate and oddly matter of fact.

"One day we'll have sex together, won't we?" had been her opening sentence late in the afternoon.

"Without a shadow of a doubt." He had not even looked up from his painting but the stirrings in his baggy trousers signalled a desire more urgent than his flippant words implied. She noticed and pointed with the painting end of the brush she was using, nearly smearing the jutting area of trouser that he could do little to disguise.

"I see something's started without us."

Her staring aroused him further.

"Can I see it?"

She wasn't looking at his painting but, just in case he'd misunderstood, he stepped back from the canvas to offer her the chance.

It was not where she was looking.

There were screens defining areas, hanging curtains to mask brick walls, poor lighting and almost no other students, so they slipped from sight quite easily and she undid his trousers with no help. She knelt, still looking, pulling everything free. Holding the penis in a confident grip, she bowed her head to surround it with her mouth. Her lips and tongue seemed expert. He came within seconds of her start. It seemed effortless on her part. She rearranged his trousers and didn't fumble when fastening the awkward buttons.

"We will have sex, one day," she whispered in a reassuring voice. Laurie was so breathless and astonished by these events so much beyond his control, that all he could say was "Thank you" as she walked calmly away.

But none of this was as it seemed. Rather than calm, there was turmoil. She was so excited she could hardly breathe. The ecstasy wasn't sexual, its main ingredient was relief. Relief after fear. She had never done anything like it but there was something about Laurie that said she could. She'd always wanted to be as daring as her mind's eye invited her to be. There was certainly a desire to be naughty but nearly all she did was proper, controlled easily by inner voices that were part parent, part society, partly her own. She was a dutiful lover, expecting little for herself. The men she had experienced couldn't know her and were either skilfully indifferent or so imaginatively excited as to be of little use, even to themselves. She hadn't minded, felt little engagement, and tolerated the act and its surroundings for the companionship it could bring.

Laurie's manner invited her to be sexual, so she'd dared to experiment, trusting to the glint in his eye. She'd never before had a penis in her mouth. She'd seen them, had her hand clasped around them by their owners, agitated the odd one, but the idea wasn't very inviting to part swallow what was often squat, ugly, rarely even neat. But, she thought her experience lacking, wanted to try a young one that probably knew the ropes all by itself. She guessed Laurie wouldn't mind and if she got it wrong it wouldn't matter; he'd probably laugh, not take it seriously or to heart. It seemed such a touchy business. The men were so serious and intent. A recent, older lover had been profoundly disappointed in her refusal to please him in this act. As he'd explained, more baffled than annoyed, he could understand his wife's refusal because it had been used to make a child. That was reason enough for his wife but not his mistress. She couldn't bring herself to do it, even with her eyes closed. It didn't appeal.

But there was lightness about Laurie that gave her confidence even to get things hopelessly wrong. She was no longer anyone's mistress, so could misbehave according to her own lights, free of anything expected in the performance of her role. Nothing was planned, it was just an idea, it was something she might do with him if the opportunity arose, and it did arise, in embarrassing splendour, behind the right pocket in Laurie's trousers that weren't quite baggy enough.

Laurie was delighted. He assumed she was an expert, or at least, this was something she did. He couldn't believe it was her first time. It would never be as good again. Perhaps it was the venue, or the suddenness of the act, the enormous daring of the woman and the delighted compliance of the male all conspiring to make this first encounter so successful, and so exquisite in their minds.

There was an element of simple jealousy in Laurie's response to the poem. He did resent the knowledge of an old man's capable fingers exploring the body of his young wife. But he dared compare thigh with thigh, whether sunburnt golden or Hebridean white. He rehearsed the assertive bravado of the youthfully intact against the disintegration of the old. He could flaunt his body's resilience, taunt the aches of age in flesh lined and diminished.

But it was the experience that informed this lesser capability that he was in no position to combat. It was what was known and already accomplished by a man of letters, children, marriage and degrees. How much more did he know that rendered Laurie naive? He and Valerie were very new. They'd had no time to make a history and just beginning made them vulnerable. Simple time would put him in the ascendent but a past he'd not been in made him feel insecure.

But there was no need, Valerie reassured him. "There's nothing for you to fear. And there's nothing in here", she laid the book of writings on the table and pinioned it with the very tip of the outstretched first finger of her right hand, "that I want to hide, from you, from me, from us. It's a part of me but it cannot challenge what we have, now or in the future." She rummaged through the corner of her upended, cardboard bookcase balanced on the table's far edge. From a pile of unused cards, still in their cellophane wrappers sealed with the dot of their price, she selected a brightly toned watercolour of pink and orange flowers filling a green and yellow garden that spanned three, not two sections of card. In the centre she wrote 'I love you' in a hundred cross-kisses. An arrow through a heart on the right hand facing page declared 'V 'loves' L'. But, the left hand portion carried the message that Laurie was reading, a smile gently playing on his face.

'THIS CARD ENTITLES LAURIE MCPHEE
To: Unfailing and unfaltering love from me.
To: Kisses on demand whenever I am in the vicinity.
To: Constant reassurance at any time of day and night.
To: Naughty deeds whenever the opportunity arises.
To: Loyalty in every way.
To: Instant obedience (This was crossed out.) 'Sorry, I forgot myself.'
To: My complete love at all times.
Expiry Date: Never.
Signed: Valerie McPhee [Mrs.]'

As he looked up she said, "Don't lose it. It's a very powerful thing."

"I won't," he promised her and himself.

He thanked her silently for this game. It had distracted him and diverted his anxious thoughts. She was so skilled in making things fun. The first time they'd made love it wasn't accidentally, late one night, after a few beers or a deliberately elegant meal. It was in the broad daylight of lunchtime, by invitation, and carefully planned. The flat was certain to be empty. He'd knocked but the door fell open. 'Come in' was written in lipstick on a piece of pink card on the wall inside. There was also an arrow that pointed up the stairs to where Valerie's room was. Along the porch floor and in the centre of each riser, a paper footprint, bare, with cut-out toes, said 'This Way' in its centre, and 'Pick Me Up' as an afterthought in tiny writing on the heel. He followed both instructions and arrived at the bedroom with ease, dropping the trail of access in a scattering pile beside the partly open door that also said 'Come in'.

Obedient and excited, he encountered Valerie in the centre of the bed. She was entirely naked, perched half lotus in the middle of a tablecloth surrounded by the ingredients of an extravagant meal.

"Red or white?"

He picked red wine but she selected the lipstick intended and drew neat circles around each nipple and deftly marked the centre of her navel before he'd recovered from the surprise.

They fed each other. Everything was perfectly bite-sized. Twirls of spinach roulade, rolls of smoked salmon, unravelling, stuffed tomatoes, olives and vine leaves, tiny brown rolls with unknown seeds, and a recognisable taste to the coating on the crust that no amount of licking could guess. They were actually coupled during pudding and managed lemon ice-cream face to face. It felt entirely natural being clothes-less. They were more self-conscious when dressed.

'How do I look?' 'Does this match?' were questions of insecurity, realising the result of dressing was adjustable. When utterly naked, nothing could be changed.

They'd already shared scars and blemishes, a mark of darker skin on her belly, a weird patch of purple on her neck. He'd had appendicitis and a stain shaped like Southern Ireland on the edge of his left buttock, which she kissed cheerily better, leaving traces of mayonnaise on Dublin.

This was an imaginative coming together. They felt innocent, childlike, oddly pure and outside of time. It was a tender, private world, a self-enclosed game with the bed as nest and they a pair of gleeful jackdaws, sharing all the trophies they had found. Their sexual loving and easy intimacy were passionate and profound but the context was playful. They weren't afraid to giggle at the most delicate of moments. It was

'Mad-Hatterish', 'Alice in Sexual Wonderland'. Separated from day-to-day existence, it was its own reality where sex and laughter mingled in blissful security and the feeling at the end of it all was entirely peaceful with eyes focussed inwards, each enclosed in a dreamy quiet.

The highlight of this meeting for Laurie wasn't the extravagance and newness and sexual delight, but a moment of sudden stop, as he mentally stood back from the scene. He had her face cradled in the crook of his arm. It was entirely framed, separate from everything else. Her eyes were flickering violet, her smile was gentle and relaxed and an access of feeling welled inside him as this beautiful face glowed with light and he could barely believe his eyes. Was this woman really his?

And still here, a few feet away, across this room? The face he'd just remembered, with its halo of joy and total relaxation, was only visible when they were making love. The sexual act wasn't needed. They had become so casually greedy they reacted to the slightest urge and performed in improbable and prosaic places: the floor, the porch, all the work surfaces in the flat's kitchen, except the one next to the sink—there was always washing-up.

What Valerie knew she needed was that certainty of intimacy achieved through a myriad of tiny gifts: touches, kisses, words, looks, situations that felt correct. Then she was tempted to give in return and relinquish a mind full of warnings, a noise of inner voices that had understood a little too much to readily trust.

"What?" she asked, puzzled by Laurie's stare.

He continued to look.

"What's wrong?" she softened her voice, a tone that acknowledged blame without any cause. She felt cold and alone in her head and craved his warmth. He said nothing but reached clumsily across the space between them, jagging the heavy table an inch across the floor. And, with a thumb outstretched above its fist, the forewarning flat palm of his other hand removing the threat of danger from his touch, he smudged away the frown that had scarred a furrow between her troubled eyes,

"Has anyone told you you're terrific today?"

"No. There's been no one to see me." She took his hand, still clasped in its fist, and uncurling the fingers in turn, spread the palm flat to her lips and kissed the smothering centre as his hand tightened to contain the whole of her face in its grip. She reinforced the pressure with the clasping of her own hands, then pulled her mouth free, gulping in air. Even in this grasping she felt freer with this man than with anyone before. Laurie could make himself invisible, disappear from an act that freed her to experience, that allowed her a space to occupy and control.

The other men seemed constantly obliged to remind her they were there. Her body felt like meat, portioned by glaring eyes, separate courses in a banquet at which she felt exposed and raw. She was to be devoured. Not all were so extreme but her exaggerations helped create the categories into which she could now place men. She thought of two painters, Pablo Picasso and her favoured Marc Chagall. She had the advantage of biography so knew more than she ought, but it seemed obvious from the actual paintings what kinds of lovers the makers were. Picasso oozed desire, the intensity of his need smacked of rape. The eyes of his models seem full of fear, the nervousness of the victim in an act of war.

His are images of possession, of devouring an object, even of dismemberment, by an egotist's eye. Body parts became weapons, so sharp, that both breasts and tongues might stab. Faces were intent, seeking their own defined pleasures. It wasn't certain he even liked women, yet he wasn't gay. He might have feared women's independence; dare not see them free.

Valerie had experienced such eager loving. She'd enjoyed it. She felt needed, so desperately important to a particular man's scheme of things. She'd been tainted but untouched by such experience for she'd enjoyed these past months a lyrical and generous loving from a man who cared for her like Chagall. Sexual loving was made easy, as simple as breathing out and in. Laurie had introduced her to this gentle, permissive way. She knew she must guard and preserve that which she could so easily destroy. Yet something perverse in her make-up dared her to do so, simply because she could.

Valerie's book of poems sat at the edge of the table like a threat. Laurie had not asked for a further reading and left alone, wouldn't look. It had been a few days now and at the end of her cleaning she always put it in its place, disappointed that he hadn't taken up her gift. Nothing was said. But then, that had been the point of the book, to obviate the need for such unnecessary explanation. Spoken words, with hurried tones and defensive sharpness could more readily hurt than her harmless sayings. She had no pretensions. They were for her and him. A way of looking at what hurt, trapped onto a white page where it could be seen clearly for what it was, or wasn't. If she had a greater skill, was truly gifted in the shaping of words, then she would have sought a public, protected from the show of intimacy by an obvious talent. But because her very best was ordinary, then this giving was intensely private and what she revealed would show in all its clumsy rawness. Another day and she'd take it back, not to destroy, but to keep to herself, where it should have stayed. She placed a flat palm on the cover, opened the book at halfway and still further to nearly the end, keeping the two sections parted by an intruding finger, let the pages flick by at an unreadable speed, closed the cover and twisted the book straight, to line up with the edge of the table.

That's where Laurie found it, minutely displaced, an hour before light on the day the book would disappear. He was wrapped in a blanket, sipping water from a cup, holding a newly-lit candle a few inches above the page. It was his, for him, about him, yet he was still nervous. Why? He supposed because it contained what he couldn't control: a past he'd had no part in, events he couldn't redefine. He always thought one of his greatest strengths was his ability to live 'now'. He stepped through problems and complications with a dismissive spontaneity that stilled other's qualms. He was good at laughter and had no regrets and tempted the most haunted to give away their guilt.

He glimpsed the book's inscription and saw it as a clue.

'I'm your wife if you will marry me.' Miranda. *The Tempest.*

He'd never had the woman who could claim the title 'wife'. That was a public statement of belonging. He would be judged by her behaviour. He needed exclusive knowledge. This one he couldn't share. She was his by statute. If she misbehaved he couldn't snigger to his mates, happy to be free of a 'wrong'un'. Valerie had to be right.

Deseo
Sólo tu corazón caliente,
Y nada más.

"Nothing more you desire, only my warm heart?" Laurie spoke in a whisper and shivered his coldness. "Doesn't she know that Lorca was gay and lusted after Dalí and Buñuel?" The quiet anger of his lips puckered the candle's flame.

Guilty? – let those
Who know not what a thing temptation is,
Let those who have not walked as we have done
In the red fire of passion, those whose lives
Are dull and colourless, in a word, let those,
If any such there be, who have not loved,
Cast stones against you . . . Oscar Wilde. 'And me.'

"Oscar bloody Wilde? What gives with all this gayness? Is there a coded message here?" He sighed, disappointed with his own thinking.

"Where are her words?" He turned the pages carefully. "She read me that. I liked that one. What's this? *Familiar.*"

'No
We will go no further.' He continued silently, mouthing the words.
'Here we stand.
Here we'll talk.
Here I'll question.
Spin out your answers.
Draw from within,
For I will know
And there shall be a
Stop to this evasion.
When I ask "Where?"
Do not cover your eyes
And shake your head.
Here I'll question.
See,
I pull the muffling
From about your
Thin throat—
And find the bones.'

"What was that all about?" He wriggled in his chair, sipped at his cup of water, as nervous as the victim of her words. "What had he done, betrayed her? It sounds like the last straw, but ..." He glanced to the top of the page and understood the title, "She calls it *Familiar*. This happened to her often, regularly, until she stood her ground. God, she was brave."

He turned the page. "What's this? Is this describing me?"

Mysterious man with labyrinthine
Depths within your eyes.

"No. That's not me. I'm the superficial one."
He turned the page.
"This is better.

Damn you! Damn a hundred times over
For entering my life and opening a door
I had thought for ever closed.

He read on to:

Damn you,
For one thing is certain,
Your stay will be ephemeral
As summer snow.

"Is that what she thought? Thinks?" He looked into the candle, squinting in concentration.

"Did she think I wouldn't stay?" He yawned and shivering, rearranged the blanket around his neck. For twenty minutes he read silently.

Scrunching his shoulders, he realised the night had turned to grey. Almost absent-mindedly, he spoke to the still burning candle.

"She's such a complex person. She's . . ." he flicked back many pages, "so passive."

Since now I dare not ask
Any gift from you, or gentle task,
Or lover's promise, nor yet refuse
Whatever I can give and you dare choose,
Have pity on us both: choose well.

"So angry:

Must it be my task
To assume the mask
Of not deserving what I may not ask?
And on a wide bed
Both arms out-spaced,
Watch the spites do battle
Inside my head.

"And so pessimistic:

For what you ask me - the
Mere arrangement of a new encounter -
Becomes a sudden
Fall of thunder, a lightning taken hard
Into my eyes. Cold indeed the sun
And deadly chill the wind,
For with that brief request
I see afar, a slow tumbling
Down the tall sky, a hauling down
Of love's bright pennants.

"And:

And, when it is over
I will avoid the corners
Where we used to sit.

"Always, when it is over."

When straw hats and sunshine and gaiety
Turn black.

He turned to the final page and pressed it open with a wide-spanned hand as if brilliantly playing more notes than an octave. "*Old Habit.* I see the pun and know it's a dress, but what you say is so sad.

Faded,
Jaded
Stitching holds it together,
Weakened and smothered by dust
Of past disappointments.
Buttons, sharp like anger,
Fashioned from Mother-of-Pearl,
Hand-sewn on life's sorrow
By me,
A foolish girl.

"And then you say you love me. I don't know how you dare." Not shivering, but really cold now, as the early light without the sun turned everything grey, he closed the book with a respectful care and set it in its place, parallel with the table's edge. He tiptoed to the bed and joined the welcome warmth that Valerie had made there.

While he slept on, tired from his vigil, Valerie kept to her resolve, and with a shrug of resignation, removed the book from the table, unread.

They adjusted to living in the light. As summer progressed the night withdrew. Between eleven and two there was a type of dusk and by three in the morning the sun was back. Not just that, the absence of dark night left the air warm. The sea was always cold. Any passing wind took the surface away that the day's sun had warmed but the shallows of their beach reached a tepid heat that they wallowed in most evenings after their meal. They rarely wore clothes. Valerie often prepared and ate supper naked. Once the tide was in their isolation was certain and no one was invited to stay.

In one of the largest sketchbooks, with blue, laminated sides, Laurie began to draw her, sometimes entirely, but more often in bits. As the pages filled, the parts of her body were depicted, scattered, like the pieces of a jigsaw not meant to fit. Laurie's observations were minute and Valerie must have complied. He anatomised her. Her vagina was often displayed, fully shown and as large as life. Her labia were surprisingly long and an object of fascination. In silhouette, viewed from some difficult angle, remembered or recreated for the sketch, they protruded free of the closed exterior flesh, like delicate ear lobes, improbably thin. Head on they closed to, ribbed, like a scallop shell fashioned from soft fabric. The vagina resembled nothing but itself. Laurie's eye was clinical, his pencil unpleasantly precise. Every joining muscle, every misaligned hair was carefully recorded, left exactly where it was. These were cold observations of an object carefully seen. There was no hint of any emotion or salacious intent.

The breasts were captured in a state of slow decline. The weeks of difficult eating meant both of them had lost weight. Laurie could afford to; Valerie could not. The earliest drawings showed her breasts as neat, perfectly rounded, with small and precise nipples at the exact centre of each round. As the weeks progressed, the area above the nipples lost the contour of its flesh. The breasts elongated, losing their fullness and developing lines. With hurtful exactness, Laurie drew each minute pucker as hairline striations in the contours of the flesh evidenced the slow removal of the fat that made them round.

Valerie's spine ran at a diagonal across pairs of pages in the book. Each segment was seeable through the skin. It was drawn like a landscape, the cracked tip of a drying furrow ploughed in a field of clay, the arc of each rib running earthwards, pushing against the ground.

There were more gentle studies of her growing hair, pages of eyebrows, others of eyes. There were noses and nostrils, ears and necks, and one long sequence of studies of the upper chest. The pronounced shoulder blades and upper ribs becoming visible above the wrinkling breasts formed a set of fan designs, as if Valerie were pictured wearing an elaborate necklace of herself.

This was a time of great permissiveness. They made love so often that they hardly noticed the act. It was never casual but they were happy to be careless, and wasted themselves in moments of accidental touching. They managed to import ample supplies of K-Y jelly to ease their greedy sexual way. Laurie had explained it was used for chapped lips, a kind of posh Vaseline and more economical than the lipstick tubes. He thought they believed him; at least, no one made sheep-bleating noises, as they would have done at school.

In the middle of the night, smearing herself with the jelly in quiet readiness for the act, she would suddenly sit across him, reaching down to thrust him home. In the half-second it took to grab it, his penis was erect, alert and fully operative, long before Laurie was awake.

"What? What's wrong?"

"Nothing. Go back to sleep. We've started without you."

"I don't know. You just can't get the staff."

"I think you have."

Valerie described their loving as 'paradisal', the adjective Frieda had used in describing her love for Bertie Lawrence. She left notes to 'Lolita Man' and, for a while, revelled in the freedom of it all. Laurie had forbidden nothing, so she dared his permission to its limits.

She loved to pinion him and despite the limits of repetition, to take him by surprise. The oars tied to the edge of the bed legs tempted her to play. Late, still light, having made love before, she would sit astride him and wriggling herself secure, locking him inside her, she would lean across him and fumble inside the cabinet drawer for a knot of tights and a tube of their cream.

"Lie still!" she would order, fending off his reaching hands.

"Don't touch!"

In full sight of Laurie's nervous eyes, she unscrewed the top of the tube and laid it open, running, on the pillow just out of his sight. Having unravelled the stockings, she would fashion one end into a slip knot noose and beckon Laurie to offer a wrist. She would slip it gently into place then snap it tight in surprise. Leaning across his face, dangling a breast into his mouth, she passed the tights around the bed, beyond the second oar and back to Laurie's waiting second wrist.

"Now!"

Pulled tight, she would secure end to end, to leave Laurie's hands high above his head. She would start to move and nudge a knee into the underside of his.

"Put your legs up."

He would.

"Higher. Higher."

She would seem to climax but that wasn't the aim; there was still something to do to him. She would reach for the tube and balance a smear of the gel that would be left, unsmoothed, at the edge, the very edge of his anus. This little bubble of cold, exquisite to feel, still felt ominous whilst unused.

She would continue to push and would whisper in rhythm, "Relax. Let me take you. Let me have this. Me."

Sensing his response, understanding a new need against her rhythm and the straining of his thighs, she would reach to the back of his legs and smooth the cream around in a diversion of gentle touching till, certain of their aim, two fingers probed for entry and then everything was thrust in this double emulation of the man, the woman, the man. And they would buckle in a flash of ecstasy and pain.

"Roll over," would end the moment. An exhausted fumbling would set him free from the restraint of this unrestrained act of sexual love.

"Laurie, I need to get off the island."

"There's no ferry."

"No, I mean Oronsay, not the whole thing."

He relaxed, but didn't ask why.

"I'm feeling a little trapped, since you ask. Sealed in 'Seal Cottage'. There's a neat little pun to describe my neat little home by our neat little beach. Don't panic. It's nothing serious. I just need to look at something big."

Laurie could think of nothing bigger than this landscape he walked in. The furthest edge of the island might well have been the end of the world. He knew that when the monks built their priory over a thousand years ago, they had no knowledge of the Americas; they thought they'd settled at the edge of the known land. It was that sense of the extreme; the limit of limits that thrilled Laurie as he painted its rocks and towering skies.

"Tell me what you're thinking? Have I blasphemed?"

Perhaps it was a kind of blasphemy to him. There was a god trapped somewhere within this land. It was beyond thinking, entirely undefined but instinctively defended. He'd gifted it all to his wife: home, history, family and place.

"I think of this island as vast and timeless. People have lived here forever, long before the monks. Those mounds behind the cottage are made from ancient shells. They're Mesolithic." He seemed to lisp. Valerie stifled a wicked snigger. She resisted the cue for a quip. He was so serious.

"And further south still are prehistoric sites. Men used to live in burrows six feet underground, with coarse-grass lids on wooden laths to close out the wind and rain."

This was her cue: "That's what I feel like, Laurie. Let me crawl out of my hole. I want a different view. These past weeks I've stayed right here, sorting out the house. You've painted and left the island while I've mended things and just read. Apart from a couple of walks to the farm for a freezing bath, I've had the same view. I want a change from staring down Jura's cleavage. That's all."

He had left the island most weeks to walk to the shop in Scalasaig. It was five miles each way and a difficult walk up to and across The Strand and the undulating narrow roads beyond. Anything heavy Robert would drop at the gate on the track to Oronsay Farm. He drove over The Strand twice weekly and there was always room in the trailer. Laurie must stand him a round. It was a while and many favours had been done in-between. Maybe that night, if they went for a walk.

"Get ready. I'll run to the farm and make some calls."

"Where are we going?" She enjoyed his sudden changes of mood. She was good at nursing a sulk and could brood over a grumble for days. He never did. Or at least, he never seemed to.

"Kiloran Bay, in the far north of Colonsay. It's the biggest thing on the two islands."

He smiled in anticipation of this new gift.

"How far?"

"Come on. Get ready."

"How far is it?"

"Ten miles."

"That's . . ."

"Each way."

"What?"

"I have a plan and a surprise. If you let me go." She'd taken his arm.

"What about the tide?"

"It's in."

"Exactly. Do we swim?"

"No. Private ferry. I'll beg a lift from the oysterman. The islands almost meet over there and he's got an amazing tractor with huge, thin wheels and a seat high in the air, and a small boat, if it's too deep to drive. And, if all else fails, we'll swim."

He ran up the dune behind the cottage, ignoring her reservations, just reminding her once more to, "Get ready" against his quick return.

The tide was rising but by no means full and would be gone on their late evening return. They skirted the edge of The Strand on a narrow track that the oysterman had fashioned to reach his newly built house high on the hill.

They were ferried across, balanced precariously either side of the oysterman, aboard the long-wheeled contraption that could almost defy the tide. Not quite, so parting was quick to ensure a safe return, as Laurie and Valerie waved their farewells from the solidity of the parking area at the landward end of The Strand. And there lay Laurie's surprise, trustingly left, with a note attached.

"Bikes!" declared Valerie, genuinely delighted at her find.

"They're from Andrew. We owe him a pint. He says he doesn't need them today, so there's no charge. He says to leave them here tonight and Robert will bring them back to the hotel in the morning. He'll be there tonight."

"Who?" Valerie wasn't listening. She was fiddling with the gears on her bike. She'd chosen the green one, leaving Laurie the red.

"Andrew. He'll see us at the hotel."

"These are great, Laurie. It's a brilliant idea. Point the way. I'm a match for anything."

Not really true. The very first hill found her out. Laurie was strong and stopped to be polite. It shocked her how unfit she was.

"I'm knackered. How far have we gone?"

"Oh, half a mile, three-quarters at best."

"Shit. I'll never make it. What's the gearing on this thing? A thousand to one?" She'd dropped to the lowest gear of the set and pedalled furiously merely to creep up the hill. But in time, she found her breath, and soon was screaming with delight, legs akimbo, as she hurtled down the other side of the same hill.

They spent no time in Scalasaig. Ignoring the hotel and shop, they rode by. They came to rest after a very steep hill, and then another and one more added itself to the climb before freewheeling to the valley bottom that opened out to a beautiful vista on either side. They sat before Loch Fada, one of Laurie's favourite places. The lake was a necklace of three, each a kilometre long, divided where they sat by marshes and a bridge and then further on by a separating spur of land that formed the horizon and implied an ocean rather than the final lake beyond.

They rested on the stones of the bridge and Laurie took the water bottle from Valerie's hand and swapped it for his hip flask, a pigskin covered concave that fitted neatly into the hand and was filled with a good malt whisky generously diluted with water from a local spring. It was surprisingly refreshing, and Valerie demanded more when Laurie had finished his modest sip.

Loch Fada filled all the distance with blue water two hundred metres wide. Coming in from the left was a row of mighty binions spilling the cliff edges of their escarpments at varying angles into the waters at the loch side. The most distant was the most impressive, barely ten degrees from sheer: the nearest approached more gently, leaving a marshy plateau between itself and the water's edge.

A mass of tall, wild grasses grew all around the water blurring the final meetings of rock and earth and lake.

The right-hand bank was flat and wide. The waters must have been shallow there because the grasses grew far into the loch. A gentle rise and a few houses promised the edge of the land. It was like the inverse of a beach scene that could only have been witnessed if they had been out at sea.

Beyond that beach, equidistant, was a companion lake that mimicked this exactly. One was enough.

"It's beautiful," declared Valerie and squinted at the distance as light played along the surface, blown into swirls and parallels by a confused and changing wind.

They rode into Kiloran and past Colonsay House and left their bikes at the edge of a track that led over the dunes to the high hills beyond. As they approached the edge of the bay, Laurie asked Valerie to stop.

"Give me your hand. Let me lead you. I want you to see it all at once."

Happily, she agreed; closed her eyes and let Laurie lead her on a good distance, half a mile or more. As she felt herself to be climbing she guessed it was near the end.

"Right. Take a look now. This is Kiloran Bay."

She cast her eye across the most magnificent of beaches. It was a kilometre long, two hundred metres wide, the mouth of a huge, semicircular bay protected by fine, craggy hills on either side. The sand was the lightest shade of ochre; she wanted to call it white. And there was nothing, absolutely nothing on it. Not a person, nor a pebble, not a footprint nor a sign that anyone had ever stepped there, until then.

"Is this big enough?"

Valerie laughed her reply. Almost nervously, they stepped on to the pristine sand. They entered a private world, a system that seemed oddly strange. All along the leeward edge tall dunes provided shelter from the wind. Either end was quickly steep and the towering jutting of both sides interrupted the full sea swell. It was peaceful, protected here. All the sounds seemed muted. The sea lapped, creeping towards them gently across the giant shore. Everything slowed down; it was even hard to breathe, as if the ocean air blew over this section of sea—just simply missed it out.

They walked a long time, genuinely in awe, until Valerie turned to look back and acknowledged, "It's miles. It's absolutely miles across."

Two thirds around the bay, the wind began to return. Jutting into the sand a spur of black rock provided shelter, if any were needed now.

"Can we make love in the middle of this? Would that be allowed?"

She had hugged Laurie close, undone his waxed-cotton coat and wriggled inside with him for closeness; the wind wasn't cold.

"Who's to forbid us? But wait a minute. This isn't our island. Others could come and there are few places to hide."

She was already unlacing her shoes. "I know. I know. I know." Each snippet of knowledge was matched with a layer of her clothing being unwrapped. Laurie joined the race. Within moments they faced each other, utterly naked, and momentarily lost.

"I don't want anything on the beach," Valerie decided, "just us. Put the clothes out of sight here."

Guessing the exact centre, they walked the sea's edge, lay on the dry sand and made love. They did this gently, with an air of ritual, as if their coming together here was an ancient gift, some elaborate way of saying thank you to the place. It was over quickly. They were more self-conscious here; after all they had been performing on a massive stage.

10

There was still a lot of island beyond Kiloran bay. The path across the high dunes curled to rest at the foot of a track so steep that in Laurie's painting it looked like a waterfall. He was working in oils, straight onto canvas, his energetic daubing resisted by his clever metal easel. To stand straight on the slope, Laurie had fiddled the legs into inelegant angles and mismatched lengths. Distorted and steady, it let Laurie respond to that moment of colour before the sun rose above *Carnan Eoin* to scatter shadows and brilliance onto the scene and so disrupt the subtle tonality of green on grey on brown. It wouldn't take long now. He'd almost caught what he saw. He mixed the paints quickly, squeezed too much ochre and then steadied, to brush on the precise platelets of colour that together would recreate the scene. It was a race against the light.

He won easily. "That's it," he said to the rocks and unmade the apparatus with all the urgency of someone expecting rain, not sun. He slipped the canvas, gingerly, into a black plastic bag, dismantled the easel and strode breathlessly to a bend in the track, steadying his progress against the ribs of concrete that served as grip and vital backstops for the crazy vehicles that braved this road. To his right, at the edge of a plateau of concrete, flat before the road went vertical, Laurie lodged his work. He'd pick it up that afternoon on his return. There was a ledge; a neat crevice and then a sheer drop of eighty feet. In the bottom of the hole, ornamented by bracken and gorse, lay the neglected bodies of two wrecked vehicles. Most of the engines had gone, cannibalised for parts. The owners survived and drank free in the hotel bar telling their stories of daring in climbing this impassable hill. A Morris Minor and a farm truck had fought for traction on the sheer road. It was the sudden shock of flatness that was their undoing. The tiny striations in the concrete, the careful rills placed there by the flattening drag of the spade, filled with water and provided a neat glissade to skid the tyres utterly and squirt the hapless drivers into space.

Laurie knew the stories well. The one was told by his Uncle Adrian the other by his cousin Mike. Each story had grown in the joy of the telling but neither contained a mention that it was they who had laid the concrete platform that was the source of their undoing. They'd braved the road to get to the farm called Balnahard. It was remote and bleak, flanked by a string of barns. They provided a roof for the livestock, shelter for a few cattle and a changing number of sheep. Scattered across all the hills, seemingly unattended except for the occasional cradle of bars nursing a bale of straw, the four hundred or so creatures scavenged a living. There was an innate defiance about these sheep lacking in the mainland breed. They would roost on the road in peaceful groups that no amount of shooing could budge. Laurie went round. If you caught the odd one unawares, it would glare, stick out a tongue in a startling bleat, urinate, then step aside. Laurie chuckled at the endless standoffs and enjoyed their punkish scruffiness as gobbets of wool dangled untidily and brown-stained bellies trailed badges of congealed mud.

Laurie was heading for a rarely seen beach in the lee of the north-eastern tip of the island. It was difficult going, from valley to ridge, across a plain flattened by marsh, past Balnahard and into the trackless dunes beyond. All the high points of the land gave a sight of the sea and vivid exposure to the Atlantic wind. For no good reason, the few cattle he saw chose to stand on the highest of these ridges, or, at best, lingered at the exits of narrow valleys that funnelled and accelerated the wind.

They exposed themselves to the greatest discomfort with eyes half-closed and a determined air. The force of the blowing combed the stubborn hair on their muzzles and cheeks to a groomed neatness. As Laurie approached he expected them to move to shelter, away from the weather and him. But no. They stood their uncomfortable ground, merely cocking an ear for a friendly word, then resumed their eye-watering vigil, a foolish martyrdom that no one admired.

The path led straight through Balnahard. Laurie opened and closed gates, crossed lawns and peered into private windows, knowing the house empty but fearful of dogs. He hated their sudden attacks and, having been brought to ground twice as a child by the wolf-like monsters that guarded here, he hoped Harriet had either tied them up or taken them with her.

The farm had descended to a friend of Laurie's christened Harriet, always known as *Harry* but spelling the name like Krishna's. Hari did mannish things but Laurie had witnessed her femininity on a number of occasions in their teens. His left buttock still carried her teeth marks, three tiny crescents of pink-scarred tissue. To this day he couldn't remember why he was bitten, and why there, but he loved Hari as a brave and daring friend and, unashamed, each would ask the other for a fuck when the need was great. Their sex was eighteenth century: romping and full of guiltless laughter. Laurie's eyes sparkled as he remembered the sparkle in hers.

She was 'out' and would be off the islands for a long time. There were deaths and pain in this family. Hari had gone to a famous boarding school in England, then to university in Wales, somewhere by the sea where she'd studied marine biology. She'd thought to do something exciting amongst warm sea creatures abroad, but suddenly, Balnahard needed a tenant.

Her father hadn't died but his elder brother had, so the family moved to a more salubrious living in Hampshire. Jane Austen spaces, polite conversation, windless fields and reassuringly nervous sheep were too strong a seduction to withstand, both for him and Hari's inheriting elder brothers. She was happy to return. Laurie remembered her conversations as he closed the final gate at the edge of a cottage garden that ended her estate.

"I count sheep once a year for the man in the moon."

They were talking in the hotel bar on one of his visits towards the end of his time at college. Hari was older than him, just a couple of years, but seemed so much wiser. He felt himself to be precisely what he was, a student, with lots of promise and a little learnt but with no plans. Hari had responsibilities. She ran a business.

"No I don't. It runs itself. Stop putting yourself down. There's bugger all to what I do. I told you, I count sheep." And she yawned expansively, nodding towards her empty whisky glass.

"By God, she can drink," muttered Laurie out loud.

"A man from the Ministry photographs the land from the air. It is a spy satellite or plane, we're not sure, but it's a real giggle." Hari had chestnut-brown hair. It flourished in a dense mass and cluttered her forehead and eyes. She was always dragging it aside to see and parting its wavy tresses to drink.

"Make them large ones, Dougie. It's getting late."

The barman looked to Laurie for approval; it was his round. With a clever nod of the head, Laurie signalled 'Yes' for her and 'No' for him. It was a manly conspiracy to cover the shame of his not being able to keep pace with this slightly built lass at his side.

"We prop up the corpses with sticks. Carl even drapes fleeces over wooden boxes. How could they tell from the air?"

"Why do they do it?"

"They're men from Brussels."

"Even so."

"The sheep are worth nothing, my lovely Laurie. We keep them for the grant money. By the time we've paid shipping and slaughter on the mainland, there's less than nothing left. They're pets. Photographic models. I wonder if we could make plastic ones." Her eyes left Laurie's as she thought through her ploy.

"No. We get eight pounds a head for every one that can stand and that's my only income, at least, from the land. Your Uncle Adrian clobbers the odd ewe and we eat all we need, but I'm not a farmer, Laurie. On the land, the best I can claim to be is a shepherd. But in truth, I'm paid to maintain the landscape. The sheep are the means, not the end. They're just

the innocent go-betweens. Same again, Dougie. Large ones." She paused
to catch his eye. "Both of them. It's my shout and I need him legless." She
grinned, and patted Laurie's chest with a flat-palmed hand.
"Stay the night with me at Balnahard. Come fishing with me in the
morning. I am good at that."

"Wake up. We'll miss the tide."
Hari's cheery grin dazzled his fluttering eyes as he struggled to lift a
head heavy after last night's whisky. She ruffled his hair, kissed his chin
and fiddled his groin into a tangle of sheet and underwear. It was still
dark.
"It's still dark."
"Time and tide."
"It's night."
"It's not."
He was shivering in the Land Rover as they nosed down the track;
awake enough to nearly scream as Hari flipped round impossible bends
and down inclines that were steep enough to be silly.
"How did you get up here last—Ooooh !—night?"
"Don't talk, I'm concentrating. Shit! What did you say?"
"Concentrate."
"It's flat now. Will you open the gates?"
"I said, how did you drive us home last night? You'd drunk a lot."
"You don't think anybody'd drive up that track sober, do you? You are
strange, Laurie."

The fishing harbour in Scalasaig was not made pretty by dawn light. At
least the clutter had a purpose. Laurie was busy passing creels for Hari to
stack and buckets of bait for her to spill with cries of 'No!' 'Now!' 'Wait!'
Her ludicrously small boat bobbled just below him, tight against the harbour
wall. Like a rowboat with a hut tacked above its pert, blue sides, the brave
piece of wood numbered CN 831 looked wholly inadequate to its task.
But his weight made it stable and the engine started at once and delivered a
surge of power that pushed CN 831 through the waves with aplomb.
Beyond the pier and the protection of the point, the tiny craft seemed
vulnerable in the larger ocean swell. But its instant reaction to each nudge
of tide was its secret strength. It never challenged the sea. It was too small
to defy. It was the marine equivalent of a dog on its back and its instant
yielding made it safe.
"The sea likes us," explained Hari. "We give it total respect and glue
ourselves to a sight of land. The only time I'm afraid is when all I can see
is sea."

Laurie was a good sailor, especially on deck. The subtle leanings of a liner or an overly large channel ferry could make him nauseous. But Hari's fishing boat bounced so violently, all his concentration was on balance and staying on board.

It was over five kilometres due south of Scalasaig to the difficult entrance of The Strand. Laurie always walked it when the sea had gone its way. To see it as intended, with islands either side, was oddly confusing and it took a long time for him to see his way.

"Those are the oyster beds and that's the car park and Seal Cottage is out of sight, just over there."

Hari stood in the stern as Laurie took the wheel and reintroduced him to a landscape he'd known all his life.

"It's so weird having water on The Strand. I've never seen it from here."

"Mostly, it's the only way I know it. There are waterproofs down there. You'll need them. It's forecast rain all day."

Laurie hardly noticed because the work was so intense. As the rain fell on the water it flattened out the tide. Hari made no stops on the flooded Strand plain but at its outer reaches the tiny flags of ownership signalled her sunken wicker pots at the end of hand-cutting lines. Laurie began by being manly and grabbed the first three or four himself. The first pull was easy—then the boat inclined. Gradually, the tension signalled that the creel was free to rise and the full weight of itself and its guessed at contents could be felt in his arms and back. It was hard. The heavy weight, invisible and long, seemed an age in emerging as the rope sliced his soft hands. Braced, his back aching in an arch, his legs were tensed to keep their balance on the movement he was creating every time the creel inched nearer to the boat. Then it was there. Lighter in the air. Surprising the lifter when free. Laurie grabbed and Hari emptied green crabs. "I sell those in Spain." White fish. "I feed those to the crabs."

"Lobster?"

"Ah. Let's hope."

This went on all day. Laurie's hands tensed into arthritic paws, bright red with cold. Hari was tireless. Only now did he see the neat muscles in her arms. She wore waterproof yellow trousers with braces and a bib. Underneath, her short-sleeved T-shirt let her forearms free to tense in a steely strength and an inexorable rhythm as she pulled the boat, dipping down towards the sea and the creel rising towards her, in a soundless march of hand over hand. She didn't blink. She was so strong. Laurie watched in awe.

"Are you planning to draw me?" she asked.

"No."

"Then take over from me because we've drifted a little too close to the land."

"Yes. Sorry." He felt a slacker until she gave him the weight.

"Shit!" he muttered under his breath.

"Bit of a bastard, that one. You'll manage."

And he did, eventually. But the final lift drew blood and an admission of defeat.

"I'm fucked, Hari. Absolutely fucked. How do you do this every day?"

"It's not every day. I don't notice the work. I just like to be out here."

They were then a long way from the land. Laurie hadn't noticed, with his head over the side, just how far out Hari fished.

"Is that Seal Island?"

"Yes. That's as far as I go." He looked all around, following Hari's gaze, and could see black streaks of land emerging from the grey sea, silvered with the grey light of a pale sky that still dropped rain. The tide was moving in giant swirls—then utterly flat places pitted with rain—then rushing eddies at the edges of rock.

"We must go," advised Hari, pointing Laurie to the wheel.

"Stand off ten metres from everything that juts up and we'll be fine."

Hari ordered the catch into its appropriate basket. There were three lobsters, black and menacing, so Hari guarded their claws with red rubber bands. To the largest of the brown crabs she did the same but the all-legged spiders and greens she bundled in a mess. The dozen and a half white fish lay in a bucket of their own.

Unloaded, back at Scalasaig, Hari rowed a tiny tender out into the opposite bay protected by the pier. She dropped the bulk of her catch into a raft of baskets that served as keepnets for the week. She'd kept the white fish, a couple of brown crabs and the odd green crab to make a stock.

"The Spanish think they're a delicacy. We don't bother over here."

"How did we do today?" Laurie asked as they walked wearily towards the hotel.

"Not bad. I do well with the small crabs. The brown ones don't have a price. The only impressive earners are the lobster and some days there's none." She blew out a long breath as she added up her day's tally. "I guess I made fifty pounds today and our supper. That's okay."

"Is it?"

Laurie didn't argue. All the islanders lived on bits and pieces. Everyone had several jobs: keeping shop, serving in the bar, unloading the ferries, making beds and making breakfasts. Hari thought herself lucky. She had more than enough. Had Laurie actually made a sketch of her when he stood and marvelled at her strength as she clung to the line of her creel, he could sell if for the same as her day's catch. It would take him an hour, cost a few pennies, unbreak his back, and use less petrol than CN 831. But he knew her response. He'd heard it once today. It was necessary to be out there.

"Two whiskys, Dougie. Make them large ones, Laurie's paying."

There were no dogs at Balnahard. Beyond the deserted farm there was little solid land, the wind had changed it all to sand and blown it into difficult mounds crowned by coarse grass. It was hard to see his way. Laurie struggled for a high point so he could glimpse the sea. The soft yielding of the fine sand defeated each determined stride. In the end, Laurie crawled, anxious to progress beyond this annoying place. The sand hills wouldn't be circumvented. He had to climb and slither and climb and trip and climb and roll into the furthest corner of the tiny bay he was seeking. He sheltered amongst a cluster of rocks that covered the beach at the top of the bay; suddenly warm out of the wind, hungry and sleepy at once.

It wasn't the beach itself that Laurie sought but what was half-buried in it. Beyond the rocks where he'd rested, exposed in the middle of the five hundred-metre bay of pristine sand, were the remains of a ship wrecked several centuries ago. The rocks that had protected him with shelter from the wind, in an unknown past moment had shattered the sides of this oak-made vessel and scattered its ruins onto the sand. What remained was impressive. On a southern beach it would be the stuff of museums, excavated, and its provenance sought. Here it was left alone. Laurie began a series of sketches. What he saw was suggestive enough to guess at its place in the scheme of naval things.

There was a giant hull rib six metres long standing proud of the sand, a metre to half a metre thick as it nosed downwards at twenty-five degrees. It was made of oak, darkened by time, and smooth even at the bottom of its deepest graining. The lines of its texture, engraved by the sand, had separated into seams, interrupted on its flank by the swirls of knots.

Throughout its top surface ugly knobs of iron extended. They must have once joined equally massive trunks of wood but, eased apart and exposed, they looked dangerous and threatening in their stubborn refusal to rust. Just in front of the beam, on the seaward side of the wreck, a whole series of metal objects stood proud of the sand. There was a huge box section, a half-melted wheel. Were they pieces of ordnance? The undercarriage of guns? They were massive, a metre and a half wide but melted. Had there been a fire? Was this a ship of war that died in a fight? What intensity of heat could melt metal so thick? Or was it just wind and sand and slow time, the abrasive nagging of tireless erosion that prevailed and prevailed and prevailed?

There was something majestic about this wreck. So much was left, to remind of what once was, that Laurie decided he must paint big. Only his largest canvas would do. He needed lots of material. He must glean what he needed now. He couldn't cart all his gear out there. And he needed to involve Valerie. She must be included. He invited her to enter the scene. He wanted her naked. She complied.

"Lie flat on your front. I'd like you draped over the hull rib."

At first he'd thought to avoid the iron rods then realised their need.

"Would it be too painful to lie across the rods as if impaled? Now your hair must fall beyond. No face, just neck and scattered hair, your belly arching away from the rods, your buttocks mimicking the roundness of the melted wheel of the foreground. Perfect."

That's how he drew her. That's how he painted the scene.

Part Three

In Vitebsk

"But I wasn't there, Iain. I wasn't there!"

"I don't understand."

"I wasn't in that picture."

"But you were. It's clearly you. I'm not following."

"Yes, it's my bum and things but I've never been to that part of the island. Ever. He just transposed drawings of me. Placed me there. He was good at blurring what was real and what he imagined. This only took place in Laurie's mind."

We had been looking at the Island books and I admit I was fretting over the beach painting and Laurie's description of its creation. I can't remember what he'd called it but it was a spectacular piece. I was only just getting to know Valerie then. It was something inane like 'The Mermaid'. Yes, it was, but with a question mark inside the inverted commas to draw even more attention to the erotic potential of the painting with those difficult iron bars. I'd never thought to sell it in Scotland. The 'Wee Frees' and every elder of every other Scottish church would have objected. I sent it straight to London. A gallery in Albermarle Street sold it in a day for a fortune. It was stunning. It must have been three metres by two. Come to think of it, it is more likely that he painted it on the mainland. It was a hell of a canvas to ferry about. But I am sure I remember him talking about the different poses he'd tried, as if the model were there. Or was he tormenting me then, as now, guessing my interest in the 'model' wasn't entirely professional?

I think I can do this, slip a filter between my feelings and the lens, create a protective layer that takes away the pain of wanting to have always possessed what comes late into a life. What I learnt during those few days was embarrassing and hurtful. In some ways, I wish I'd never begun. In most ways. But I knew I had to face it all. I couldn't leave Laurie with anything to taunt me with, no point of leverage from which to topple me over. I confess that, had I read these earlier, with or without Valerie to explain, I would have found it harder. I felt less vulnerable with that handful of years now between us. The greatest comfort was Laura. I don't think a baby has ever had so many hugs. The reassurance was all for us not her. I know Valerie was doing the same as me.

"What you've got in miniature there is the source of our problem."

"Ours?"

"Not yours and mine. We have no problems, do we? I meant Laurie

and me. It's here. I wrote this. This is where I start to come in." She turned a few pages and pointed to the sentence that she then spoke:
" 'When I gaze at you, it is as if you were my work.' Underlined, you see." She pointed to the sentence.

"Who said that?" There were quotation marks.

"Marc Chagall—who else? —Talking about Bella."

"Who else?"

It was Valerie's uncompleted thesis that brought us together. In all honesty, she probably knew as much about his work as I did; in the end, more.

"When Laurie took my body to that beach and draped it all around the wreck, it was as if he'd come to possess me. He had assumed the right to place me in any context that he chose. I felt that I wasn't the subject of my own life any more but an object in his. All right, a very special object, The Object, finally, but nevertheless, I'd become a thing."

"Yes, but . . ."

"Sorry. Yes, I know what you're going to say, that I rarely stayed in the pictures."

"Stayed in? Were you ever in them?"

"In nearly all of them and then he painted me out."

"I didn't know. Why?"

"Ask him. You're his agent. Apart from the death-on-the-beach thing, which was never shown in Scotland, everyone assumes he painted landscapes. Well, that's how they ended up. But most had contained me. Then they didn't. For a long time, a time so long it annoyed me, he wouldn't draw me at all. It was so strange. Before he ever knew me he'd made half a sketchbook of drawings. He'd ignored the intended model and chose to draw me instead. Weird. Then, suddenly, without any explanation or real cause that I know of—my haircut? Hardly likely, but he can't stop. Every day he would add to the pieces. You've seen it. It's here." She pointed to the sketchbook in question as evidence. "Whatever I was doing he would capture it. Capture. That's when I started to wonder how an artist relates to his model. That's when I began a serious study of Marc Chagall and Bella Rosenfeld, not out of idle curiosity, but as an attempt to understand what was happening to my marriage."

"You wrote about Chagall as the precursor of Surrealism. Yes? You began with Apollinaire's visit to the studio in La Ruche, by the Paris abattoirs, when the great man described Chagall's early paintings as *surnaturel.*"

"He was good at inventing important words, wasn't he, Apollinaire?"

"Wasn't he just?"

"I tarted it all up, later, with your help. Then, I was using my studies for personal reasons. Too personal to make theses out of."

"What were you looking for?"

"Good question. Understanding, certainty and, I suppose, some kind of sanity."

"Did you find it?"

"Sort of. It was a twofold quest, really. I was trying to understand Laurie. I was close, intensely close to a committed artist and I confess, I didn't understand him at all. His involvements, the way his mind would deflect so readily from me into his blessed landscape, bothered me. And he wouldn't or couldn't articulate what he thought. He had no objective understanding of what he did and I desperately needed that to begin to understand him, to begin to tolerate the life his art was forcing me to lead."

"But you'd fallen among artists before."

"No. I'd been around students; nice middle class lads and lasses getting their jeans dirty for three of four years. That's why I concentrated on the History of Art. The actuality of art students was too tedious. They took themselves seriously, certainly, but not their work. I'd never been close up to the real thing. Laurie was the only one that just did it, you know. The only one who didn't break stride. From student to practitioner: from studio to gallery. Nothing in between. No hesitation, not a moment's prevarication. I both admired and resented that sureness, that absolute certainty of self. You must understand, I never envied his talent, just the hold it had over him. I'm a woman, for God's sake, and I wanted to be paid due attention. The closest I was getting was to be swallowed by his creations. I felt bleached, wrung out. I was losing a dimension. I was becoming art. Then I heard a new voice: 'My name is Marc, my emotional life is sensitive and my purse is empty, but they say I have talent.' And I fell in love with this honest voice. It spoke the words that Laurie never would. You remember the opening sentence of *My Life*, his autobiography?"

"No. I only dipped into it."

"It's here, isn't it? We still have a copy. Or did I leave it on the island with Laurie? If so he'll have it. It wasn't easy to come by. He'll keep it safe. Ask him. You should. It's important."

"I do know it. I've read some of it." Very little, in fact. I couldn't get into it. I'd been required to provide provenances for a number of paintings. I knew a great deal about specific moments in Chagall's life, very little about the rest. Odd to remember, it was Apollinaire who suggested Chagall should offer work for exhibition in Herwath Walden's gallery in Berlin. I began my searches in Potsdamer Strasse, just as Chagall had, when he returned to Berlin in 1922. The paintings had all gone. Sold, apparently. Walden had banked the money for the painter but German inflation had rendered the proceeds worthless. A few paintings were recovered for the artist, as a kind of compensation. And I'd found a number of the others, in the way of business for a client at the bank.

"It's here." Valerie offered me the spine of a hardback notebook. She was reading from the pages open to her.

" 'What I first set my eyes on was a trough: simple, massive, semi-hollow, semi-oval—a junkshop trough. Once I got in, I filled it completely.' Isn't that amazing?"

"Amazing."

"It invites so many responses. Look at all these equal signs."

She'd written 'Trough' and, equally, a page-long list, beginning with 'womb'.

"There was a painting in 1925 called *The Watering Trough*," Valerie explained patiently.

"Ah. It all makes sense, now."

"Stop being so sarcastic. This is exciting for me. I haven't seen these for a while."

"I'm sorry."

"Anyway, you should be more sympathetic."

"Why's that?"

"Because you were both born dead. Stillborns."

"Oh."

" 'I did not want to live,' he says. 'Imagine a white bubble that does not want to live. As if it were stuffed with pictures by Chagall. They prick it with pins, they plunge it into a bucket of water. At length it gives a feeble whimper.' Did you whimper?"

"I guess I must have."

"They stuck you with pins, too."

"Yes, they did. At least, with one." I'd had to share this bizarre beginning with Valerie because I carry a distinctive scar. Something collapsed inside my mother before I could be born. I emerged a mess. I seemed to be dead, so they began my first and last rites. Fortunately, an enterprising doctor injected my heart with adrenaline as a final attempt to kick start me into life. It worked, but the syringe used must have been as big as me. It left a puncture hole, exactly above the heart, that grew. It's now more than a centimetre across and, in its adolescence, grew hairs. It's impossible to miss, a perfect target for a firing squad should I ever be executed in the nude.

"It's such an honest voice, after a while I thought I could hear it, even recognise its changes of tone. 'My father had blue eyes but his hands were covered in calluses.' He sold herrings and often smelt of their brine. Chagall talks of his family; he remembers gifts of little cakes and frozen pears, magicked from a pocket and popped straight into his mouth. 'He worked, prayed, and kept his peace. Like him I was silent too. What was to become of me?' He had to find a special occupation. 'Some kind of work that would not force me to turn away from the sky and the stars, that would allow me to discover the meaning of life. Yes, that was what I was looking for. But in my home parts I was the only one who had ever uttered the words 'art' or 'artist'. What is an artist?' he asked. I wonder when you know that this is what you are? It never arose for you and me, Laurie. We stand on the edge of artistry. It's our life. It was something I could nearly do. But it wasn't something I was. That's what college did for me. It let me see that no amount of skill could penetrate to the centre. Did you ever think to make art?'

"No. No, I never did. I came very late to it and entirely as a voyeur. I like the world it creates, and I'm a willing onlooker to all of it. But no, never any inkling, ever, that it might be a calling for me. And I should say that I do both admire and pity those that are 'called'. It's such an isolating state."

"He was so poor. There were times in his life when he starved. He lived on a cucumber one day in Paris."

"That has no nutrition."

"Shush. Leave the romance. Vitebsk, his hometown in White Russia had twenty-five thousand Jews. It was practically a shtetl. But he loved it. The wooden houses, the ritual, the simplicity. 'Here is my soul. Look for me here; here I am, here are my pictures, my roots. Sadness, sadness.' It's Laurie and his islands, isn't it? Everything is there . . . for him. Just as the grandfather's house in Vitebsk was full of the sounds and smells of art for Chagall, so Oronsay and the other islands of the Hebrides are full of art for Laurie. Was he ever opposed? Laurie? Was he ever baulked in his wishes?"

"I don't know. It would seem not."

"Chagall was. That's what isolated him, pushed him to the edge of everybody. I suppose in the process it's also what defined him. I could never get Laurie to intellectualise what he did. He seemed to have no distance on his choices. They seemed all unexamined."

I just shrugged. I didn't agree with her. I prefered Laurie's way.

"Neither of his grandparents thought anything of his art: 'What an art, that does not even convey a likeness.' Apparently they set a very high value on meat."

"Very wise."

"But he's so generous. Listen: 'If my art had no place in my family's life, their lives and achievements greatly influenced my art.' And this: 'I stammered that I wanted to go to a school of a . . . a . . . a . . . art.' I think that's why this struggling, this apparent strangeness makes his work so original, whereas Laurie. "

"Is what? Traditional?"

"Yes, that's a nice word for it, traditional."

"Does Laurie even like Chagall's work?"

"No. Probably not. As you say, he is more . . ."

"Valerie, he is no different to Chagall. Their traditions are different, that's all. You're right to compare Laurie's need of the islands to Chagall's love of his Jewishness. Nearly all the paintings I have acquired have been totally immersed in his tradition: the fiddlers, a wedding, Rabbi's with little prayer boxes glued to their heads, sheep and goats and the circus. Peasant things."

"Maybe. But the images are his means, not the end. He had a manifesto. A love of life, sure. 'Clamorous' he called it. He wanted to be a craftsman. Silent not famous. But, above all, he wanted to paint in a way that no one else did. 'Someone give me the power to breathe my sigh into my canvasses, the sigh of prayer and sadness.' I think that's a beautiful aim. 'May God help me shed real tears only before my canvasses. My wrinkles, my faded complexion will remain there, there my fluid soul will be imprinted forever.' There's so much to puzzle out. What was it André Breton said?"

"Far too much about almost everything."

" 'Chagall and only Chagall provided painting with the triumphant advent of metaphor.' He's right, I think. The paintings are poems. Difficult, hard to decipher, but visual poetry."

"They don't appeal to all, Valerie. Most lookers don't want a set of notes to give a picture meaning. What's hidden can stay hidden."

"He didn't aim for that. He argued that if a picture worked, if it came from the soul, the 'upright heart', then any symbolic meaning would be achieved automatically. Here it is." She flicked through her book of notes. " 'If a symbol should be discovered in a painting of mine, it was not my intention. It is a result I did not seek. It is something that may be found afterwards, and which can be interpreted according to taste.' Like I said."

There was no air of triumph, just a sudden sadness.

"Don't you like him either?"

"That's not the issue. Of course I enjoy a great deal of his work. He is clearly a pioneering genius. He lived for nearly a century and was massively important to the world. You can't blame Laurie for being less."

"I don't."

"Nor for failing to intellectualise his gift. That kind of self-consciousness can be so arid."

"Oh no. No. You miss the point. Read this page here, to yourself, quietly. Please."

I did. I must admit, Chagall's assertions did seem to contradict my idea of him.

'It seems to me that art is first and foremost a condition of the soul.'

'Perhaps my art is the art of a lunatic.'

'The entire world within us is reality, perhaps more real than the visible world. If one calls everything that seems illogical "fantasy" or fairy tale, all one proves is that one has not understood Nature.'

I whispered through these words. By the time I confronted a poem dedicated to the painter written by Blaise Cendrars, praising Chagall because:

He paints with his thighs
Has his eyes in his behind
There it is Your face
It is You dear reader
It is I
It is he

I remembered my happy bafflement of earlier encounters and handed the notebook back. One word, unexplained caught my eye.

"What's *chimie*?"

"Where? Show me. Ah. It translates as 'chemistry', but that's not what it means. It is to do with magic. Chagall believed that his images had some special power in them. Jewish tradition actually outlawed religious image making. They were afraid of its ability to influence and persuade, as if by some innate, dangerous force. Chagall called that energy *chimie*. He thought a painting contained something of himself, but also had an integrity of its own, an authority. The ones you went looking for he remade, you know. At least, some of them. He was trying to recapture those parts of himself he had lost. That's why, for a while, he made two versions of every painting, just to guarantee he stayed whole. I suppose you think this is lunacy?"

"No, I don't. At least it was a madness Laurie shared."

"How?"

"In removing you from his pictures."

"Maybe. I always feel as though I'm still buried there, trapped beneath the surface of the landscapes. But, as you say, he must have felt threatened, else why bother. Anyway, I don't suppose I thought I had got any closer to Laurie, despite my wanderings through the thoughts of Chagall. But I did accept the daunting need of place. I did understand that. Chagall said he needed Paris as much as a tree needs water; that the city was his teacher, every minute of each day. Oronsay was as necessary to Laurie, even if it had only one tree. It was his Paris. But he didn't leave a homeland to find this intensity. He simply went home; returned to the light and freedom. And he left me. Or so it felt. Seal Cottage seemed such a tiny world. It was my Vitebsk and I was his Bella. It was such a beautiful story of love and gravity and I wrote it all down. Look. There are drawings and writings. When Chagall first saw Bella he was afraid. She hardly looked at him. Not surprising. He had a meeting with her friend on a bridge at the edge of the town. But he knew everything from that moment.

'Her silence is mine. Her eyes mine. It's as if she had known me for a long time, and knew all my childhood, my present, and my future; as if she had been watching over me, reading my inmost thoughts, although I had never seen her before. I knew that this was she—my wife. Her pale face, her eyes. How big, round and black they are! They are my eyes, my soul.'

"Is that how you felt when you first saw me?" Valerie smiled to soften the challenge in her question.

"No. I wouldn't have dared."

"Why? Was I so frightening?"

"No. Just out of reach. Your man Chagall had the greater daring of youth. What was he then, in his early twenties?"

"Yes. The same as me."

"Ah." There was nothing to say to that. It was true.

"Bella came to his studio."

"Did he paint in the nude then?"

"No. That was later, in La Ruche. He kept everyone waiting at his door while he got dressed."

"Why didn't he wear clothes?"

"He said he had no dress sense."

"Unanswerable."

"Imagine this. Bella knocks timidly at the door of Javitch's house. She's bought him a huge bunch of mountain ash, a bouquet of branches, green splashed with red. He says 'Thank you' and regrets it. He feels inept. They kiss. Then she takes off all her clothes and poses for him in the still life that is magically taking shape in his mind. He is afraid and nervous. Astonishingly, he confesses that this is the very first time he has seen a nude. Not just her, but anyone. She is practically his fiancée but he is still afraid of going any nearer. He dare not touch all that loveliness. She seems to him like a feast spread before his eyes. He makes a painting and hangs it on the wall. His mother sees it. 'What's that?' she demands, pointing at the breasts and forbidden dark patches. 'Take that down!' He obeys.

"To avoid future embarrassment, he moves to a policeman's house where Bella can come and go as she wishes. One night they go to leave.

The door is locked. There is a lamp that smokes, a few empty saucepans, and a stock stillness. How will he get her out?

" 'The window!' They were seen and became an object of gossip. This is down town Vitebsk not central Paris. But they are innocent, at least, so he claims. She is purer than Raphael's Madonna and he; he is an angel. Do you believe them?"

"Why not. It's your story. When's the gravity?"

"Well, if I were Bella, I think I'd be experiencing a sinking feeling about now. After all that virginal nudity, her beau disappears for six years to have his expiatory bath in Paris. I wonder if she felt as abandoned as me?"

"Abandoned by whom?"

"By Laurie."

"When?"

"Every day. For every moment of daylight. Unless it rained. But, we had remarkably fine weather that summer and autumn on the island. Each of my months felt as intensely lonely as Bella's years. It seemed she minded less. She remembered his eyes, 'oblong like almonds'. She'd never seen such eyes before, so she says, except in illustrations to tales about beasts. What an odd analogy. She compared his movements to those of a 'lurk-beast'. Don't ask, I don't know. I suppose she thought there was something feral and never to be tamed in her Chagall. 'Chagall' means 'to have walked' in Russian. We all tolerate men with a clear direction and difficult women, like me, can't stop themselves trying to deflect them from it. Bella was more dutiful, I think. She claimed that the face of her boy lay inside her like a second ego. His voice sounded in her ears. It wasn't because he was so unusual. She had met artists before but nobody had appeared such as he. She thought him as strong as a peasant, taking his force from a steel river. She had been calm before him. Lived in peace in her house. Read books, avoided people as evil ghosts. But at one moment a young man had come and broken the calmness of her days. She wrote to him and Chagall feared that after these years abroad all feelings would have evaporated; that all that would remain was a bundle of letters. He wouldn't dare another year of separation, so he rushed home, to go to his sister's wedding. Oh, yes, and to see 'her' again. And now there are problems."

"Good."

"Why good?"

"A hint of realism?"

"This is a true story."

"A truth told by an artist."

"No. Told by me. On to things of weight. What is heavier than a disapproving family? The Rosenfelds disapproved of Marc Chagall utterly.

'His father is a simple store man.' They would never climb from herring brine to diamonds. Bella's family was rich. They owned three jewellery shops in Vitebsk. Bella had graduated from a fine girls' school in Moscow and studied at the university there. She was intelligent, a talented writer, much travelled with her mother—and there was Chagall.

" 'He's an artist. Whatever's that?' they cry. They dazzled him with the many-coloured fires of their rings. They braved him with brooches and bracelets that glittered. Three times a week they tormented his empty stomach with enormous mounds of apple cakes and poppy cakes and cheesecakes that they attacked furiously in an ecstasy of greed. Their father ate grapes like his ate onions, and poultry, a once a year sacrifice chez Chagall, was always on their table. The only distraction was a crazy old grandfather who hated all things Russian. He prowled the apartment behind a long white beard throwing everything Russian he could find (books, pictures, passports) to burn in the stove. Doing nothing but pray all day, he wanted everyone to be rabbis. He disapproved of the world; Mrs Rosenfeld has focussed on Marc.

" 'Listen,' she tells her nervous daughter, 'I think he puts rouge on his cheek.' He did. 'What kind of husband will that boy make you? He's as pink as a girl. He'll never be able to earn his living.' 'He does,' she'll reply. He didn't, was the truth. Bella would not be convinced."

"Good."

"Oh. Changing sides now are you?"

"There's nothing more reassuring than a family row."

" 'You'll ruin yourself with him, my daughter,' cries Mrs Rosenfeld. 'You'll ruin yourself for nothing.' And the strongest of all: 'What will people say?' All that gravity bound them closer together. Never attack an unsuitable mate; it recreates them in their lover's eyes. Chagall wrote the most beautiful words for this time of their life together.

" 'I only had to open my window and blue air, love, and flowers entered with her. Dressed all in white or all in black, she has long been flying over my canvasses, guiding my art. I never complete a picture or an engraving without asking for her "yes" or "no".' "

"Did Laurie always ask you?"

"Yes. Surprised?"

"No. I . . ."

"Yes. Since you asked, he always did. I think he valued my opinion more than yours."

"That's understandable. I was there to buy, not admire."

" 'Was it worth it?' Chagall asked himself, to be entangled with such high-class people. Nevertheless, despite his protests, he found himself standing under the most authentic of wedding crowns, like those in his pictures. He'd arrived at his wedding late. Important looking stomachs were aching in anticipation of his arrival and dinner. Without him there would be no food. The agitation amused him. Soon, without music, against the yellow background of the wall, without stars and without sky, under a red canopy, he would be married. There were tears, smiles, confetti.

'Such an embarrassment, being an artist.'

'It seems he's already famous. He even gets paid for his pictures. Did you know?'

'All the same, that's no living,' sighs another.

'What do you mean? What about the honour and glory?'

'Who's his father, then?'

'Ah.'

"They made him so shy he didn't even touch the mountain of grapes and fruit that decorated the great wedding table. It was over in half an hour, less, the 'sanhedrin' was in a hurry. It was driving him mad. All he wanted to do was clasp Bella's slender, bony hands and run away to the country with her, to kiss her and to burst out laughing. But, to be ritually perfect to the last, they were separated; he, escorted home by her brothers: she, to remain with her sister in the family house.

"But they did come together, at last, to be alone in the country. Woods, pine trees, solitude. The moon behind the forest. The pig in the sty, the horse outside the window, in the fields. The sky lilac. As pretty as a picture by Chagall."

"Who else, indeed."

"There are three paintings I love from this period of happiness. They're all anti-gravity. *The Birthday*, *Head over Heels*, and probably my favourite, *The Walk*. Before the wedding ceremony, on his birthday, Chagall visited Bella. She wrote, let me find it, I want to quote it exactly. It's here, beside the relevant picture. See?" Valerie had made tiny but exact drawings of the pictures she was referring to.

" 'I suddenly felt as if I were taking off. You too were poised on one leg, as if the little room could no longer contain you. You soar up to the ceiling. Your head turned down to mine and mine turned up to you, brushing against my ear and whispering something. I listened as your deep, soft voice sang to me, a song echoed in your eyes. Then, together, we floated above the room with all its finery and flew. Through the window a cloud and a patch of blue called to us. We flew over fields of flowers, shuttered houses, rooves, yards, churches.'

"Then you look at the paintings. In *The Birthday* the artist floats above Bella, who in turn treads the air above the vermilion floor of the kitchen. She receives the whispered kiss she'd written of. Then, in *Over the Town* they complete the journey described. Bella floats, completely horizontal, arm outstretched, grasped by the painter's supporting arm, as they hover above the rooftops and yards.

"Were her words the literal basis for the painting? Do you think that he has precisely 'pictured' what she has written? There were few times when Chagall painted so precisely. The exactness of the pattern on that cushion, the seeds of the (is it a melon, on the table?) her purse with its metal clasp, full of change, the view through the window they are floating towards: everything implies the real. This feeling of floating elation, of weightless joy, is rooted completely in the now, an actual, describable moment of time. Not a dream, not a fantasy—a fact. This is painting poetry; a magical world of word and feelings made real. This is a genius that is as split as a peach.

"My favourite is *The Walk*. They've been on a picnic. There is a crumpled tablecloth on the left foreground with a decanter of wine and a goblet. The cloth is bright red and floral-patterned. They are just rising above a Cubist, patchwork landscape in various shades of green. Rooftops, a pale pink synagogue, a single cow in silhouette, a branch with purple leaves fill the bottom half of the painting. The rest is a pale yellow sky. To left of centre, in a black suit with an open collar, clutching a black dove, is a happily smiling Chagall, his left arm fully stretched upward, palm flattened. Resting on—no suggestion of clinging, this is a most delicate linking—the down-turned palm of Bella's right hand. She is floating in the air. Her bright red dress and contented, smiling face fill the whole of the top right-hand corner of the sky. Her outstretched left hand has already left the painting. They are happy acrobats on the moon, defying the weight of life. I think the painting is a triumph."

"Do they ever come back to earth?"

"Yes. With quite a bump. They eventually move to Moscow. Bella preferred large towns. She loved culture. Chagall agreed with her. For a time he didn't paint, sooner playing political games at the college where he worked. She saw him neglect his painting. Bella wept. She warned him it would all end in insults and snubs. So it did. As he acknowledged, she was always right. When would he learn to take her advice?

"These were years of famine and cold. Rejected and hurt, he left his home. His town was dead to him. The Vitebsk road was run. He did not return for his Mother's or his Papa's death. He told his wife his sufferings. She suffered in silence. Everything was destroyed for her too. One afternoon seven cars drew up in front of the dazzling windows of the Rosenfelds' shops and soldiers piled the entire contents into them. They went into the apartment and even took the kitchen silver that had just been cleared from the table. Failing to open them, they laboriously loaded the shop safes into their cars too. That night, Bella's father tried to eat with a tin spoon the maid had bought for him in the town. Tears ran down that tin spoon and fell into his tea.

"In Moscow there were hungry mouths and the howling of October. There was no need of money; there was nothing to buy. The militia arrested Bella. She was trying to exchange her rings for a quarter of butter. There was a child to feed. Idotchka, Ida. Chagall claimed they were cheerful and empty. So they slept and dreamed and one day woke up in Paris. Soviet Russia didn't need him but the rest of the world did. They were to be affluent for the rest of their lives. And he said of her: 'Only you are with me. The only one of whom my soul will not speak a word in vain. Everything you say is right. So guide my hand. Take the brush and, like the leader of an orchestra, carry me off to far and unknown realms.' Which is wonderful. Then this, where I began: 'When I gaze at you, it is as if you were my own work.' And that disturbs me."

She closes the book, with a sad reluctance to let her story go. Then opened it once more and showed me a half-page sketch, quite charming in the simplicity of its line. It was almost a cartoon. There was an outline of a house, windows half-drawn and in the foreground two lovers kissed on a bench. From the profile, Bella's face was easily recognisable; the lover's face, one assumes Chagall's, was hidden behind hers.

"It's lovely."

"Yes. It was from the autobiography. Look at her."

I did and I saw nothing odd. "It's obviously Bella."

"Yes. You see her head and shoulders and two outstretched hands as she offers her cheek to be kissed. What else?"

"Nothing else. There is nothing else."

"Exactly. That is the finished drawing. I didn't leave it half made. She doesn't exist from the elbow down. She's just suggested in space. Her skirts and legs are implied by the presence of his. She's becoming invisible."

"Yes." I could see she was right.

"And that's what I felt like. That's something I learnt about being a painter's moll. All that presence finally leaves you invisible. I didn't even continue to exist in the actual paintings. There's one work, it's called *Bella with a Collar*, a *White Collar*, something like that. She's a giant, straight from Brobdingnag, looking entirely serene. She is pointing down to the top of the woods that barely reach her knees, and tiny in the foreground, smaller than the finger pointing, are Chagall and Ida playing in the garden. It's . . ."

"Magnificent. She was his muse, his goddess to worship. He feels humble before her." I interrupted her.

"But that's not right, Iain. That's not a good place to put him or her. You become weary of being looked at. You crave; at least, I craved to be looked into. In the end, your very body functions as a kind of mirror, reflecting back the looking eye. I longed for some transparency. I needed to be seen through, at least some of the time."

"Did you feel no resentment?"

"For what?"

"For no longer being in the pictures."

"I don't. Yes. Yes, I suppose I do."

"Did?"

"Do. Anyway, I'm still present, archeologically. I don't think he ever scraped me off, he just painted over me, buried me in impasto. One day some nosy curator will see my grinning face as an X-ray image beneath the surface paint. I hope I terrify him for his intrusion. So there I hide, timeless me. An immortal. Never ever real, like a genie. The stuff of fairy tales.

'Bella, Bella, on the wall
Were you ever that fair at all?'

"A rhyme for me now." She didn't pause.

'Valerie, Valerie, quite ill-manneredly,
Was buried when her beauty palled.'

"Yes, I resent it. Why not? It was so hard to sit still for all that time. I pose. I oppose. I disappear."

"Or, he disposes," I added, cleverly.

"Very witty. And so precise. But it's still an unfair declension, isn't it? Surely, I was always more than a surface, whether beneath it or on it?" She smiled. "Now there's an irony."

"Why's that?" I asked her.

"That's what Laurie accuses us of well, you, of doing. Just trusting to the surface of me, of us."

"When?"

"Sorry?"

"When did he make this accusation?"

"Now."

"Now?"

"No, not immediately. Around the time of the divorce. Of course we talked, he talked, even wrote to me."

"And?"

"You know the kind of thing: 'We can never be strangers.' 'Only I know you.' It was he, and he alone that introduced me to myself. He was the man who made me whole."

She rattled off the phrases.

"Did he?"

"If he did, he dismantled me afterwards. But he always maintains that you know nothing of me. He thinks you and I are strangers. I would guess that's why he gave you and not me the Island books. He says that we play superficial niceness games, glossing over the darks, not noticing the depths."

"But . . ."

"He says we wear human make-up. Quite poetic, really. Is it true? No. Don't answer. He says that by obliterating the past and suppressing these 'depths' we have relinquished the 'now'. Do you think he's becoming a Buddhist? Or just simply sour. It's all right. There's no need to answer. I was being . . ."

"Scurrilous?"

"Rhetorical. And anyway, we continue to confront the past. At least, that part of it contained here." She pointed to the Island books.

Part Four

The Island

1

It was late autumn. There were no leaves to fall. The change of season was signalled by the angle of light as it glanced off the waters of The Strand. There was no heat in the sun to raise a haze but Valerie must squint to peer through the dazzle. The evening light, almost parallel to the land, skimmed the thin surface and burst in a million events, fragmented at the edge of each ripple of the advancing tide. The ceiling of low cloud seemed to stand on wide columns, as the distant crags drew the sky down, then beneath, into reflections of themselves in the water. The vast plain, bleached of colour, shimmered in tones of grey, empty as a desert, a cold mirage at its surface, where nothing moved

Valerie stared. She was on Oronsay, at the landing point, perched on a rock. If Laurie didn't appear soon then he wouldn't return that night. It was already too late, she knew. The tidal level had passed critical. Her blurred seeing made rocks move, raised then dropped her hopes. She was looking to the far edge, anticipating his start. It was a shock when a rock nearer than the middle quivered upright, flattened, stood solid against the light. A thin voice travelled on the wind. It wasn't shouting to her. She doubted if she could be seen. In this open land, the key to survival was stillness. You only became visible if you moved. Very slowly, Valerie withdrew behind her rock and walked back to Seal Cottage. Laurie would be a while yet. She didn't want him to know that she'd waited and then withdrawn when he'd been seen. As she climbed the road, out of his sight, the faint sound of his singing reached her ear. It was a folk song, something in Gaelic.

Back inside she readied the rooms. Laurie was always excited when he returned from Colonsay. There was the exhilaration of the walk, with its mild sense of triumph over the encroaching sea. The trophies of fresh food packed on his back added to his sense of well-being. Valerie teased him about the tins he had shot, but if he hadn't hunted he had gathered, and that was primitive satisfaction enough. He enjoyed the self-sufficiency, temporary and unnecessary though it was. He felt secure in their isolation. It made Valerie nervous, even after all these months. That was the reason for her vigil. As the winter approached the tides grew awkward. Access was offered only in the dark. Twice now Laurie found himself outwitted, begging beds on the Colonsay side. They were his tribe so he was welcome everywhere, and invitations for Valerie to join him, though offered, were usually turned down. He thought she was happy to stay alone in Seal Cottage and congratulated himself on finding such a self-contained wife. In fact, Valerie felt acutely unwelcome amongst Laurie's relatives on the other side. She hated the totality of the isolation when on the island alone. Daylight made it tolerable; the views distracted her mind. Darkness shrank it to a spot, a tiny focus that if acknowledged could release a vivid sense of fear, a litany of 'what if's' that endless self-assurance failed to restrain.

But, she preferred this to the cold eyes that probed in judgement whilst the smiling mouths welcomed. She had felt an outsider in territories where she supposedly belonged. Here she was a stranger, and would remain so for a thousand years. There was the endless examination of her surname.

"A Kinsell, you say? Is that right?"

"Yes. Valerie Kinsell. But now I'm a McPhee, I'm Laurie's wife. One of yours?"

"A Kinsell, you say?"

"Yes, a Kinsell."

"And would that be one of the Kinsell's that ...?"

"No. No, it wouldn't."

"Ah. Still, you're always welcome."

"Am I?"

The fire in the stove was laid but not lit. The lamps were open ready and fully filled. The candles had been checked, replaced where low, straightened where adequate. Boxes of matches were in place but she would begin nothing until Laurie walked in. She would even feign surprise rather than let him know that she had watched for him anxiously. This bravado was a mystery to her. Why not acknowledge her fear of being left alone on Oronsay? Why not simply explain or angrily react to his abandonment? Some hidden wisdom warned her to say nothing. So she complied.

"Honey, I'm home!" Laurie shouted from outside the door. He mimicked Jack Nicholson's crazy greeting in *The Shining*, pushing into the lobby of Seal Cottage wearing the same manic grin.

"Let me help." Valerie was quickly there, lifted the full rucksack from his back, eased a canvas from under one arm and an easel from under the other. She knew the routine. Once fully packed, Laurie locked everything in place and with Sherpa-like stoicism, trudged his journey. He didn't relax until arrival and by then, he barely could. The muscles of his arms and the gentle curving of his back provided too rigid a structure and it took several minutes of weightless ease to let the blood flow again. Valerie kneaded his shoulders beneath the straps whilst Laurie frotted his forearms into life.

Quickly recovered, he delved into the sack that Valerie had eased open but left for him to unload. He liked to hand over the goods, like a prosaic Santa Claus. The wrappings were brown paper but fresh carrots, round cabbage, pears and tomatoes were as welcome as perfume or jewellery. The edges of his pack were laced with sketchbooks. He was aware of the approach of winter and feared this loss of light. He had started to make sketches, dozens and dozens of them, to be used as a substitute for outside when forced to work indoors. He was keen to order his day's observations so, having scattered his gifts of grocery, he lit the chandelier candles and the lamps to the side, making quick use of the table before Valerie could lay a supper made with the fresh food.

She was quickly ready. He offered to move but she settled in the window and invited him to so the same

"Leave it there, love. We can sit here and watch the last of the day."

She offered him a colourful plate of very plain food. It was such a treat to have fresh things; there was no need to make a sauce. She'd steamed a portion of all the vegetables and edged them around a few pieces of chicken that she'd poached in a stock that had produced the cooking steam. It was a very simple way to preserve the taste, and as the chicken remained moist, it passed the only culinary test set in Britain.

Valerie ledged her plate on the windowsill and returned with a basket of bread-wedges, butter and cubes of cheese balanced on a chopping board that she set between them.

"Where did you go today?" she asked.

"Hmm. This is good."

"Thank you."

"Not far. No time . . ." Now he swallowed. "I left the list at the shop to be made up and worked by the old fishing village, just north of Scalasaig. It's on the road to Loch Fada. You turn off before the cattlegrid."

"I've not been."

"Not much to see."

"You did a lot of drawing of nothing, then." She'd wandered to the table, still holding her plate. One large sketch spread across the centre pages of the largest book there. In the distance were craggy headlands, jutting out to sea. In the foreground stood the twin gable ends of what was once a cottage. It was made of local stone and the points still stood but there was nothing in-between. No roof, gables or timbers, no windows, side-walls or doors. Everything perishable had done so, only the stubborn rocks remained. What had clearly fascinated Laurie was their gradual reversion to type.

"You've made it a new part of the landscape," she observed. "You can hardly tell it was a house once."

"Yes. Yes. That's what I saw there." He was excited she had noticed and quickly rose to stand alongside her, absent-mindedly handing her his empty plate.

"The rocks of the building have weathered in tandem with the formations of the shore. It seemed that the very strata, from which the original bricks had been taken, had somehow visually reclaimed their own. Do you see?" He pointed to the very centre of the drawing, and running his finger just above the marks, traced the layers of rock from the far distance, to the middle, to the near and somehow hid the vertical outline in the matching textures of the horizontal forms.

"But people once lived there." There was sadness in Valerie's voice.

"Yes. There was a complete community, a village. It would have run right to the shore."

"Doesn't that make you sad?"

"What?"

"The end of all those dreams?"

"I just saw it as a surprising beauty, you know? That the landscape had taken something ugly, broken, and somehow had slowly reformed it, made it its own. It's as if the weather is sculpting it into a natural form."

"Doesn't the human story interest you?"

"Not as a painter, no." He interrupted her quickly, and his answer was not meant to appear so abrupt. He had paused to swallow in the excitement of his thinking and left a gap in a sentence that should have been spoken as one. "But as a man . . ."

Valerie had already stopped listening. She was shocked by an aesthetic that could so override any compassionate response.

"Will there be no ghosts in your paintings?"

"Ghosts?"

"Yes, ghosts. The spectres of the people that died trying to survive on Colonsay and this speck of land."

"I can think like an historian, Valerie. I can imagine these islands when huge communities thrived here. There were thousands once. Most were my ancestors, so I'm unlikely to forget them. And it saddens me; of course it saddens me, to think they've all left. The fish never came; the kelp lost its worth, the mainland beckoned more and more persuasively. It was the land that drew them here and it's the land that I love. And no, I don't see their ghosts. They didn't die here. They just upped and left."

"Just like you did." The intensity of her remark waned as she stepped into the kitchen. "Fruit?" she asked, cheerfully.

114

"Sorry? Yes, I will. What did you mean?"

"Cream? We have cream."

"No, plain. What did you mean, just like I did?"

She hadn't sought a battle, just a glancing blow.

"No. Come on. There was something behind that remark."

"I meant . . . it doesn't matter. I was just being mean."

"I didn't leave the island." He frowned, perplexed, scanning her face for meaning or intent.

"I thought it island policy to educate you all on the mainland," she began, matter of fact.

"From eleven."

"From eleven."

"There weren't enough children to fund a school."

"So you left at eleven."

"Well, no. We weren't here when I was little."

She already knew this.

"But, you were born on the island?"

"No. No, I wasn't."

She knew this too.

"And before you make some smart alec remark, no one was."

"So, no one was ever born on this island?"

"Well obviously, in the past. I meant in recent times."

"Where were you born?"

"In Oban hospital, like everyone else."

"Everyone?"

"It would have been pretty irresponsible to have a child so far away from", he sought for a word and came up with, "facilities".

"I don't quite see the connection, Laurie, when there are no rights of birth or upbringing. I just don't see how you were ever on this island. Until now, that is. I wonder if I've already been here as long as you ever were in the past."

"This is my spiritual home." He accentuated each word separately, making the statement to deflect Valerie and to reassure himself.

" 'Spiritual' is good, 'chosen' is good, even 'favourite holiday destination' will do, but actual 'home'?"

"Yes, home. This 'speck of land', as you call it, is entirely my home. I belong nowhere else."

"So, your heart doesn't belong to Glas - gee?" She grinned as she split the final word.

"No."

"Even though it schooled you, colleged you, housed you?"

"No. These are the landscapes of my childhood, not the city."

115

"I see."

"No, you don't see. You're smirking now and making fun of me. You can do that. I know you're clever. I have liked that in you. But what I find here has got nothing to do with cleverness."

"Nor reason."

"Nor reason. When I clamber over these rocks, and step across these fields and marshes, I am known. Can you understand that? I am known. The land recognises me. If it is my chosen place then it is a two-way choosing. This place calls to me wherever I am on the earth. It seems to want my presence, and I yearn to be back. I breathe a sigh of relief when I step onto the jetty, no, before that, when I first see the line of the land. I can draw it from memory. It's seared behind my eyes. This is my Grail, Valerie. My Holy Land. As a tiny child at Oronsay Farm, with absent parents having to work away, my Uncle Stuart, who by your lights was a simple man holding unreasonable beliefs, pointed me to every secret corner of this place. I greeted it on hands and knees. I touched it and smelled it and put it in my mouth."

She signalled him to stop.

"No. You released this. You set this going. On purpose, I suppose?"

She didn't answer.

"What purpose?" He persisted.

She didn't entirely know.

"Do you think I betrayed my island?"

His sudden anger licensed an unkind response.

"Betrayal?" She laughed and, by repetition, made this choice of word seem absurd, even to Laurie.

"Betrayal?"

"Well, you know what I mean."

"Okay, Laurie. Let's try resentment. Do you resent their defection?"

"Whose?"

"The islanders. The deserters of villages."

"We weren't talking about that. You were denying my right to belong here."

"I think you're more pleased now the place is empty."

"No. It's dying."

"You seem to believe there's a purity in the absence of humans, that the island, the actual island, is more significant than the islanders."

"In some ways, I do, but . . ."

"Laurie, I'm sorry. I didn't mean to hurt you. It's really wonderful that you feel so rooted to a place and a people. I envy you that. I still have a secret suspicion that it's bogus, the whole Hebridean 'Och hi the noo' bit. Maybe that's because I don't belong here . . . or anywhere. The only landscape I feel comfortable in is the one inside my head. Those outside,

116

especially here, I find dark and threatening. It doesn't know me. Or, if it does, I'm not sure it likes what it sees.

"Do you give it a chance?"

"What?"

"The place. A chance."

She sat at the edge of the table, put their plates down in the middle of his books and, leaning forward, clasped the crown of her head in the palm of her hand. She turned towards Laurie. She was very earnest, no longer playing her disruptive games.

"I have a major problem with this, Laurie. You see I don't believe there's such a thing, being, entity—creature as 'Place'. I don't think the rocks have minds or the grasses intention. I don't believe the wind whispers, it simply blows, the effect of an unavoidable molecular rush from a place of high to low pressure. That doesn't mean that I don't see beauty here. I do. I most certainly, excitedly and utterly do. Really, really, my love, I adore the views. But such beauty lies for me in form. It is the pattern, the shape and the association so that when that effect of wind happens—the dynamic of all those accidental objects occurring together—I see it as an intellectual experience. I see it through a pair of educated eyes that have been trained to appreciate and taught to recognise. There's nothing untutored in my response. If a scene moves me, I examine my feelings so that my mind can understand what it is undergoing. It's not left to chance. The artist," she paused and touched him gently on the hip, "at times, just with a nudge, reshapes what is found, and he does so according to a gamut, a whole chromatic scale of preconceptions. He uses his judgment."

Given a kind of cue, Laurie shifted his gaze from the glare of her eyes to the grey blur of the night sky beyond the cathedral window. Valerie turned towards him. Not quite alongside, she spoke the rest of her words over his left shoulder. Her focus was the same opacity he stared into.

"As I understand these things, there are rules and assumptions. Some, at the surface, change with fashion and taste. I have tried to learn about such things, because I think they exist." She moved closer. "But knowledgeable granite, or millstone grit with a mind. No. I can't manage that. It's a leap of faith too far for me. It belongs among the shell-mounds and the people that hid in holes in the ground."

"In that case, so do I." He smiled, ruefully.

"I know you do."

"Do you mind?"

"No. I've always wanted a pagan lover." She paused. "Do I disappoint you?"

"Not yet."

2

To the north west of Oronsay are the only significant buildings on the island. Barns, a farmhouse, a priory and church play impossible games of chess with the Atlantic Ocean. *Beinn Oronsay* itself, the highest of the hills, keeps the north at bay. Walls within walls, cloisters, covered ways and inner cells contrive to escape the endless wind and winter rains. The barns shield the house that deflects the weather from the walls that shelter the inner priory and church. But this stone and concrete babushka fails.

"It can't be done," Valerie whispered as she sat on the face of a medieval knight lying proud in the carving of his tombstone on the floor of the innermost of the priory's rooms.

"It's even raining in here." The thought made her giggle. The impossibility of shelter troubled her more than this sudden laughter. She was wandering through the ruins of the Augustinian priory built God knows when. It was something to do with St Columba, she knew, and knowledgeable visitors had the friars worship St Oran. But the locals knew better and they and now the Ordnance Survey, spell things with an 'o' : Oronsay.

Enough of the afternoon light found its way through the glass-less windows, following the scudding wind and sprayings of rain, to make visible the tranquil face of a stone-carved woman just beneath Valerie's gaze. It was a nun or a widow with a homely stone pillow beneath her wimpled head. There were no features left. She once had been outside and not much could survive that. Valerie ran her fingers across the missing face. There were still contours enough to feel a cheek and the chin was clear and firm. What surprised her were the fingers, the hands in general, but the fingers most of all. In relationship to the length of the face, the hands seemed exaggerated, impossibly long. To the right of the cheek, resting on the stone pillow, bent the fingers of her left hand. But, stretching as far as the ear, invisible beneath the cloth wrappings, an elongated forefinger, three-quarters of the face in length, pointed to someone or something outside the scope of this death. Lying on her side, her right arm was crooked across her chest. The right hand, although seeming too big, was anatomically normal, until an improbably outsized thumb burst from the row of clenched fingers and signalled us to look. At what? Valerie was fascinated. The figure looked like a lazy hitchhiker, snoozing at the side of the road. Despite the digital distortions, there was something oddly pleasing in that missing face, something tranquil and knowing in the gestures. There was a story here that now could never be told.

"Sorry. I didn't realise." Valerie apologised to her seat. She hadn't known the bump she sat on was a head. "Sir," she added, in mock-formal respect. There was nothing left in the blob of stone to hint at any feature in this face. Valerie's respectfulness was based on the more obvious sword clasped flat to the stomach, cutting a neat diagonal across the pleated skirt of armour and dinky mailed feet. All the stone trophies collected here lay or leaned with neither historical order nor local significance. The priory had served as a collecting point for headstones and monoliths from all over both islands. Valerie rather liked the haphazard clutter and cheerful absence of any declared provenance for these mysterious pieces. She knew that the highest cross was built for a prior called Colin. She found the unholiness of the name amusing. The cross, with its central crucifix and patterned traceries was majestic, its tip visible in profile through the top corner of the mitred window in the end wall of the room she crouched in.

"Is this really yours?" she had asked Laurie, in total disbelief, when she'd first visited the priory.

"Well, not mine, but my family's, yes. It comes with the farm. It was my playground when I stayed with Uncle Stuart. There was less in it then. They have plans, I think, to make a proper museum. They'll label things and make it a bit neater, I guess."

"I prefer it like this, don't you? It seems so wonderfully careless. A great wedge of history left to decay. It's almost Greek in its abandonment."

"No. It's not abandoned. Everything has a name. I've drawn each slab, every piece of stone. I've copied the runes and mapped the designs. We've dated the High Cross and know when the small one came. There have been a lot of claims for significant burials here, ever since the MacDonalds relinquished the Lordship of the Isles. That was when it came our way."

"When was that, exactly?"

"Well, to be precise, in 1493."

"Of course. It had slipped my mind."

"It was an important date in our history." His laughter acknowledged her irony and his pedantry. "There's so little happened in recent centuries that the past seems closer. We were brought here as school children and introduced to each relic. Uncle Stuart told me a story about every rock. One morning on Colonsay, we were walking near the sea and he stopped and bowed and doffed his cap to a standing stone. He introduced me to it in a solemn voice: 'This stone is called *Balaruminmore*. Look at it hard, young Laurie. It watched our family man die, murdered on the exact spot

119

where you're standing, by a MacDonald, in 1623.' If it hadn't been mid-morning I'd have glanced at my watch to see if he meant that very day."

To her surprise, Valerie sensed no history in this place. It was a black day and she was waiting for Laurie to light the stove and start the generator, any necessary thing that would take the cold, dank edge off the farmhouse. She had been shown the secrets, and surprises here that only a local would know, or better still, an inquisitive child with no playmates. At ankle height, beneath even a careful visitor's looking, was a tiny hole, protected in recent times by a sheet of plastic that had become tarnished to a tobacco-stained yellow. Pressed behind its grubby window, the skull and cluttered bones of a man were visible, the neat round of a leg-end distorting the edge of the plastic, where the disordered remains had been scruffily trapped inside. Knowing it was there hadn't lessened the shock of each re-encounter.

But to Valerie, this 'burial' seemed symptomatic of the place—tawdry and inelegant. She even wondered if it was legal. Moving above the sad bones, she glanced down and slipped past. She shuddered in the damp air and recoiled as the cold rock of the ceiling touched her neck as she crouched beneath the lintel of a low door that led into the central cloisters. There was no roof, no paving; the crumbling sides let all memory and atmosphere escape. There should have been the echo of chanting, some spiritual lingering from the time of holiness. The exposed gable that ended each cloister reminded her of another place on a much grander scale than this. Her mind's eye filled with a picture of Fountain's Abbey set against a vast mackerel sky, scaled in crimson and grey.

Much of the abbey was lost but what remained reminded you of what once had been. The magnificence of the pointing of that high gable end invited the eye to complete the roof space, fitting crossbeams into the deep holes that once held them in place. There was the imagined sound of plainsong. The spirits of the monks lingered as a perpetual praising of their God. Was it just a matter of scale? Laurie had made a distinction, calling his a 'Monastic House' not a 'Friary'. Was it too domestic, too little to lift the soul? It was worse than that. When she gazed at the vast walls of the Yorkshire abbey, foolishly separated from any crossbeams to bind them in, she longed for their survival. There was something magnificent in this precarious standing, a daring that filled her with awe. She wanted to scare the weather away, wave puny arms to defy the erosions of time.

But here, in this dark, low place, she would urge the wind on to complete its half-achieved purpose. She would welcome an end to this insignificant lurking. Fountain's Abbey stood proud as a celebration and extravagant gift of man to God. But this monastic house, to give it Laurie's title, was an image of grim survival, a testimony to man's determination to grind out an existence in the most improbable of settings. It was Man celebrating Man. It seemed trapped in its own lack of ambition. This small-scale aim fell short and would soon disappear entirely. The wind was welcome to it. The only reaction of Valerie's that bordered on the marvellous was her sense of wonder as to why anyone would want to build such a place in such a place. Whatever the privations, there were few witnesses. Whatever the gains, there were even fewer to praise. If it had a purpose, it was lost on Valerie. To her it seemed pointless and despite their historic sufferings, she found nothing to admire in them.

Nothing here had escaped the eternal intrusion of water. It had eaten into the very fabric of the farmhouse. Inside, there was a dank, underwater smell. It was like being in a cave. The kitchen walls were a pale blue, mottled like a bird's egg. Crystals of salt glistened beneath the paint. The Aga gave off a faint heat. It ran on solid fuel, greedily.

In the distance, a Walter Mitty-like "Pocketa! Pocketa!Pocketa!" announced the presence of a generator that, filtered through ancient Bakelite plugs with two prongs and worryingly crowded sockets, provided electricity. This could make the light they craved. Not the gentle, soothing kind that candles and lamps emit; they could make that at Seal Cottage. It was bright, uncomfortable, generated light that they wanted, a glare to work by. There was too much dark for Valerie and Laurie's days were frustratingly short. They decided to invest in as much fuel as Robert could bring to wake up the old house a few times each week. They could share or divide the space. What mattered was the artificial extension of the day. Laurie could complete what he had begun: Valerie could encroach on the range of the night.

3

In the first light of day, dressed ready for a walk, she left a note for Laurie to read alone. She'd made it funny to disguise its serious intent. She just wanted him to laugh and forget. To desire him was easy but, last night, she'd pushed him away. With alarm she realised that when everything is permitted there is no room for games. Laurie offered her the intimacy that every woman craved and she realised that if she allowed it, too much of her would die. She couldn't stand all the bliss. She didn't want to be this well-known. She needed thwarting. Did she secretly prefer her careful men with their controlled sex? Being abandoned didn't necessarily set her free; at times it left her desolate. She resented the absence of veils. She needed a third party, a bigger audience to hone her human skills. What wiles could be used to see off a night sky? She needed a rival she could touch. Right now she needed Laurie closer. She would write some words to reassure him all was well.

Sorry I was odd last night. I'll make up for it later. How many times can you make love in an evening? A lot is my favourite number. I wrote you this.
I everything you,
V.

Perhaps we can work this out
As long as you're mature about it
And I'm mature about it
So we can both be mature.
Perhaps we can achieve a kind of maturation
Which may develop into maturiosity.
Hell, lets try!

When she returned the note was gone and so was Laurie. She was happy he'd read it, relieved there was no reply. But she'd wanted to see him, to ensure he'd understood and reacted in the way she'd arranged for him. She looked outside, climbed to the highest point beside the gable end of the cottage that cut into the hill of sand. She thought she glimpsed him, a bobbing head amongst the dunes on the south side of the island. She thought to call but the scudding wind would mask even the loudest of her cries. Was that him?

"Laurie!" She shouted anyway as a blast of wind blew his name back into her mouth. There was a storm at sea, out of sight. These were the winds at its edge. They blew past her face at such a speed a seeming vacuum robbed her lungs of their air. She gasped and cowered, wanted to shout out at conditions this extreme. She was standing on sand rendered firm enough by the lattice of roots underneath. Sprays of coarse grass had matted together to form stubborn overhangs. Tussocks of sedge, like heads of wild hair, flopped and bounced at her feet. With a faint whistle, not a roar, a giant breath of wind found her.

There was no buffet or blow. With alarming care, and a human-like touch, the wind pressed into the small of her back and lifted her into the air. It was such a deliberate force that Valerie laughed out loud, like a small child on a swing calling to be pushed higher than was safe. She fell with a clump down the four or five feet of cliff worn concave by the sea. She landed heavily on her shoulder and left her head unprotected to bang on the sand. She'd been so surprised, almost delighted, to find herself pushed into the air. She lay still for a long minute. Dazed, a little nervous, she asked mental questions of all her limbs. With deliberate care, she rolled onto her side and adopted the recovery position. She was rescuing herself according to procedures remembered from some First Aid course at college or school.

From where she lay she could look out to sea. The ghost of Jura stood above her head, a hint of hills behind a bank of grey cloud. But out to the west, for a distance beyond guessing, the Atlantic Ocean spread away. For a self-pitying moment, she felt unutterably alone. How had she let herself become as vulnerable as this? To fall, unseen, in a deserted land, tossed aside by the wind, was totally absurd. This was nonsense.

Now on her knees, she flexed her back and sat down before daring to stand. She put her head between her knees and located the bruising on her cheek.

Finally she stood up and limped carefully towards the cottage. Her legs were fine; the halting walk was a defensive gesture to keep any serious injury at bay. She breathed deeply and tried to overcome a profound sense of shame. She felt ridiculous. Made fun of. The stooge, pushed over by the Invisible Man so everyone could laugh. To finish its game, the wind blew sand in her face, an invisible bully she couldn't defeat.

"Bastard!"

The cursing helped.

"What would have happened if I had been more seriously hurt?" she asked of Laurie, on his return later that day. He was concerned. Her face was swollen into ugliness and, by now, the pain in her shoulder had stopped her using her arm.

"You weren't."

"I know. But what if? It could have been my leg. Then what?"

"Luckily, it wasn't."

"I need luck to survive here? Is that it?"

"Not entirely. It was unfortunate, what happened. And freaky."

"A freak?" She pointed to her puffy face.

"Not you. The wind that did it to you. It must have been a massive storm out to the west. We caught the worst of the edge of it here. I wonder what speed it was blowing when you flew."

"I wonder."

"It must have been huge."

"It must have. I'm glad you're fascinated but would you think for a moment about what I'm asking? It's a serious concern of mine."

"Of course. I'm sorry. It was just so . . ."

"Just so. Can we speculate?"

"What if?"

"Yes. What if?"

"So, you've broken your leg, in two places. No, more. We could have you in Oban Hospital in an hour, maybe two."

"What? I was being serious."

"Me too."

"And how do we perform this miracle . . . Fly?" They spoke "Fly," together.

"Fly?"

"Yes. There's a small airport at Oban with several light aircraft. Nothing grand, but Air Ambulance material."

"There is?"

"Yes."

"But, where do they land? That's all very well but . . ."

"On the airstrip."

"The what?"

"Airstrip. There's a landing area between the dunes, beyond the shell-mounds."

He was pointing, almost carelessly, through the bedroom door and beyond.

"You're joking."

"No."

"I've never seen it."

"Nevertheless, it's there. I've used it myself. A few of us sometimes flew in from college. We said it was convenient for an urgent need but really it was to make a grand entrance. There's an airstrip on Colonsay as well. And if that isn't good enough, there's a helicopter dedicated to the islands. I think it may be stationed on Skye. I'm not sure. It's part of the Coast Guard and Mountain Rescue. That could take you further afield. All the way to Glasgow, if you want."

"Oh."

"Reassured?"

"Yes. No. Who's to know?"

"I'm sorry, you've lost me now."

"Who's to know I'm hurt and they're needed? Who will tell them, assuming it can't be me because I'm hurt and not walking? Who will know?"

"I will. I'll ring from the farmhouse. And if it's dark, I'll light beacons on the dunes."

"But what if you're not here?"

"I'm always here."

"Not always."

"Very rarely am I away. Even at worst, it could only be twenty-four hours. One day."

"What do I feed on, rock food? Can this geology nourish me?"

"Use the pantry for supplies as normal."

"I was guessing myself in a remote part of the island."

"Don't. That's enough. Be happy you're safe."

"I was worried. Take me seriously, Lolita Man. There was a moment out there when I was really afraid."

Last thing, before sleeping, guessing Laurie would be up first next day, she left him a note on the table by the breakfast plate she'd already laid.

Please remember,
Although I'm legal,
I'm still a kid and I cry easy.

They worked through the darkest of the winter evenings, often apart. Laurie painted at the farmhouse: Valerie studied at the cottage. She pinned a note to the door, copied from Apollinaire: "Please don't waste my time." But the urgency was waning. Her mind wandered from her task. She envied Laurie his art, it seemed much more absorbing than scholarship. She allowed her studies to drift more towards the personal, seeking solutions to her life in those she studied for her degree. She sought to understand the artist through the mind of Marc Chagall, and the nature of her own position in the life of Bella Rosenfeld. In comparison, Laurie disappointed her and she disappointed herself.

125

When he wasn't there, she missed him. When he was, she didn't know what to say. He mistook her silence for contentment. The simple rhythm and endless creativity of his days left him peaceful and serene.

It was at the early end of the day, towards the end of winter—too soon to think of spring. There had been storms to the north and west. Laurie had gone to Colonsay and Valerie was hoping to see him return. The Strand looked desolate, steely grey and bleak. The wind rippled the surface. No one was coming across. He wasn't secretly hidden. Valerie knew she'd be alone. She waited until the tide was in and stumbled home in the dark.

The Island

4

The following morning Laurie had found his way to the lee side of a southern spur of Colonsay that thrust furthest into the Atlantic. He'd borrowed a bed for this one night, the tidal times for return were difficult, falling in the dark and he'd wanted to finish painting a rocky point called *Aird Alanais* as seen from the lookout hut on the small cliff above. He'd left a number of unfinished canvasses there, a useful handful of oil tubes and a pot of brushes. No one ever came to the hut or if they did, they acknowledged it was the painter's and touched nothing. He had worked fast that morning. There was an odd energy in his being that he couldn't account for. It wasn't entirely creative but it had urgency and a desire to be out of him. He reworked all the canvasses: blocked in the darks, picked up first one, then another, adding and blurring, looking quickly out at the promontory with its nearly symmetrical spurs to each side, adjusting his line of sight fractionally to include new pieces of land in each. Wet, nearly covered, certainly in need of respite, he let the canvasses alone.

Instead of taking the longer, much easier way to the made-up road, he'd shuffled to the front of the hut and saw his painted scenes unguarded by glass. With extreme care, he scrambled down the one hundred feet of rock that rose sheer above the beaches. It was a quarried cliff. With typical carelessness, a huge metal basket on flanged wheels had been toppled from its still existing rails and left to rust, not quite fallen, its top lip some thirty feet from the ground, resting dangerously against an unquarried outcrop of rock. The rails ran along concrete sleepers resting on flattened rock and came to a sudden end still a distance from the sea. Fallen pylons and tumbled gearing were still entangled in surprisingly thick cable that was fraying and unravelling in the eroding sea air.

He turned his back on this accidental sculpture. He'd determined at some stage to find beauty in elements of its shape but today its incongruity made it ugly. He stepped down to the bay, a precise shark bite, semicircular and neat, made of sand ribbed by the sea, where no one had walked. Under foot it felt hard and resisting. He could feel the presence of the ridges, harsh, even through the thickness of his boots.

Promising to resist, he pushed against the ridges, only to feel the whole substructure recede in a spongy absorption. Each step was robbed of its thrust. The misleading crust of the surface yielded and sapped the energy from his legs. Weary and feeling insecure exposed in the middle of the bay, he took the quickest way to land and scrambled through the dunes, treading on the certain stepping stones of tussock grass. Soon there were rocks and he clambered up a steep mound. The effort of the climb, with his face to the rock, demanded his attention and emptied his mind. Near the summit there was a track and his descent to the bay below was clear. He removed his rucksack and sat staring out to sea.

Here there was an uncertain line to the coast. Two kilometres of rock belonged to the land but were continually hidden then revealed by the sea. These secret shallows explained but didn't entirely remove the mysterious beauty of waves breaking way offshore. He watched now, as cloud-edged sunlight lit the bay and heightened the drama of huge waves curling and crashing, seemingly, against the sea itself. The noise of the collapsing water reached this height. The sudden streak of white cutting the metallic blue drew his eye.

The path that dropped to *Plaide Mhor* point was difficult and steep. But the beach at the bottom rewarded him with complete shelter. The edge of the whole spur of land that led to a house and a peninsula called Ardskenish, was protected by a cliff of sand, topped and matted with coarse grass. Here was peace. The howl of the wind was stopped. The noise of the sea was gone.

He squatted on a rock seat just inches from the water and was instantly mesmerised by its gentle motion. In the single centimetre swell a flat piece of seaweed rolled languidly in the invisible recession of water. On edge, a minute black triangle rose above the surface like a shark fin then wriggled to new shapes in the moulding waves.

The shock was waiting in the next bay. If the wind blew from the west or south, all this spur of land was sheltered. Offshore rocks could deflect the north wind but not here. An unguarded channel was open to the sea and stacked on its sand was the debris of the recent storm.

He sank to his knees and studied one of the monstrous stalks in front of him. His mind knew he was looking at kelp but his sketchbook drawing seemed more aptly sinister. The one tuber he drew was two metres long. At its widest it was as thick as a wrist. Flat leaves crinkled and bent at one end but the wrenched root, swollen to the size of a fist, was pockmarked with suckers, like a diseased penis or the grotesque socket of a limb. That was the one he drew. Looking up, the full calamity emerged. There were thousands of these tubers. They lay scattered and laced, a metre high mess, with stems oddly solid, like cold flesh to the touch.

He stepped back and sketched the scene across two pages of his book. The giant kelp stems wrenched from the seabed and tossed onto shore began to look like so many severed limbs, the remains of a mediaeval battle. The cry of the boys, treacherously slain by the defeated French on the fringes of the Battle of Agincourt blended with the words of Marlon

Brando's Kurtz as he praised the heartless act of the Viet Cong soldiers returning to teach a village not to collaborate with the West by cutting off the inoculated arms of all the newly healthy children. This was that pile: thin, pink and cold, with tuberous sores at the wrenched and severed ends. Intrigued, he'd stayed to fill a sketchbook at the kelp atrocity. He clambered up the sand cliff and saw from above. He inched into the water and looked from the sea. He changed his own position, not the object of his gaze. As always, he left what the island gave him in the position that sea, wind or time had first presented it. In homage to the gift, he'd sooner adjust his seeing. He refused to replace carefully, according to an aesthetic that prejudged what would be pleasing to a guessed at audience. Such a wilful recreation warped his skill and damaged the integrity of what the island offered.

The darkness was complete when he arrived at Seal Cottage. He left his boots and bag in the entrance, gently lifted the book of sketches from its pocket in the rucksack and didn't actually speak until he entered the warmth and gentle light of the living room. Valerie wasn't immediately visible. She stood to his right, backed into the corner at the edge of the mantle shelf, the body of the stove between them. He looked ahead, through the window and out to sea. He saw her reflected image in the squared panes the moment before she spoke.

"Where in hell have you been?" She retreated from the vehemence of her greeting into the complete shadow of the corner. He couldn't see her face as he turned to look. The candles of the chandelier above her lighted only her hands. The fingers were interweaving nervously, stretching, interlocking—forming fists.

He proffered his sketchbook by way of explanation, hoping to share his excitement for the day's work.

"It's two days and a night you've been gone. What was I meant to think? What were you thinking?" Her face leaned into the light. Her eyes shone with anger. "What was I meant to do?"

"I couldn't make the tide. No one was crossing The Strand."

"And?"

"I stayed at the oyster man's."

"Did you think of me?"

"I thought you would have guessed. I thought you might worry for an hour, at the end of the tide, then realise I'd stayed."

"Were you meant to be my only concern?"

"I don't follow."

She sighed in cold annoyance and took a step into the room. To avoid his gaze she turned her eyes sideways to the line of framed drawings on the mantle shelf. The two nearest her left hand were early pieces. They hardly qualified as pictures, just sketches, the one nearest her had actually been torn from a sketchbook and cheaply framed for its words rather than its drawing skill. She'd lent him a book, one that had excited her. What was it called? A man whose mind was disappearing in dementia wrote it. The narrative voice was damaged and had fought for its understanding whilst it watched the world go mad. She'd been enthralled by the writing and made deeply sad. They were not together then. He'd been leaving a difficult relationship and occasionally confided in her. The book was a sympathetic gift. Some witticism had caused the exchange. He'd said something trite like, 'She's driving me out of my mind,' and she'd replied, 'No. This is going out of your mind.' Something like that. Maybe it wasn't witty after all. He'd made a drawing of how he'd imagined the main character would be. An elderly face full of pain, balding, forehead scarred with a frown, eyes looking two ways, full of an inner fear. She'd said she liked it, particularly because he'd written lines from the book as borders to the sketch. 'I am the last survivor of my own language.'

She'd just glimpsed that line across the top of the page as the first finger on her left hand lazily flicked the picture into space. She didn't follow its descent so jumped in shock as the glass shattered noisily on the stone flags of the hearth. He looked at the debris. The picture was face down, the cardboard flap that would enable it to stand freely had jagged upwards like a fin. Slivers of glass protruded from beneath the edges of the frame. She believed the picture was still intact and knew the frame was commonplace and cheap. She looked across at the artist. He said nothing. He was staring at her, not his damaged work. She wanted to hurt him more and looked at the picture next in line. He followed her gaze, understanding her intent.

He recognised a collage he'd made a few years ago. It represented the haunted face of Jason recounting his losses. He deliberately produced it to complete a trilogy with a pair of paintings he already owned. A fellow student, the girlfriend and eventually wife of a good friend had made the first. They'd actually been married for a short, disastrous while. It was such a bizarre end. She'd lived in rooms painted black, then retreated to a closed order of nuns. She'd asked for, and been given a 'Cap and Candles' divorce that meant all her marital sex could be removed. They didn't take her in the end, despite her new virginity. She lacked the vocation. She should have painted; she had a calling for that.

She'd given him a poster-sized painting of Medea. The carefully drawn face had been used for the front cover of a poetry magazine she'd edited. The eyes didn't really look at you. They were black and deeply cynical. There was a hint of a smile around a pretty mouth. Her breasts were exposed—'withered dugs'—he'd always thought of them as that, despite their roundness. The triangle of skirt was patterned in a biological tracery that described capillaries and the endings of nerves. As if this weren't disturbing enough, emerging from the space to the left of the skirt, eerily suggested in various pastel greens, was a shadowy replication, magnified, of the eyes, nose and mouth of Medea's face. It was his muse, staring, unamused and all knowing, larger than life-size, from the back of the picture. He'd taken it everywhere, except Seal Cottage.

Once, revisiting the art department at his school, an image made by a very young pupil caught his eye. It was a print called *Playground Incident*. Against a dark background, a young girl in a blue party frock, with a white lace frill, lay dead. Her head and arms were separate from the pretty torso. The gaps were small, just far enough away to suggest death. It was, he'd thought, a perfect accompaniment to Medea. This would represent one of Jason's sacrificed children.

She knew he was remembering as she pushed the collage into the air. She was more wilful, less nonchalant the second time, so the initial movement was forward not down. The top edge of the frame caught the corner of the stove and caused the picture to pivot and swirl before landing on its back, unbroken, with the pained expression of the face looking up. She smiled, oddly relieved. Still he said nothing. She must be told to stop. She needed that and he knew. Looking across at him and not at her feet, she still trod precisely into the centre of the glass. She let her weight descend and heard the glass groan as it cracked. There was no shrill, breaking sound, just a creaking, like ice cracking.

It was an anti-climax and dulled the effect of her act. Both knew this was a sacrilege. She was daring to spoil what was sacred. This wasn't just his value system or hers—she certainly shared it—it was universal. The work of art is so vulnerable and protected by its own integrity. Sooner maim a human being than vandalise a work of art.

She stooped to retrieve the broken pieces, careful to extract the still undamaged works from their shattered frames. She hoped he'd retreat so she could hide them and when back in civilisation, frame them once more, with fresh mounts and carefully chosen wood, to make amends for their exposure.

But he stayed and dared her further. He knew she couldn't damage the actual work easily. He guessed she wanted to spirit them away and put them back in place, reframed, as if this moment hadn't happened. He ought to have let her but he felt as compelled to stay put as she did to go on. He only finally looked away as she began tearing the pictures in two. The cardboard of the collage resisted and all she managed was a torn corner and a buckling of the layers. The face of the old man tore neatly in two.

131

She put all the pieces of glass, frame and mount, in the rubbish bucket by the door. The remnants of the pictures were placed neatly on top where he saw them next morning. He was indifferent to the work, even though it couldn't be remade, but he knew that she had crossed a barrier of behaviour that was irreversible.

"They were horrible images, Laurie. From a time when you were sad. All the senses in the picture of Jason were damaged. Did you realise that? Had you ever noticed? The eyes were blind, or at least, empty. You'd given them no centre. An ear was missing and the mouth had a difficult crack in it. It's not like that now. You're with me, which must be a kind of madness, I guess." She laughed, unconvincingly.

"Maybe you're right."

"Maybe." His lack of reaction thwarted her. She was being forced to absorb the shame of her act.

No witty message of 'luff' or 'wild strawberry' could paper over the cracks she'd just made. A fuck was out of the question. He'd found control over their all-healing urge. He tried to warn her: "Don't take this loving for granted. It isn't as robust as you think. We've been blessed with this endless pleasure. With no effort, we can make love for hours. That's because our bodies are always listening. They know when to push, when to stop, where exactly to touch. It's an instinct and it's based on trust. And by simply reacting we always get it right. Always, love. But if you bring games to the bedroom, if you make us think and try, if there's a hint of an effort, of the deliberate or the thought out, it's dead. We'll lose it. It's as fragile as ashes. We'll never clasp it back. It'll be dust. Just dust on our fingers. Don't play games there. Not there."

But she did play games. In the absence of a rival she invented one—at least, for a very short time.

"Where do you stay when you stop over? . . .

"Does this Oysterman have a name?" . . .

"Have you wasted your best already? Is that why you can't do it again?"

"Why are you doing this, Valerie? Do you believe any of these things to be true?"

"No, not really."

"You don't?"

"Why so surprised?"

"Not surprised, just angry. I have nothing to feel guilty about. Why are you spoiling what has been so lovely?"

"I'll stop. I promise. It was a mistake. You don't really deserve it."

"No, I don't. You're my wife and I love you more than anything there is."

"That sounds nice, Laurie, and I'm happy to be reconciled but I still don't think you're telling the truth."

He sighed with frustration. "How many more times. There aren't even any women on the island."

"Not women, no. Of course there never were, that was me being . . . perverse."

"So, what else can trouble you?"

"This place."

"How do you mean?" He was nervous.

"How much do they mean to you, these little pieces of land."

"Well, you know. This is my home. It's fundamental. This is the basis of . . ."

"Would you say you 'loved' these islands? Would you use a word like 'love'?"

"Yes. Yes, I would, but . . ."

"And this 'loving' would have an emotional content?"

"No."

"Think for a moment. Just think before you answer."

"I've always thought of my responses here as spiritual. I know it's a word you don't like."

"I've nothing against the word."

"Okay. It's the concept, the fact that this landscape moves me in ways I don't really understand."

"Or want to."

"Sorry?"

"Or want to."

He puzzled for a moment and agreed. "Or want to. No, I don't want to understand, just to experience. And I've always feared that if I pried too deeply, I might just damage something. I take it all on trust."

"Like us."

"Yes. There are similarities."

"Tell me some more similarities."

"I can't. This is your way, Valerie, not mine. I don't question everything. I'm content to respond and accept. I don't need reasons, just the right to celebrate."

"Is celebration an emotion?"

"Partly, yes."

"So, your love of this land is emotional?"

"Yes. Very clever. Well argued. You should become a barrister. You prosecute well. Am I on trial?"

She paused and smiled before she answered. Her eyes were cold.

"Yes. I think perhaps you are."

"And what's my crime?"

She thought, choosing deliberate words.

"Bigamy. No, trigamy."

He waited for her to explain, smiling.

"One day you will have to choose between me and these island mistresses of yours."

Laurie was standing outside the cathedral window, sheltering under the overhanging gable end. The wind and wall of sand kept the rain away from the sketchpad open on his left arm. The paper was black. He was working with chalk and occasionally white crayon. The scene before him he thought spectacular and would fit well into the series of night paintings already completed in the artificial light of his farmhouse-kitchen studio.

There was no colour in the scene before him, everything was black or grey, except on the horizon, left of centre, and another tiny area to the far right where shafts of light from the rising moon had eked a passage through the dense black cloud. The reflections from this breach lit the whole surface of the sea, like a clever piece of spotlighting on an empty stage. The hint of white to the right edge revealed the vertical rods of rain linking sky and sea at the horizon in a vast rolling chain.

At first the eye would want to look at the dab of brilliant white to the left but, the focus of Laurie's gaze were the swirls of sea near at hand. There was an apparent centre, flattened by the rain, and a whirl of waves escaping, as if something huge had risen, not fallen to create this rush. The route of the tide was contrary. Beyond the rock tips of a distant reef, the pattern of the movement changed again. The whole surface was a maze of chaotic energy rushing to and from it. There were bits of debris scattered and everything that was happening seemed slow. The movement wasn't that of water, it was denser, more unctuous, like the snaking flow of oil.

"What on earth are you doing, Laurie? There's nothing there to see." He didn't argue. "Just a minute. I've nearly done. I just want to catch this event of the light." He reached out to the horizon as if he could grasp the lit piece in his hand. Valerie watched him work. His intensity was unnerving. His breathing was short, like a runner's; his movements rapid, of both arm and head. Then it was over. The sky went black, the pad was snapped to, and Laurie rushed inside gladly, happy now to escape the air made cold by the rain.

"What so you see in the dark, Laurie? What is it you can see?"

"It was the patterns of the surface. That's what caught my eye."

"Nothing more than that? That's all you saw?"

"That's all there is to see, Valerie. That's the mystery, I think. Or at least, it is for me. The ever-changing scud of the surface, where the light is always different, not just daily, but by the second. Nothing fixed, a constant flux. It's like a celestial . . ."

"Kaleidoscope?"

"No. I wasn't thinking that. I was going to say painting. It's like a major canvas that keeps revealing itself."

"And what's your role in all this?"

"To trap a moment. To try and remake just a fraction of what's to be seen."

"I was watching you work. Just a minute ago, you know. Do you know what you look like when you work?"

"No I don't."

"Possessed. You look like somebody possessed."

"I doubt that but, certainly, I need to concentrate."

"It's more than that."

"It's very intense, sometimes. It had to be tonight. The light was only present for a few moments. I had to rush to capture it. That's why I looked intent."

"Does your eye control it?"

"What?"

"Can your looking slow it down?"

"I don't understand. I don't make any of this. I'm just a witness."

"That's a very humble claim."

"It is. I feel humble here. I'm not worried to say that. I look at some of these skies that are so vast and so magnificent that their beauty fills me with humility. I'm not to be made fun of for that."

"No. I didn't mean to. I'm sorry."

"What did you expect to find here, Valerie?" He finally asked the question she'd anticipated since the day they'd arrived.

"I'm not sure."

"I didn't mislead you. I described what was here. I saw it as a gift, the greatest gift I could offer—the beauty of this place. And I know you hate it and blame me for bringing you here. And I don't know what to do."

"Of course I don't hate it. And I certainly don't hate you. Oh Laurie, I don't know. No one was misled, you are right. It's not even that you knew what to expect but you seem to be having totally different experiences to mine in exactly the same place, at exactly the same time. It's baffling."

"You're the one that's baffling. I never know what to expect. The things you say, it's like having the pieces of a jigsaw but no picture to help slot them together, just pieces that contradict and change their shape."

" 'Heads are round so that thoughts can change direction.' "

"You see. There. I can't understand these utterances of yours."

"Not mine. Too good. I was quoting."

"Don't. Speak straightforwardly."

"I envy you your certainty. You have no doubts."

"I do. I just don't . . . I am a painter, an artisan. I have no grand ideas. I'm not clever or on the cutting edge. But I have a gift and I have a responsibility. I think it's my . . ."

"Mission?"

The irony in her voice stopped Laurie for a moment. Then he offered his word, "Job. Nothing so grand as mission, just my job, to capture on canvas the natural wonders of this island. That's what I wanted to do this year. I don't know about the next or the one after. I had the money and you and there was an urgency because, as you've so often said, all this is dying, so I have to work fast and I have to work now."

"I'm so sorry, love. I truly am. I do admire what you do. And I don't know what stops me from enjoying now, and why I have an urge to spoil what's so noble in you."

"Maybe it's your mission."

She laughed and left him with the last word.

The light was returning. It was the beginning of spring. Laurie left early. He was meeting a cousin for lunch in a cottage in the grounds of Colonsay House. It was a long trek and he might be gone overnight. Valerie knew and raised no objection.

She filled a hold-all with clothes and a pack with unread books and left Seal Cottage without locking the door. She arrived at her rock that could survey The Strand and saw the last view of Laurie on the other side. She waited until he'd climbed the hill and was totally out of sight. If she crossed now she might be seen as a tiny distant speck that could only be her. There was no one else who could be leaving Oronsay.

She'd left him some words, not as an explanation but an end. She wanted to draw a line under this experience. She couldn't cope any longer with the isolation. It was time to rejoin the world.

"I'm so sad,
Lolita Man,
I have to leave.
This loneliness has left me desperate,
And nothing can be born out of desperation.
Hope comes from change and growth
And I have withered in the sameness of this place.
I have dismissed all my conversations
And have ceased to study all my plans.
My dreams are on the run.
Once, I laughed and painted meadows.

Listen.
There is a voice whispering back to you.
Hear it.

"I'll finish with another's words, at the risk of annoying you further. Paul Eluard carries more authority than I ever could. Believe him, even if you can't believe me.

We lived well,
We lived courageously."

Part Five

The Outskirts of High Wycombe

1

"I caught the ferry that afternoon. I was noticed, but ignored. There were polite nods yet no one actually spoke to me. My rehearsed explanations were not needed. I've no idea if they were happy or sad to see me go. My leaving seemed unremarkable to them. I stayed the night in a huge bed and breakfast that promised views over the harbour, but I couldn't see it. The next morning, I took the train to Glasgow and as soon as I arrived, I rang you. Do you remember?"

"Yes, I remember."

"I don't come out of this very well, do I?"

My mind still held the picture of her face on that particular day. I was so shocked I panicked. I couldn't begin to imagine what had caused the way she looked. I thought she was dying. That may seem melodramatic, but that's exactly how reduced she was. She looked tormented, wracked. Precisely that, in great pain and stretched to the point of snapping. The flesh had gone from her face and left it lined and tense. The hollowed cheeks made her eyes too big, the thinness of her lips protruded her teeth. He eyes were dulled; her hair was lifeless and unshaped. Her skin was sallow, but with a waxy glisten, like the melting basin of fat in the top of church candles that gutter when they burn. She looked like a prisoner of war unexpectedly released on the doorstep of her home. She was glad to be there, ashamed she had come, had no idea how she looked, but needed to apologise for having stayed away. It was a complex mess of signals reflected in her face.

"What's happened to you? What have you become?"

That's how I phrased it. Something warned me not to touch her. Had I been kinder, I think she would have lost all self-control. I just saw her, in that moment, as right at the edge, the absolute furthest edge of rationality itself. And the message of her eyes, even in this extremity, was one of defiance, or more fairly, a desperate self-defence. And I knew her greater need at that moment wasn't for the gentleness of compassion, or a dry shoulder to cry on, but for a patient, preferably intelligent listener to whom she could justify her present state.

"Why are you here?"

"It didn't work out."

"Where's Laurie?"

"Still on the island. He'll hardly notice I'm gone."

"What's happened?"

"It was a terrible mistake."

"Have you left him?"

"He's certainly not here."

"Are you going back?"

"Not in this lifetime."

"What can I do for you?"

"Help me with this."

'This' was her unfinished thesis. The emotional neutrality of the document was the chosen route to save her self. She came to me as her teacher, an adult with supposedly attendant wisdoms and a direct link with the husband she'd left behind. I confess to being anxious about him. In one tawdry moment of materialism, I did remember that my bank and I had a financial interest in Laurie's continuing success.

"Tell me, Valerie, is Laurie still painting?"

"I'm hopelessly lost in the private detail. Could you suggest a new approach?" She was flipping through the handwritten pages of her emerging thesis.

"Would you sooner I didn't mention him?"

"I thought something theoretical, something pretentious and vague . . . In time." She paused. "Let me do it this way. I must look elsewhere." Ironically, this whispered coda was delivered with her eyes shut.

Mine weren't. I confess to a host of misgivings. My friendship with Laurie was genuine. I admired his talent and the work it made. I was also acting as his agent. I couldn't steer an easy passage between husband and wife. But Valerie surprised me that day and Laurie disappointed me in the days to come. She didn't scream: she schemed. She sought practical solutions to her pain. After those first difficult moments, we found neutral areas on which to stand. I became her partner in a careful and deliberate reintroduction to the world.

She was damaged in body and mind. It would take a long time for her body to readjust. She'd lost so much weight she'd begun to ingest her own muscles. She started a carefully monitored set of exercises that would eventually leave her fitter than ever before. The cycles of her body had collapsed. She ceased to menstruate in the middle of the last winter and the limited diet, undermined by anxiety, had left her deficient in those mysterious chemicals essential to proper life.

I joined her in this rebuild and benefitted just as much. We swam and jogged, even played a little squash. It was public and social, gradual and overt. Even in our private selves we believed there was nothing to hide. We focussed on the surface, what was obvious between us. The running pretext for our union was her evolving thesis on Marc Chagall. It also provided a context—the college, with its facilities and social functions amongst common friends. But most pleasing and surprising was the subtext, the subtle undertone of meanings and things felt that gradually emerged between us. This was never quite acknowledged. That was our strength: still is. The growing bond between us was never referred to at all. We began loving at a tangent. And that oblique, unquestioned way has worked for us. Never obvious, never discussed.

Laurie's visits, meanwhile, were characterised by a difficult mixture of self-pity and a desperate need to explain. He shifted all his paintings to a rented studio overlooking a yacht marina on the Glasgow road out of Oban. When each set of pictures was finished, he moved them in with me, until they filled one whole room of the apartment in the centre of Glasgow. The work was stunning and I tried to turn his mind to that and the details of the exhibition I was putting into place. Most times it succeeded, this deflection into work—for them both.

Valerie's sudden collapses into self-loathing or anguish annoyed her more than me. She was really cross if she allowed herself to whine.

"You have my permission to beat me with your hockey stick if I say anything so wet again."

"I haven't got a hockey stick."

"Use mine."

"You haven't got one either."

"Buy me one. Then I'll lend it to you to hit me with, just in case."

I like people that cope. It doesn't mean they have to be tough or insensitive. As a young man I thought that the woman was all that was needed. I found her, so I married her, and was complete. I don't think that now. I loved Valerie's competence. I admired the way she fought for new beginnings in knowledge, in people and in place. She was so young but so magnificent, at least in my eyes, in taking on her own shoulders and in her own cognizance the responsibility for the way she lived her life.

2

We still live on the outskirts of High Wycombe and now my wellies are green. We pretend at stability for Laura and there's usually one of us in the house despite the need for travel in both our careers. I don't suppose Valerie would consider what she does as structured as a 'career'. She works to fixed-time contracts doing various kinds of research. They're all based on art history: the life of painters, '-isms' and movements, buildings and places made significant by art. She loves it. She's very good at it. She has the zeal of an amateur despite being held in high professional regard. I, well, my bank has used her for difficult provenances. She did our catalogue for the Scottish Collection and has started writing something of her own. She's still drawn to that time in Paris when Chagall was the least famous person there. We sit together in those Left Bank cafés, have lunch in the Latin Quarter and coffee in the *Café Procope* and recreate in imagination actual meetings between Diaghilev, who's brought along Nijinsky and Cocteau, who happens to have with him Picasso, oh, and Stravinsky, just in case there's a need for music in the new ballet to be made.

And there's Beckett and Joyce, Hemingway and Pound, and Eliot's just gone to the loo and you look up in disbelief at what is actually Napoleon's hat, preserved in a glass case and left by the young lieutenant in payment for his unpaid bills. Such an attractive time and such an intriguing place.

What she's writing is another thesis, this time for a doctorate, a PhD. She's looking at André Breton and his odd little circle of friends. I was disappointed she chose to do that because I don't like him or, to be precise, I don't like what he did to people of greater talent than himself. But the fact that she's doing it at all, amongst all those other demanding things—jobs and husbands and Laura—is admirable. She has amazed me.

We thought to buy a room in Paris but decided we'd sooner vary the places we stay. We're often there on business and we didn't want to live in a place we use for escape. We go most years, together, around my birthday in the spring. My favourite place is the Marais, that unfashionable district around the Place des Vosges. I love its faded glory. Francis Bacon had a studio there and Victor Hugo made it his home. I think Céline lived there also, that writer of weird prose.

I enjoy the live music in the cloisters and the galleries at the square's edge. You eat outside at all times. Even the cold is overcome by those clever hot umbrellas, giant Calor-gas-heated mushrooms, with polished lids that send the rising heat back down.

There's a little restaurant we go inside, on the way to the Picasso Museum. It's called *Un Piano sur le Trottoir* and that's exactly what it is: a piano blocks the pavement and, intrigued, you peek inside. The walls are painted purple, feather boas dangle from a hat stand, theatrical paintings complete the theme. It's charming and crazy and although in a tiny back street, it seems always to be full.

We do have a place in France, though. Have done for quite a few years. It's kind of an apartment, one vast open space with a few private corners off. It's in the south, at a place called Grimaud, an artificial port built out of unusable marshland near the peninsular that leads to St Tropez. It's grown to be very touristy, so we don't go as often as we did. It's owned on a long lease that ends in a few years. I don't think we'll renew it. I'm not sure. We'll wait and see. The freehold belongs to one of the early wives of a film star; an original investor in what must have seemed a crazy plan. It's a miniature Venice, at the edge of the Cote d'Azur. When I first saw it, I loved it and I had a bank bonus, so we bought the place we'd actually rented for our holiday that year. Its address was Rue des Artisans, and for some reason that seemed auspicious and tipped the scales. It was very expensive then.

I like sailing and the great draw to buying there was that you can keep your boat at the bottom of the garden where only other sailors can approach. The roads are waterways. There are a few bridges that visitors can cross but your private spaces are at the water's edge.

I don't have a sailing boat now but I did then. I wanted Laura to grow up loving the sea as much as I did. Eventually, I'm sure she did. There's still a little rowboat with a giant engine out the back. It's so much quicker to go to St Tropez across the bay. After ten in the morning the peninsular road is one continuous jam. It takes twenty minutes across the harbour, especially if you go early to shop at the market in the central square. St Tropez is charming at the right time of day. It still manages to be original. I can remember Laura's astonishment, one early morning in the bay. It was midweek and in office hours and we were moving slowly towards the town. Laura was at the helm where the sudden power of the engine made her nervous, so we pootled along if she drove. Ghosting past us, completely self-absorbed, was a man in a business suit, wind-surfing across the bay. His shoes were in his left hand; his right directed the sail. The man's utter confidence in his ability not to get wet was totally convincing. This was the only way to go. I was sure he'd have a following, but he's the only one we've seen. What panache. So very St Tropez.

The apartment was just an excuse to be there. We spent all our time outside, in the patio area beyond its huge glass doors. There was a pergola to create shade, latticed with the leaves of a vine. Grapes did grow, but were inedibly sour. I think they were of a variety just for making wine. There was a bamboo screen between us and next door but the thing I cherished most was a beautiful mimosa tree with its spray of tiny yellow flowers. It always looked chic and cast delicate shadows across our dining table near the water's edge. I have memories of barbecues, others and our own, the smell of charcoal-cooked meat that wafted tantalisingly on the evening wind.

We holidayed there eight, nine times in a row. We've flown; we've driven. When Laura was very small we even put the car on a train. It was Europe's version of the Orient Express. It began in Boulogne and we got off in Avignon. We had a little area to ourselves, a small dining/lounge with two cabins at either end. Each suite had a steward—ours even cooked us a meal. Laura loved it. I don't think she slept at all. She'd demanded a top berth and could see straight into each brightly lit station throughout the night.

Laura and I have been very close. We've always been able to talk. I think my being that much older helps. There's none of the rivalry between us that seems to exist between Valerie and her. We rarely row. I enjoyed her as a baby and I enjoy her now.

Well, did, until the recent past. We've grown apart this year.

It's more hurtful because unexpected and unexplained. Last year was tremendous for us. We spent a lot of time together whilst she was studying for G C S Es. She let me teach her, a privilege I understand few parents enjoy. She's at a good school. We pay fees but many don't. It's like an old-fashioned grammar school. I don't mind the means testing. The standards are high and set by the girls. Laura's not the best but she tries hard. I think the word 'determined' featured on every single report.

She's a nice person. She's sensitive and has a lot to give. I taught her maths and physics and history, an old favourite of mine. I read law and I'm a banker but all my interests tend towards the arts. I'm good at sums, as she calls them, and have the knack of making things understandable and clear, so she says.

She did well. Mostly As and taken a year early. It's this past year that things have been hard. She's made new friends in the Sixth Form and I think they believe being close to your father's not cool. It makes me sad. I miss our closeness. She's doing an odd mixture of subjects, diplomatically chosen, I fear, to satisfy both her parents' worlds: economics and art. Valerie's helped with the art. There's something gone wrong there.

Laura had to do a special study of an artist that's still working. Valerie had a brainwave and thought the perfect subject would be Laurie McPhee. After all, Daddy has easy access and can introduce her to both the painter and his work. So, Laura's met up with Laurie more than once in this past year.

It's a long time since Laurie's actually had a studio. The isolation used to drive him mad. That's why, despite his success, he decided to become a teacher. He could have lived as a painter but his solution has been very neat. He's created a studio within his art room and offers endless access to his pupils to join him when he works. He's got everything he needs. A music system, a library, all the technical apparatus, even a printing press and kiln. But, above all, he has company, young people who admire him while he works. The school is delighted and praises the hours he keeps, while Laurie has a permanent space to pursue projects of his own.

His meetings with Laura were in London, at a gallery where he's routinely shown and I know that they met at the bank, in our private gallery, to see the work of his I had bought, set in the context of his peers. I still organise his one-man shows but they are less regular now. I wander in more splendid worlds. The bank's Scottish Collection has really taken off. I don't deal in millions, nothing quite that grand, but the paintings I seek now can easily go for over a hundred thousand pounds. The Peploes and the Hunters have really caught the eye of serious collectors all over the world. And I, with the bank's money, often with private capital to assist, do my best to keep them here, out of America's golden grasp.

I travelled to the Midlands recently to assess a private sale. It was a portrait of Cadell's *The Poet* I remember it was called. It was attractive, small scale, quite charming but a long way from his best. Even that would have cost thirty thousand pounds. I didn't buy it, as a matter of fact. Even at his best and biggest, Laurie cannot command such a price. Nevertheless, we nurture all our emerging talent; therefore Laurie is important in his way. And for as long as he wants me to, I will organise the showing of his work.

Part Six

A Private View

Missing

Why did I go to the island after all these years? Sarah deserves a straight answer but I don't know where to begin.

I start with: "I . . ." and let my thoughts trail to a silence that is conveniently interrupted by the arrival of Sarah's eldest son.

"You'll remember Duncan, Iain?"

I don't. If we have met, I've forgotten or, the years between have changed him beyond recognising.

"This is Mr Stewart, Duncan. He organises the selling of Laurie's paintings."

Sarah cleverly prompts our dull memories and sensing the boy's awkwardness, I offer to shake his hand. There is a momentary confusion and, anxious not to embarrass him further I pull my hand away just as his nervously stretches into the space mine has left.

"Hello, Duncan."

He doesn't reply but signals a nod of acknowledgment. He's a nice looking boy, overly tall, needing to grow into his height and his outsized collar. His mother has clearly dressed him for the occasion, and despite his social reluctance, Duncan is doing his best to please.

"Is it Year Nine or Ten now, Duncan?" I ask him, proud of my knowledge of current school jargon.

"Ten," he tells his shoes.

"You'll be doing your G C S Es then?"

"No." He looks alarmed and glances to his mother for reassurance.

"It's a different system here, Iain."

Relieved, Duncan repeats his mother's words. "It's a different system here, Mr Stewart."

"Of course it is. Tell me, in what way is it different?"

I've totally confused him now. He stands in perplexed silence for a long moment and a hand secretly reaches towards his mother's arm.

"He'll know soon enough, won't you, Duncan? He's barely begun yet. Find your brother and get yourselves a drink at the front desk there."

They exchange reassuring nods and with the faintest of eye movements she reminds him of me.

"Nice to meet you, Mr Stewart. Excuse me now," and off he goes.

Sarah smiles. "It's a difficult age for the lad. So terribly self-conscious."

"He's charming, Sarah. And a credit to you and . . ." I don't want to add Laurie's name even knowing he deserves to be included " . . . your mother."

"Thank you. Now are you going to tell me what's wrong or not? There's something on the tip of that tongue of yours that's eager to be said. So?"

"I went to Colonsay looking for Valerie."

"Is she lost?"

"Just missing." I'm smiling, inappropriately, at Sarah's choice of words.

"Well, you don't seem too worried."

"I am, Sarah. I'm very worried. I'm relieved to have told someone."

"How long has she been gone?" Sarah has moved closer. She finds caring so simple. She is sincere.

"I don't know."

"Oh."

"It's hard to describe. You see we lead busy lives. We are often separate. That's not a complaint. We love that, the freedom to be fully apart and fully together. So, it's not unusual for me to hear nothing from her for a week. No, in fact, that's commonplace. We're very intense in what we do. Our work. You see? A week is not a long time to us. On occasion, especially if she's gone somewhere awkward, like St Petersburg or Moscow, it could be two weeks. On rare occasions, that is."

"How long has it been this time?"

"Two whole weeks and quite a few days."

"That's a long time to worry. So, do you think she might be trapped in Russia or somewhere like that? No, you don't, do you?" She pauses. "Laurie's here. Right here." Sarah physically turns me towards Laurie, who is busily chatting in the far corner of the gallery. He doesn't see us looking.

"I know she's been in Denmark. I spoke to the curator at the museum in Louisiana. She was only there for a couple of days. We leave our diaries by the phone, you see. There wasn't anything else. No more entries."

"So Colonsay wasn't in her diary, then?" Sarah looks arch, oddly knowing.

"No."

"But it was in Laurie's," she adds.

I don't know what to say to Sarah. This is very difficult for both of us.

"You should understand, Iain, Laurie is free to do whatever he wants. I don't have any hold over him. But I'm absolutely certain that if he is planning to go back to Colonsay, he is planning to go alone. What were you thinking of, trailing after Valerie there?"

A Private View

Colonsay

There were quite concrete reasons to suppose she might be there and with Laurie but I judged it best to leave things unexplained. I felt that Laurie had featured much too largely in all our recent lives. If I acknowledge any jealousy or emotional fear, I would have to admit that his sudden arrival in Laura's life was more troubling to me than any renewed acquaintance with Valerie.

I enjoyed the first week empty of family. I had no pressing work and I chose to eat out as often as I could to pretend to an independence I didn't entirely feel. I knew Laura was with 'friends' but just how many and in what circumstances, Valerie made it clear, was none of my concern. I know she's in the Sixth Form. I am to assume she is sexually active and I'm meant not to mind and not to pry. Nevertheless, I marvel at Valerie's relaxed attitude towards such things.

In lax times I tend to become tidy. My office was a mess and I'd filed absolutely nothing for weeks. With two writers of interminable reports in the same household, each with the responsibility of reference, therefore retention, our house was always full of paper. We'd converted the loft into an overspill library, an archive of our personal and professional lives. The Island books were up there somewhere and copies of all our completed tasks.

It gave me great pleasure to clear the decks. I took a couple of days leave and began carting box after box of papers up the rather dangerous ladder-stairs that gave access to the roof space. The attic was floored with varnished boards and kit-formed metal shelving that offered perhaps fifty feet of storage. I still had my college trunk, old-fashioned in cabin style, with bamboo trim, metal feet and a laminated plastic label declaring all within the property of Iain Stewart. This was where Claudette lay trapped in her shoebox of letters. I surprised myself. I wasn't curious or in need to be reminded of her.

I don't pry. I am a respecter of people's privacy. I've never had access to gossip. I seem to be left out. Even at school I was never party to the collective secret. Mine always was common knowledge and came last. I didn't mind. I had no prior intention when I entered Valerie's study. She was being included in my tidy up. Almost two weeks had passed without a word and I was anxious but, in a conscious way, I was looking for nothing.

Her desktop wasn't overly cluttered. I placed the mail that had arrived since her absence in an over-elaborate letter rack that she'd brought back from some exotic travel, Morocco, I remember. Hers is a pretty desk: Victorian, kneehole, with matching, bow-fronted stacks of drawers. The inlay is still exquisite around the edges and in the centre of the bows. The brown and gold-bordered leather top is looking warn, scratched.

She keeps her work diary in the top, right-hand drawer. I did look for that, wondering if there was an entry I'd missed and my growing concern could be shown to be unfounded. The diary wasn't there but what I saw at a glance remained as a vivid after-image even when I'd closed the drawer. There was a tumble of letters and a card in familiar handwriting.

That Laurie should write to Valerie wasn't strange but what puzzled me was that Valerie's writing was evident, on more than one letter. They were addressed to him. What were those letters doing here? The most recent postmark on an envelope of hers was dated less than six weeks ago. The envelope used by Laurie was large enough to have contained the letters written by Valerie. His envelope contained a card. Typically, it was one of his own, or at least that was my first thought. On closer inspection, the print had been made from a painting of one of his pupils. It was the prize-winning entry in the Christmas competition, so the little paragraph of blurb explained on the back.

There was this note, written on the shiny white interior of the boy's card. Laurie liked to use a fountain pen. Some of the letters had smudged, not drying evenly on the glossy surface.

'We came together and the island drove us apart. It is entirely possible, as you suggest, that one day we may unite again and the island could be a home. What is certain is that we two will grow old together. I have none of the safe places you require, so keep the words secret yourself. I'm not to be trusted with them. Laurie.'

I didn't like the boy's painting. The colours were a little brash. But on reflection, that might be the fault of the printing, not the original work.

Valerie's writing is alarmingly neat. It is almost upright, entirely clear, with few embellishments in the script. Nevertheless, the curve of the tails of the 'y's and the 'g's suggest a certain flair, an artistic intent.

'To understand what happened between us, one must have had the experiences we had, and thrown away as much as we did, and gained as much, in knowing the fulfilment of body and soul. It's not likely that many did.'

There were too many 'ands' in this sentence and most of the words sounded familiar, nearly quoted but not quite—a difficult habit of hers.

'Why was a gift of a pair of earrings made from Ferrero Rocher wrappers so moving? I've no idea. I really can't answer your question, but when you gave them to me I wept with silly gratitude. They could have been diamonds and pearls.'

Valerie said to me that when married to Laurie she was playing truant from her maturity. I didn't read all the prose. To do so felt prurient. Oddly, I had fewer qualms about the poetry. It felt acceptable to read that.

To Lolita Man. My Sin.

I was wise in different ways to you,
But not very knowing.
The lessons have been harsh
And ill taught.
I'm no longer innocent
But what you knew was better.

What have I learnt?
That you have a lot to give
And mostly we just take.
That they couldn't empty us
But that left me sad
And wary.

I taught you fears you never had.
In losing me you lost those
At least.

I possess nothing in you,
Ask nothing of you.
If you can give to me,
Reach through the hurt
To a peace

Then we can smile
And trust
Beyond the critical
Putting an edge, one limit
To this map of loneliness.

'You say you still experience a slight frisson when you see my handwriting. What strange creatures we are and everlastingly perverse.'

That was my wife talking. Those are snippets that Valerie has written to a man she'd once married then left to come to me. I slipped the folded letters away, inside their envelopes, and then into the drawer that concealed them from sight but not mind. I sat at her desk to make the call. Laurie's answerphone invited my response. I sat in silence until the second beep prompted me to put back the phone.

A local travel agent that Valerie and I always used gave me details of the only hotel on the island of Colonsay. I rang. They were charming and clearly not busy. Even without asking I was offered a full-board rate that provided my dinner free. I would stay three nights to be met from the ferry. Angela at 'Getaway' booked my flight to Glasgow that included a hire car for the drive up to Oban. I'd nearly asked the proprietor of the hotel if they were staying there. The nearest I dared was to admit that Laurie McPhee had given me their name. She knew him well—the whole island did. A charming man. They'd a painting of his in the lounge.

Still I didn't ask. The parting niceties settled it all.

"We'll see you Friday, then, Mr Stewart. Laurie should still be here."

I should say immediately that he wasn't. Laurie had left on Wednesday's ferry and, unless she was hidden with miraculous skill, there was no evidence of Valerie, either accompanied or alone. I hadn't imagined a confrontation. Absurdly, I hadn't even thought that far ahead.

I once saw a play with a college friend and one scene had a profound effect on us. An older man was breaking eggs on his own head, goaded into this humiliation by a beautiful young entertainer barely half his age. She was a Lulu, a black-stockinged fetish and she robbed him of his pride. Afterwards, whenever we feared the other might be treading dangerous ground, risking folly for love, we used the shorthand: 'Be careful, it's eggs on head time,' to create the necessary distance between humiliation and need.

As I travelled on the ferry, watching the thin line of the horizon grow into land, I whispered that warning to myself. I was going to Colonsay not to fight or confront, not even to reveal, simply to know what I faced so I could conduct myself afterwards with an element of pride.

I was met on the jetty by a bus without a door. I was its only passenger. Also waiting was a blue Transit van ready to take a small party to 'something' cottages, the white name once painted on the side had peeled to anonymity. My two bags—one was canvas, filled with sturdy boots, anorak and waterproofs—and I were dropped at the hotel entrance after a slow pull up the long hill from the fishing port of Scalasaig.

There was no one in the hotel. I pushed open the door of a conservatory that served as a porch to the front entrance. The wood of the door jamb was swollen with weather, the door itself, rotted through. They could only lean together, not close. To my left, a drying room gave out its moist heat and I wandered into the hotel proper calling out my own name.

Eventually, someone came, a young cleaner who happily gave me a key and explained that I had the freedom of the place.

"The bar's open at six. Everyone will be here then. Dinner is at seven-thirty. There's you and one other so chef's not doing a choice. But you're the only guest so use all the bathrooms and things. Do you want tea? I could do that, not very well, but I would, or you could try 'The Pantry'. That's better than me."

"Where's the pantry?" I asked, thinking it might be within these walls.

"It's the café by the harbour. It's very nice. I meet people there for tea."

" 'The Pantry' it is then."

"Thanks." She looked relieved. "I'll get on."

"Please do. And, thank you."

My room and its view were quite splendid. The hotel boasted AA rosettes and several centuries of history. It was beamy, thick-walled and old, but the interiors were modern, my shower excellent and the beds firm and new. Ungratefully, I went in search of a proper bath and found one three doors down. There were piles of sweet smelling towels, herbal bubbles and wrapped soaps. The curtains were bunched like tarts' knickers, the description Valerie gave to this crumpled, modern style.

With a growing sense of the geography and reassured that all my wishes could be fulfilled, I quickly unpacked my handful of things, that included a bottle of Bowmore, a malt from the island of Islay to the south. It was too early for a whisky and I needed some good water to thin it so, I decided on 'The Pantry' and tea.

There was something amiable about the clutter of the harbour and its small scale added to its charm. The pyramids of creels, the upturned dinghies and the tiny fishing boats high and dry had a painterly quality, a sense of deliberate order even though accidentally left. Looking out to sea, the concrete harbour and ferry facilities to the left seemed rather ugly, in scale if not in shape. It was difficult to reconcile the tower block size of boat I just arrived on and those frail craft up on the beach. There was absolutely no activity. If there were fishermen, they'd been and gone. If this was a local industry, then it had failed.

'The Pantry' was sign-posted to my right behind long sheds where boats had been built and repaired. It was a bungalow-sized place, with misted windows from the warmth inside. There were three or four tables crowded together, with pretty tablecloths and crockery already laid. There was one other group sitting nearest the counter who had the confidence of regulars and did't stop talking because of me.

I took the chance to wander round. There were shelves and alcoves full of local goods: sweaters and pots, cups and scarves, even some local honey that seemed very expensive. I put the pot carefully back in place and asked for help from the people there. A wide-armed lady with greying hair and the kind of pinafore my grandmother used to hoard, quickly stood up and left her chatter to offer me:

"Tea? My scones or her cake?"

The one referred to was a splendid sight. A look of wonderful scorn crossed the wrinkled face. The tiny eyes, rheumy and dull, suddenly shone with hate. What hair there was, was improbably trapped inside a peaked baseball cap in sandy-coloured beige, with a bright red logo on the crown. The hair escaped in angry tufts, dyed an unconvincing blond that the inherent grey tinged yellow. Quickly on her feet, she took two unsteady steps in outsized trainers that curved like boats. She sported a café-bought sweatshirt with Colonsay on the front and a baggy pair of joggers that couldn't disguise her sparrow-thin legs. She snatched at a stick that had been ledged in her chair and pointed a spindly finger at the cake.

"That's mine," she grinned. "Have mine, it's much better than those." She didn't even look at the neat little pile of attractive-looking scones hygienically secure beneath a glass dome with a huge glass knob on its top. "I told her it was Auntie Kate's, and fooled her, you see. It was mine all along. Been fooling her for years. Auntie Kate's my foot. That's mine."

With that she sat down, much to my relief. Her gloating made her even less secure on her feet. I thought to order both but I knew I had to choose so, wittily, I asked for Auntie Kate's cake. Both smiled, the old lady winked, as if she'd carried off her deception after all.

The cake was good, I didn't have to lie, and the tea was perfect, in a big china pot with an ample cup by its side. I ate in silence and was quickly ignored. I had nothing to say, I just wanted to overhear.

"What can we do when the corncrakes come?"

"I'm going to throttle mine." The baseball cap quivered as bony hands enacted their threat.

"The one in my garden sang all the summer. It was hoarse and voiceless by August."

"I'll borrow yours then."

"Once it was quiet, it left."

It was noticed that I'd been listening and was about to leave.

"You'll have to understand," the cake counterfeiter explained, "we do love the birds, we really do. I wouldn't hurt one. It's just that they keep us awake. You do understand?"

"Yes, of course. And can I thank you for my beautiful tea and cake. Will you tell Auntie Kate?"

"Oh yes, I'll tell her," and she winked a goodbye.

I left feeling oddly happy and to my shame hadn't the vaguest idea what a corncrake looked like, let alone the sound of its song.

I walked up the hill to the hotel, felt fine and kept going. The sky was darkening and in the absence of falling rain, the air itself seemed to trap a wetness that left my jacket and hair damp. The land continued to rise in a gentle but eventually tiring slope. At what seemed the top, the road turned right and I followed it for a short while, just far enough to glimpse the coast, below me, to my left. There was farmland, a small cottage, then a marshy plain that ended in an inlet, a narrow fjord that glistened silver in the disappearing light. It looked chill and remote and certainly suggested an edge. Where the long narrow bay opened, the Atlantic Ocean began. The evening breeze carried a chill that scurried me back, my collar upturned to keep my neck from this cold wind.

There were lights en route, a few noises off, the sudden scurry of a vanishing sheep, but everything seemed to centre on the hotel. Now there were people. The small lay-by opposite was full of cars. As I went in there was a sudden noise, and a haze of cigarette smoke from the bar. I was greeted cheerily by my hostess, a very attractive lady with dark hair and eyes, round neat face, and an elegant tallness that she used like a dancer with a straight back and careful stride.

"Hello, Mr Stewart. I'm sorry I missed you earlier. Do you have everything you need?"

I readily said yes and disappeared for a bath, promising to be down for dinner within the hour. She gave me the wine list to take away in case I chose a bottle of quality that might need time.

My bath was superb and necessary to get me warm. By the time I got back I felt really chilled. An insidious damp had seeped out all the warmth of my walking. I poured myself a good measure of Bowmore in the toothbrush glass from my shelf. I topped it up with water from the tap, realising after a quick trial that its source was the very highland spring that the supermarkets put in bottles.

The chin-high hot water, the bubbles and the seeping warmth of the malt whisky inside, made a delicious mix. I chuckled with pleasure and, impossibly, still shivered. I was only now becoming warm.

Dinner was excellent. There were two single tables, not side by side, but separated by a large chiffonier that sported a half Stilton, a slice of Cheddar and an already decanted bottle of port. Each diner had a window and, although we conversed, we did so in parallel, staring outside not at each other. We could see to the bay of the port and across to Jura, its twin hills, the Paps, just in view to the right. A hint of evening sun, or more likely, the moon, lit the tips of the hills a light grey. The base and the coast of the island were unseeable, already lost in the twilight and mist.

I'd eaten a fresh tuna salad and guinea fowl with sage. There was lemon soufflé for dessert that was lightly textured, bursting with lemon flavour, an after tang and a refreshing zest. It was delightful. My dinner companion was called Donald Andrews. He was ten years older than me, retired and had the confidence of having completed a successful life. He was an engineer in some big way of business, travelled, but culturally, had remained stubbornly at home. He was thickset, solid-stomached, opinionated but prepared to withdraw.

He was building a house on the island, had practically finished, in fact, and was making this short trip to chivvy things along.

"The finishing is so slow, don't you find? And they will try to blind you with science. I mean, you think of the things you've built, the plant, the people, sometimes the governments one has involved, and to be stymied for a widget, to lose a month for a wedding, the making of a garage for a storm, not here, but miles away from where everything must come."

He explained, in exact detail, the extent of his plot. How he'd bought land first, with nothing certain in mind, but was deflected when his wife fell ill and eventually died. His children, two sons and a daughter, all within hailing distance, as it were, had encouraged him to proceed, promising long visits to him or for him to them, if things became tough. In this gap of time, someone else had built and, as far as Donald and his surveyor could see, hadn't played fair with lines of sight, ease of access or other neighbourly concerns.

The absence of any building was something of a limitation for the accusation of apparent encroachments but compromises had been reached, plans somewhat changed, and thin strips of land exchanged for useful triangles elsewhere. There were other plots below his, over the road and still for sale, the remnants of a derelict fishing village, with borders that ran to the edge of the sea. He would keep a weather eye, to protect his view. All in the name of fair dealing, you understand.

He was a fastidious man with many things he never did, including drink my offered glass of red wine, a superb Rioja that I'd highly praised. It was too late or too soon, too strong or not strong enough, before ten or after nine or some other restriction he'd self-imposed. Despite his punctilious ways, I liked him. He was profoundly earnest and quickly learnt my name and anyone else's that came his way. He was determined to belong. He was highly clubbable and despite appearances, as ready to learn the rules as lay them down.

I remember him for a repeated phrase that intrigued me at the time. He was looking for a boat and quickly discovered this was an interest of mine. I'd never sailed these waters but knew of others who had and offered what snippets of knowledge I could muster.

"But it must take the ground, you understand. It must be able to take the ground."

He pronounced this need with gritted teeth, as if talking of some painful thing. He explained the problem of the annoying refusal of sea and land to comply with his or any boat's need.

"When the sea is deep, as it often is, then the nearest land is sheer. You could anchor off, some do, and ferry back and forth by dinghy. But, anchors creep when tide and winds change. Your shelter can become your grave. When there is sand, a proper beach, as there are many such on this island, you can't get near. The shelving is too steady, the water not deep enough. I want a boat with courage and twin keels. I want us to sail in with water and then stand our ground when the tide takes it away. The boat must be sturdy, able to withstand high winds, high waters, anything 'Atlantic' at all, and still . . ."

"Take the ground."

"Precisely so. I can see that you're a man that understands, Iain Stewart. Would you take a glass of port with me? It is after ten."

I ate a memorable breakfast. There was a pot of tea, triangles of crustless, buttered brown bread and (a totally new experience for me) a Loch Fyne kipper. If the word 'kipper' brings to mind the radioactive brown object, in plastic wrappers with the air sucked out, or sporting secretly inserted knobs of butter, then think entirely again. What I experienced was a magnificent fish, succulent and subtle in flavour, a plate-filling delight, lightly smoked, filleted, opened and cooked flat, with central bulges of flesh that parted into translucent flakes. It was astonishingly good.

I dressed for the weather, a fine drizzle from a drab, grey sky, and carried a lunch packed by the hotel in a small rucksack they also lent me. I'd forgotten mine. I thought to walk the length and breadth of Colonsay, taking all day for the task.

I would go anticlockwise so stopped at the shop beyond the harbour and ferry dock and not far from the site of Donald's new house. I asked advice about Oronsay and the possibility of going across the following day. I was given a slip of paper lifted from a pad on the counter with 'Strand 10.30 am - Back 3.00 pm' written in a bold, clear hand.

"Will you walk it, do you think?"

"I'm not sure. Is it too far?"

He looked me up and down and quickly reached the judgment: "It'll be too far."

"Ah."

"But, you should try Archie."

"Archie?"

"That's right."

"Why Archie, will he give me a lift?"

"No. Not Archie."

"So, why?"

"But he can help."

"Ah."

I waited and tried again. "How will he help me?"

"He'll loan you a bicycle. You can cycle to the hard and cycle back. It'll make your journey easily possible in a day. That could be your answer."

"Thank you. Where do I ...?"

"You'll be wanting Archie, now."

"Probably, yes."

"Good. I think you're wise. It's a fair walk."

"To Archie's?"

"No. To Oronsay."

"And Archie?"

"He's in the back."

"The back of what?"

"Well, the shop, of course, where else? He's my son."

Archie would leave me a bike at the hotel in the morning, immediately after breakfast. I could pay via the hotel, that seemed both usual and the least complicated of the difficult options on offer. I bought a few things that I didn't need and a bottle of water that I did. This seemed to cheer them up and, as I stepped out into the rain, I heard their mumbled exchanges of bemusement that anyone would be walking on such a day.

It was surprisingly refreshing. I have never smelled such air. It had a sweet, heady, pine scent with not a tree to be seen. There was nothing to pollute it. The worst taint was wood smoke and that added to its allure.

As I climbed higher and the wind blew the rain in my face, I found it oddly gentle and I began to snort in each breath. It was invigorating but eventually palled.

I started a long, slow, meandering descent that ended in a bridge, a gap in the rain, and the magnificent presence of Loch Fada. I sat and stared at somewhere familiar: the range of hills, escarpment to cliff, that formed the southern edge of the lake, the plain to the north, the water growing sedge, the browns and ochres and blacks. I'd looked at this scene in Laurie's canvasses and now I was actually in place. It was beautiful but try as I might it remained his. The place was quiet but I was not. I was not precisely thinking of Valerie or him, but my mind wasn't entirely there. I was looking, merely. The scene pleased my eye.

A squabble of geese out of my sight couldn't challenge this peace, the profound stillness that blew in with the wind and scudded the clouds that rustled the grass in and at the water's edge. But the island didn't invite me in. I was there and not there. I seemed unable to belong. There was so much emptiness, I felt like an intruder on the scene. It was not a comfortable place. It was grand not pretty. The sky loured.

At the top of the hill on the left, by a few houses and others promised up a track, there was a village hall with an open door and a poster that caught my eye. There was an exhibition inside of local scenes by local people for their own enjoyment—or so it said. I peeked inside. It was like a set from 'Whisky Galore!', so simple, with a pre-war charm. The pictures were totally disarming. They were made out of love, not skill. Many were by children, one as young as eight. Most scenes were utterly local, the precise point, bay or rock that could be seen from their door. There was a surprising parochialism here, a proprietorial claiming of each element of space.

'My rock.' 'My bay.' 'My bit of this coast.' Perhaps this was the reaction to a place so small, with such tiny parcels of land to go round. Perhaps the naming of territory and particular claiming of land was a grasp for individualism, a signpost to declare self. I couldn't tell a rock apart, and most strips of coast looked the same. Nobody had made anything grand. There were no pictures of Loch Fada down below, nor the stunning place I was about to see.

I approached the sea with my head in the air, staring at the drama above me. A pair of mature buzzards was teaching two youngsters how to hunt and kill. One had something alive in its grasp that it dropped through the air into the flight path of a juvenile who missed and the other parent caught the hapless prey again. It was vile and fascinating. Almost carelessly, the pigeon, gull, whatever it was, was allowed to fly free, its purpose served. Then, in improbable manner, the four birds perched in line on top of a convenient row of telegraph poles that trailed away up the hillside.

Then I looked down and turned to take in the grandeur of Kiloran Bay. I gasped in wonder. Even on this dull day the white sand created its own light to present a view that was breathtaking in symmetry and scale. The giant crescent beach was fringed with dunes and protected by an immense alley of hills. The Atlantic was to the left so its sway was deflected. Even on this day of disturbed seas the waves lapped in with lagoon-like gentleness. This was South Sea Island, Bahamian, somewhere exotic or grand. And it was empty. Not a foot nor paw mark in the place.

It was a secret to be kept. Access should be forbidden. No one, not even Laurie McPhee could do justice to this place. I walked to the middle of the bay and back, ate my lunch at a picnic table by a stile on a raised area that took in all of the view.

Through the early part of the afternoon, I trailed along the road above the northern shore of Loch Fada, or Fadas—there appeared to be two separate waters. As the road turned south there were a number of cottages, a group of people and some welcome animation.

One of the buildings was a shop. There were bicycles leaning outside. The hours of opening were minimal according to the card in the door but I was lucky, though the owner wasn't there. All the books related to this island or others nearby. There were tiny production reprints and an in-house label of novels, fictions that were set in the Hebrides, Inner and Outer.

I browsed for a contented half hour and left having merely purchased an Ordnance Survey map, Pathfinder 375. I now knew I stood near *Port Mor* and, alarmingly, there were at least five squares left to the hotel, and each one was a kilometre to walk.

It was dark when I got back and, having left all my outer clothing to dry, I practically ran to my bath, with a grin of anticipation and a glass of Bowmore. Everything ached. I must have walked ten or twelve miles during the day. It had mostly rained, the wind had never dropped and abetted by the whisky, my cheeks glowed a healthy red. In fact, they were sore, a little chafed. Later, I would beg some cream. For the moment, I wallowed and allowed myself to dream, not of reconciliations or misunderstandings happily understood, but what that ingenious man in the kitchen was creating for my dinner that night.

I was down the stairs early and ducked into the bar to drink a beer. I was really thirsty. There were a few people standing, a group in the corner eating potato crisps and, below my gaze at first, Donald Andrews mumbled a noisy hello through a munching of steak pie and chips.

"Last night was a treat, I should say. I don't normally dine so well. Once in a way. This is good tucker. I can recommend the pie if you wish to eat in the bar. Are you taking part in the quiz, by the way? You should."

"What quiz?"

"Here, in the bar. Join us after dinner. Any team will have you, I'm sure."

"Thank you." Released from his stare, I moved to the opposite corner of the room and perched high on a stool in front of that night's barman, Michael by name. He'd just introduced himself.

"I'm new, you see. Aren't you meant to shake hands?"

I must have looked askance and confused him.

"I don't see why not. As a matter of fact, I think you probably should."

I ordered a lager that he poured with the same kind of care, and patient interruptions, as his Dublin equivalent pouring a glass of stout. He stayed to confide. He wasn't needed elsewhere.

"I was glad of the work. If tonight goes all right then I could have a night in the week as well. It's good to keep the Australians out."

"Are you local?" I asked when I finally got to sip from my drink. It was more of a gulp so I spluttered over the beginnings of his reply.

"Yes. No."

I wasn't sure which he was but he went on to explain.

"I was born on the island but, like all the others, I left. My dad went, then my mother too."

"Where, to the mainland?"

"No. They're buried here. Right opposite. The graveyard up the track."

He was pointing with energy as I hid my confusion in long sips of lager.

"I came back to settle things and I stayed. I'm still here."

He had doleful eyes and an air of customary defeat that reminded me of Eeyore.

"And you make a living?" I asked, encouraging him with raised eyebrows and a smile.

"No. Not yet. But I will. We all do lots of little jobs, you know. I work a few days a month at Colonsay House looking after the sheep. I tend to things in the harbour. I help with the staircase when the ferry comes in."

He was of an age so I asked: "Did you know Laurie McPhee?"

He grinned for a moment in happy memory.

"No. But of him, we all knew of him. He was a lad, a real lad. One for the ladies. There were tales enough then. He's a painter, you know. Quite well-to-do. But he remembers the island. He always comes back. He was here last week looking for something to own. It's the houses that bring us back. If you own a house then it kind of waits for you. But you have to come back to inherit. That's the catch. Another?"

I said yes when I meant no. It was difficult being with Michael. I couldn't drink it and left most of a glassful on the bar. There was a commotion in the room opposite the residents' lounge where we drank more tea after breakfast and coffee after dinner. Our hostess and a group of five were crowded into the window seat to the right. The lovely Helen beckoned me over, conceding her view on this intriguing sight. They were watching the light of the rising moon play on the Paps of Jura. Back-lit for a moment, precise edges in silhouette were defined in the clear night sky. A fanned array, a moment of blurring, then the moon took all its light to itself, bleaching from pink to white and quickly climbing up the sky.

Helen looked me earnestly in the face: "The light on Jura changes every twenty minutes. This is a special place."

Everyone was looking. Donald had joined us: "And that's why we come here," he added, with a certainty no one would challenge.

The lounge party was to join me for dinner. Two were local, the others their visiting friends. They sat at a table behind me placed in the exact centre of the room. I still had my single table with its customary view of the dark. I still looked out at the water and glimpsed sudden contours when the lighthouse flashed to the south.

We began with a vegetable terrine, its subtle flavours implied in the colours of its stripes. Spinach? Carrot? No one was finally sure.

The main course was wild salmon, rod caught in Loch Earn, with a watercress sauce to die for. Strawberry shortcake, Stilton and port. This was unbelievable. It was as good as the best in France.

We were few so we finished early, in time for the evening's quiz. I was a reluctant participant in any such event when knowledge is to be displayed. It's not from incapacity; I'm quite well read. I'm just not a competitive beast. I'd be as embarrassed to win as to lose, to show I knew or didn't know what I ought to have known.

Fortunately, the teams were set and most places at table filled. As the only paying guest, a seat was found for me and I spent the time in between the rounds chatting to the challengers, getting to know a few. My immediate neighbour was called Christine. She was probably seventy, looked healthy and well preserved. Yet, there was a nervousness about her. She was never entirely at ease.

"Have you always lived here, Christine?"

"No, mostly not. We always used it as a summerhouse. They were my husband's links, on his mother's side. It was only when he died that I came. It's only, what, four years since I've lived here full-time."

I shuffled a little closer and asked: "What is it like in the winter here? What is it really like?"

It was clear my curiosity was serious and she took an age before she answered with one word.

"Uncivilised."

"Then why?"

Before I could finish my question she asked it of herself.

"So why stay? You get used to it, the mud. And there is always the view. Did you see the moon light up Jura tonight?"

I said I had but wondered if that were compensation enough.

"I am content, Iain. Make no mistake. I don't think it's fashionable anymore to accept one's lot, simply and without complaining. I have no television. I could, you know. There is that hideous great dish on the hill above the port. I could pipe it to my house, but I refuse to. I prefer a fire and a good book. Can you accept that? When it's rough and wet outside, when it's really wild, I sit safe within my walls. I'm warm there and I'm dry and I'm protected. Does that sound smug?"

It sounded more like bravery to me. I suddenly had this vision of dozens of stubborn widows and widowers sitting by their fires alone, awkwardly surviving. It seemed the island was a place for these simple heroics, where merely to be was the challenge. You dealt with what was available; did what was possible to be done. If goods and opportunities were limited then it was justified to live in this limiting way.

I could still smell a whiff of penance in this. As if to be here was in expiation for some unlocatable wrong. The years passed had the air of a sentence, something endured, for however long. Nobody seemed to be here by choice. It was what was left when the rest of normal life ended. Each story was full of justified excuses, the very nature of life here allowing all kinds of failure. Every journey seemed to have been prompted by a loss, and residence here was a subtle punishment for daring to live on. This was an island where death, not nobility obliged.

"Where is your house, Christine?"

"Lower Kilchattan, overlooking *Port Mor.*"

"I was there today. There's a bookshop."

"There is indeed. It's his."

Almost opposite, close enough to touch, was a splendid figure surrounded by red hair. A robust Bertie Lawrence, with blood-red cheeks and beaming smile, the burst of hair and spray of beard looked more manic Irish than Scot. But Scot he was, Douglas his name, with an out-stretched, freckled hand and enough bonhomie to fill the isle. He was clad in tweed and tartan and an utter enthusiasm for this place. He quickly explained that he once owned this hotel and its outbuildings and lettable barns. It seemed a gold mine to me so I couldn't help asking:

"Why did you sell such a marvellous place?"

"Ah. A good question. This is my wife."

A carefully dressed, quietly contained and attractive woman sat expensively by his side.

"A need of funds to put me into retirement. A need for time to do other things. A need to spend precious days with my lady." His arms outstretched in an expansive gesture that didn't quite end in a touch. He screwed up his nose before adding: "A need to write and bury my head in my books. I'm a publisher, you know, but every copy is at my expense. Now I've a magnificent stock and can sell for years, but there's this desperate need for capital to go on and grow and, and . . ." His eyes fixed on private horizons of tome on tome on tome.

I loved his enthusiasm and said so. He beamed his delight. I hinted at my involvement in things Scottish and with a pat on the leather bench, I was invited to his side. Suddenly, there was a whole bottle of malt whisky from Jura. And with equal suddenness, there wasn't a drop left in it.

What a talker, what a drinker and what a fool I was to try and keep up. He didn't even hiccup and I felt fine seated amongst the noise but the second I tried to stand I stumbled, my head filled with private whooshings, and it took a lot of diluting water to become still enough to sleep.

The next morning I wasn't too badly hung over, but Helen grinned when she wished me good day, so I hoped I'd done or said nothing to embarrass myself or those people and things I'm meant to represent. I rarely drink. I enjoy being in control and I'm outspoken about drunkenness and its effects.

"Did I?"

"I thought the full breakfast," was her reply.

"Oh. Was I bad?"

"No. Not at all." She was genuinely laughing, a happy chuckle that echoed in her chest. "You were fun. It was a great evening. You got Douglas really fired up. I've never seen him in full flow. A magnificent man."

"Indeed. An example . . ." I left the comparison short, my breakfast was arriving on what looked like a platter to serve a family of four. Shamefully, I ate it all. White pudding, black pudding, sausage in circles as well as sausage shape, potato cakes with eggs on, tomatoes and full bacon rashers and triangles of fried bread in a fan. The oatcakes were a roughage too far. I'd actually eaten a bowl of cereal before I began. I felt set up for the day and any residual alcohol had been scared away.

"That was magnificent. How do you manage this?" I asked Helen. It was she who actually collected my plate.

She shrugged her shoulders. "I just order it from the mainland, like everybody else."

"Is it that simple?"

"With a little organisation, yes. I mean, our chef is special, obviously, but he decides what he wants and I telephone the order to Tesco and it's delivered by ferry the next day." She opened her palms like a magician showing how easy the trick was.

"By the way, your bike's outside. Archie delivered it first thing. It's pretty straight forward, just . . ." She wove patterns in the air by way of explanation and pointed to the hallway table, through the open dining room door. "You lunch is there. You know the hours of the tide?"

"Yes, thank you."

"Give yourself plenty of leeway. I understand it can be tricky, no matter what they say."

"Have you not been?"

"No."

"You've never been to Oronsay?"

"No. This island is more than enough for me."

A Private View

Oronsay

Archie's bicycle was technically splendid. I'm not. There were several cogs and levers to work them on each handlebar. I knew how to cycle, everyone does who was once a boy, and I set off with minimal wobble. But I first learnt on bikes you stopped pedalling to change gear. With my first racer, I mastered the running change, but the array of tackle on a mountain bike was beyond me. Its sole object seemed to be to pedal as fast as you possibly could in all circumstances. It was like the low gear option on a Land Rover, perfect in boggy off-roads, but I was on tarmac going gently up hill and it took a dozen or more clicks to get any feeling of progress at all.

I needn't have worried. My legs quickly helped out by ceasing to have any push. I couldn't believe how unfit I was or how quickly I'd run out of steam. I'd barely begun, turned left off the hill, run into a valley and up towards a house standing back on the right-hand side, when the pain in my thighs caused the muscles to knot and I leapt off my mount in humiliating pain. I'd got miles to go and I was done in.

With rubbing and rest and performing the more familiar act of walking, my legs slowly recovered. I remounted and pedalled in a tiny gear that kept me balanced going nowhere at all. I was reluctant to over stress my pathetic body but, after a while, it woke up and recovered from its state of shock. I'd never thought of cycling as exercise, just something you did, like a swim. No longer, it seemed.

This part of the island was empty and oddly drab. There was marsh and tussock grass and, even though my new map promised mysterious remains of chapels, burial grounds, even a fort, the most elaborate event to be actually seen was the Gothic script on the Ordnance Survey itself.

I freewheeled to the bottom of the hill through a narrow valley and spilled out onto the vast plain of The Strand. The gap between the islands was massive, my guessed at point of landing a good mile away. Water glistened on the surface of this giant sand lake and breaks in the cloud spilled blinding sunlight onto the water still lingering there. I hadn't realised it was so big. I fell into a momentary panic and realised I needed a strategy to cope with this.

There was no one visible on the sand, not for as far as I could see. There was a small lorry on the concrete platform to my right, but no driver to ask advice. I re-scanned my paper from the shop. It was after 10.30 so I was safe.

With a deep breath, I began to cycle across. The surface beneath me was solid. The water was only visible when squeezed beneath the tyres that sizzled as I pedalled along. My confidence of not sinking grew in line with feeling totally exposed. By halfway I admit to being frightened. This was drying sea but felt more like a desert to me. It was a gauntlet I had to run. The sudden wind and surrounding emptiness made me feel vulnerable and totally alone. I was waiting for an attack from some invisible and impossible foe. This was nonsense, but it was how I felt. Imperceptibly, the water was getting deeper. By now it was over the bicycle wheels' rims. The sight of dark weed under the water and eddying patterns on the top were evidences of a depth I couldn't manage in, so I looked right and left to find a shallower tack. I veered to the right and realised I'd lost sight of my landmark on the island ahead. I'd hugged too close to Colonsay itself, not sure where Oronsay began. I decided to go back to the middle and rethink my final approach.

By now I was quite breathless and the wind was blowing a gale. It brought me to a standstill and I stopped, dry-footed, on a plateau fractionally higher than the surrounding sand that harboured tidal pools from the not yet fallen tide.

I checked my watch. And decided to wait. It was after eleven, a quarter of an hour could do no harm. Standing and doing nothing, I was calmer but losing heat. This was stupid. What was my worry? At worst I would just get wet. Self-chastised and self-goaded, I began again and headed directly at the rock, the high point of vantage that hid the track that led across the island at the proper landfall on the other side.

I went quickly and quartered the ground. Suddenly, my front wheel was being buried, with water half a metre into the spokes. This was alarming. I couldn't manoeuvre. The resistance of the water, the clotting of the weed, and the deepening of the hollow would topple me, I was sure. The pedals went under water. With a shout, I wrenched the wheel and rushed in a fury back to my previous island of high ground.

Panting and feeling stupid, even with no one to see, I had no choice but to wait longer. Then, I suddenly realised, perhaps this is as dry as it gets. Perhaps as you get closer to the island these channels never entirely disappear. I looked around for confirmation. There wasn't a soul on The Strand. Why? If this was prime time crossing, the perfect corridor, why was I entirely alone?

Then I looked up at the island, Oronsay, the object of my quest, and wondered what perversity drove men to such extremes to want to live there in the first place. Wasn't Colonsay remote and difficult enough without having to live on a blip beyond, that is only accessible at low tide for a few hours each day, at least, so they claim? Maybe this tension and urgency came from my need to be there and back in a day. To be denied an hour of access seemed crucial whilst the desire to live in such a place was for its timelessness, its reflections of eternal things.

I wondered if I thought nice things about the island would it allow me to get across. It was certainly making things difficult. Wasn't I welcome? Was anyone?

Right. I'd decided to be decisive. If I got wet I got wet. I lined up my front wheel on the landmark and determined not to be deflected at all, even if my feet had to go under water to complete the task. But, I'd just check the time, rearrange my pack and get ready for the assault, keeping calm.

And away.

Fine.

Fine.

It was getting deeper. The weed was thicker. I couldn't turn the wheel. Oh, sod it. Keep going. Keep going. It couldn't get worse, could it?

I was over.

With a triumphant laugh I pedalled to high and dry ground.

It was too steep to cycle, so I pushed the bike along. I decided to leave it by the farm gate that opened on the track that would lead down to Seal Cottage. My first idea was to carry on up the hill and visit Oronsay Farm. It had changed hands since Laurie's time and was now owned by a wealthy American lady whose family fortunes had been made in whisky amongst other, less exotic things. Everything was restored and embellished beyond recognition. Rumours talked of millions spent, but clearly, all necessary expenses had been met. The house had grown conservatories and outbuildings, the garden, protecting walls. I peeked over and saw a suburban layout of box hedges and covered walks.

There were letting cottages and the priory had been upgraded, its treasures now catalogued and roofed in. I wondered if anything had been gained by this over-nurturing and huge expense when the sound of an engine and a lot of voices made me suddenly alert. I'd no real sense of where private and public ended and felt an intruder if these were the owners newly returned.

I half-recognised the faces. They were my dinner companions of last night, stepping out of the rear of a Land Rover, painted Post Office red. The shopkeeper, wearing a postman's cap today, drove it.

"Ah. You'll be the man that's using Archie's bike." He recognised me before I him. His disguise was convincing enough. "I hope that's not it abandoned by that gateway, down the road away."

165

"Yes, is it not safe? I thought."

"It's not a question of safety. No one is likely to take it. You're right on that score. On the rest, you're wrong. It shouldn't be here at all. You've brought it through the water. There's weed amongst the spokes."

There was.

"There's no point in denying."

I hadn't.

"You should have left it on the hard, like I suggested, when you first asked to hire it in my shop".

"And then?"

"Walked it."

"I wouldn't have got across. I think your tide times were wrong."

"That's not really likely, but I'm happy to stand corrected. As for Archie."

"I'll clean it up".

"Good. So, I'll be back at three, then? Will that do you all?"

All nodded yes. I stood, bemused.

"Why did you bring them over?" I accentuated 'them' to imply 'and why not me?'

"Oh, it wasn't a favour. We paid. He's a taxi," explained one of the ladies, anxious to set things right.

"You're a taxi?" I asked, still confused.

"Of course. It's a service of the Post Office. I'm able to deliver people and mail with my specially adapted vehicle. There are seats in the back, as you can see."

"But why didn't you offer to take me?"

"You didn't ask. And anyway, you seemed determined to cross by bike."

"Yes. That's what is must have been."

"Well. At three then. I'm afraid I'm on the limit, so I can't take you along as well."

"No. Thank you anyway. I'd much sooner ride. It's much more fun."

"It's also corrosive. You take good care of Archie's bike."

Sufficiently chastened, I quit my unexpected companions, who had come to claim some long standing arrangement for tea at the main house, on offer, should they ever happen to be passing near. As improbable and vague as everything else here, I left them to their chances and wandered in land.

I headed south, not on the track, but across the undulating marsh through the middle of the island. Each clumsy step kicked up sand and threw a skylark into the air. I have boyhood memories of their constant presence, the distracting singing and landing a disguising scurry away from the nest. But here there were so many, with their grey and yellow markings, shrill calls and inelegant punk tufts of feathers behind their heads. There were plovers and sea birds. I thought I saw a cat. More natural life than I imagined was keeping company with the nervous sheep.

I was almost standing on Seal Cottage before I saw it beneath my feet. I retraced my steps from the dune beside the roof and approached it from the side. Someone had stuck a stone gargoyle, an ugly, horned face, with a distorted devilish grin, high above the entrance porch. Several sea mines, rusted a bright orange, cluttered the area to the left of the doorway. One had rolled to the seaward side, in front of the cathedral window, just behind a small retaining wall.

I peered through this and the side window, and to my astonishment, the cottage contained all the things Laurie and Valerie had left behind. Nothing was changed after all these years. I could make out the shell mirror, the iron fireplace and fishing float chandelier. There were even pristine candles in place. The windowsill still sported its bones and the wooden furniture carried no dust. It was eerie. Not left but waiting; ready to begin from the moment it left off.

I ate a late lunch sitting on a sea mine, my back to the cottage, staring out to sea. Two skylarks squabbled on the wall before my nose. It had started raining but still the sea was calm. It lapped gently at the foreshore on the beach immediately in view, an archetypal sound of water sluicing over sand; and despite the clouds over Jura that removed any shape of paps, I felt entirely peaceful, for a moment, at one with the place. I succumbed to the illusion that the island was entirely mine, a Man Friday, though it was Sunday, hoping no Robinson Crusoe would call.

A roll of thunder broke my daydream and the falling rain hastened my retreat. I retrieved the bike and freewheeled to the rock and found dry sand all the way to the shore. The wind blew fiercely at my back and made progress easy across The Strand. I didn't look back. The rain was heavy, abetted by the driving gale. Nevertheless, I felt quite secure, slowly moving along. I was aptly dressed, with waterproof legs and jacket and headdress to match. I was compact and secure, a little knot of defiance being deliberately blown along.

I was across The Strand in very quick time and even managed to cycle up the first of the hills. It was only then that I allowed myself to look back and, all I could see was rain and cloud. Oronsay was merged in the mist. I shuddered and rushed away. A clear drop of rain had found its way inside, to land on pristine flesh. It was a shock and made me cold. I was actually pleased to start riding again.

Back at the hotel, before anything else, I set about cleaning Archie's bike. Sprays of green weed had stuck to the forks and dangled in neat fans, like those plastic hoods ladies used to fix across their back wheels to protect them from the spray. There was a convenient hose, and despite the rain, I sought out every vestige of hidden seaweed and seawater, any clue that could give my game away. Conscience clear, I claimed my bath—a refilled indulgence of nearly an hour. I'd puckered, gone pink, relaxed and drunk a whole pot of pre-ordered tea, fortified with Bowmore.

I dined on medallions of pork, covered in Calvados cream, and afterwards took a glimpse at a Ceilidh that was taking place in the village hall. It was a gathering of a clan, Macleod, I think, and I'd been invited to go. I looked through the windows and saw a kind of dance to the music of the Scottish accordion. Most stood around the edges, listened or watched—a group of men drank beer at a bar. A few did dance, in organised lines, to steps pre-rehearsed and confidently made. I felt totally outside, unable to relate to the earnest social fun in there. I really didn't mind. I'd seen enough. It was time for bed, one more Loch Fyne kipper and civilisation once more.

I wondered if I'd ever be forgiven for taking Archie's bike across The Strand.

Together

"Can you believe I've never seen this place you all talk about?"
Sarah has surprised me. I was sure she had. She can see I'm puzzled.
"The boys have been, not me. Laurie has taken them to Colonsay."
"Ah. It's that I'm remembering, then."
"I don't know."
"No." There's a long pause. "I had leave owing, you see. I thought I'd use it up there. Instead of waiting."
"If you say so, Iain."
"I liked it. The people are interesting. The food in the hotel is superb."
"Good."
There is another pause. I don't know what else to say. Sarah ends our silence.
"I'll go check on the boys. Make sure they've found each other."
"He's a fine lad your . . ."
"Duncan."
"Yes, a fine lad."
Sarah is shaking her head at me. "Don't fret so, Iain. She'll come back to you and she'll stay, you see." Her kindness doesn't reassure me but I'm grateful all the same and lean down to kiss her cheek as though in greeting instead of goodbye.
I can't believe this turnout. I think it's the busiest it's been all night. Still, I'll be glad when it's over. I'm tired.
"Hello, you."
"Laurie, you made me jump."
"You were miles away."
"Yes. I was on your beloved island."
"Really? What made you think of there? There aren't any pictures . . ."
Laurie is looking around the walls to accentuate his point.
"No, not in pictures, nor mind. I was there, on terra firma."
"What are you rambling on about? You need a drink. Hey."
A conveniently passing Sixth Former has offered two glasses of white wine to Laurie from his tray.
"Here. It might wake you up."
"I was on Colonsay."
He's sipping his wine.
"When?"
Now he looks confused.

"Just a couple of days ago."

"You're kidding."

"No."

"I'm just back myself."

"I know."

"How?"

"Sarah."

"Of course. You silly sod, why didn't you say?" He's reached out and touched my arm. Laurie doesn't do that very often. I'm surprised and strangely pleased. "We could have gone together."

"Really? Wouldn't that have been difficult?"

"No. It would have been brilliant. I could have been your guide. Shown you the wonders of the isle. If I'd have known you would go, if I could have counted on your company, then I would have gone back to Seal Cottage."

"Back?"

"I never have, you see. Can't seem to find the courage. It's seventeen years since I last saw it and that's a long time to be afraid. But if you were with me."

"What have you been afraid of?"

"What's locked in there."

This wasn't a question but I replied as if it was. "Everything. Nothing, as far as I can know, has changed. The furniture, the mirror—everything. What you've drawn, it's all still there. It's like the *Marie Celeste*."

"I've never been to fetch anything, you see. I got the books, Valerie's portables. But the rest, the big stuff, no."

"There's a gargoyle. Is that new?"

"Yes. I've been told. Meant to be a joke, I think. They kept it closed. Looks like some sort of shrine, I understand."

"To what?"

"A good question. A very good question." There's a pause. "It's going well, isn't it?"

I nod a yes and finally, I dare to ask: "Laurie, do you plan to spend time with Valerie?"

"When?"

"It's just that . . ."

"Have you seen her?"

"No, of course I haven't. That's the problem, isn't it?"

"Why is it a problem?"

"Don't be ridiculous, Laurie."

"Well, I'm sure she'll come over."

"What do you mean, come over? Is she here?"

"Of course she's here. I saw her two minutes ago. I should imagine she's gone to the loo. Trust her to arrive late. Trust her to arrive at all."

"She's here?"

"She's there," and pointed to where she was.

She's surrounded, talking to a group. She is looking at her best. Healthy and animated and just over there. I watch her.

"Laurie?"

"Hmm."

"Why did you go to Colonsay? Sarah said something about a house."

"Well, sort of. No house but a bit of land to put one on. That's the idea, or might be."

"Is that by the old fishing village, past the shop?"

"Yes it is. How lovely that you've been there. We can talk Colonsay together."

"Yes, I suppose we can, now."

"I just thought I ought to own something there. Even if it's never more than the land. It's a real siren voice, you know. Never stops calling, never stops inviting you home. So, I thought I might build a new house there. Nothing too grand and at least I belong. I wouldn't be one of these endless newcomers, bossing the natives around, looking for boats that can 'take the ground'."

"I think I've met that one." It was a good impersonation.

"The busy Donald. I'm sure he means well. He tries so hard but what a bore."

My opinion was kinder, but I still keep talking to Laurie. I'm nervous about Valerie's eventual approach.

"What will you do with the house, if you build it?"

"Let it."

This is a surprise.

"What?"

"I could reserve key weeks in the summer or any special times when I wanted to go. But, no, it'd be a holiday home. Add a bit to the pension. I'm missing a few years, you know."

"So you wouldn't live there?"

"I've already done that. Once was enough."

"Does Valerie know?"

"Valerie?"

"She said something about . . . made me wonder. In old age?"

"Oh, that old chestnut." He's sighing, as if impatient. "I think we're meant to be each other's safety net. You must remember that Valerie is much younger than you."

"I never forget."

"And I'm Sarah's plaything, so when time has flown, who knows? He who lives longest? We can't control futures we don't live in, can we? Hello, stranger."

"Hello, Laurie." He takes both the hands he is offered and steers her elegantly to a kiss on each cheek.

"Hello, Iain. Do I get a kiss from you too?"

"Of course, any number." I kiss her with nervous politeness, carefully, on the lips.

"I'll catch you two later. We'll have dinner somewhere, to celebrate, after all of this."

And he's gone and left us alone.

"You're here," I say superfluously.

"Yes, I'm here." She moves closer and pats me on the chest with the tips of her fingers. "Will you get me a drink, darling? This is a long way from home."

I wave a boy over and she helps herself from the tray. I see the backs of her fingers appear brown. I wait for her to sip, followed by an excessive 'Ahh' before I ask the only question I want to ask: "Where have you been? I was worried."

"I know. I do know that. It was in a good cause."

"Tell me, then."

"I've been to France with Laura. We've been to Quai des Artisans."

"France?"

"Yes. I wanted to spend some time with her. We should spend more time there. It's very beautiful. We should renew the lease."

"You've been to France?"

"Yes. I've already said." The calmness of her manner was exasperating. I so, so wanted to be cross but I was relieved to see her, safe, looking well, and on her own.

"I thought you'd be glad of the peace, so I didn't get in touch. Anyway, I knew you were hurting."

"And still you didn't call?"

"Oh dear, stop being so melodramatic. The hurt I'm talking about is more important than us. I mean you and Laura. The gulf between you was growing. That hurt me as much as you. I thought she'd been treating you badly and I'd never seen you look so lost. The friendship between you has been too special to let a few silly months ruin. All those years of love and being able to talk, lost for some fad, some fashion, some temporary mess. I keep telling you, my honourable man, stop believing in women, we're not worth all the fuss. Nor the decency."

"Did you bring her?"

"Yes, I did. Three line whip. But she wanted to come anyway."

"She's here with you now?"

"Yes. Foisting beer on Sarah's Duncan and leading him astray."

"What did you two say?"

"Well, that's best kept between us, Laura and me. But she needed time away from that group of friends. They are going nowhere that Laura is. I wanted her to come to understand what kind of person she is, what tribe she belongs to. That it's not disloyal to be different, that being clever or talented is a gift, not to be ignored. And that a father like she's got is the biggest gift of all and that she was an utter fool to spurn his offer of friendship, even if it comes with greying hair. Get me another one. I fancy getting drunk."

She's given me her glass.

What can I say to her? I'm so grateful. I want to laugh with pleasure and sigh with relief. I want to appear in control of this when I feel an utter fool. Thank God for the need for role-play. Here's Laura and I've got to play Dad.

"It's great, isn't it?"

"Hello, you. You're so brown."

"It's a French tan. And it's all over, if you were wondering."

I wasn't, but she does look well. She takes my arm and leads me round, telling me her opinions of the pictures that come into our view. We make a good couple. People step aside to let us pass. There's never any confusion, she really does look like me. I'm no sugar daddy, just a proud father with his daughter on his arm.

"Will you take me to Nottingham?"

"Whatever for?"

"To see the university. They're really good at biological sciences. I've drawn up a shortlist. I know you're busy but we can go weekends."

"Of course I will."

"And maybe Southampton. They've a huge marine biology centre. It cost . . ." She pauses and shivers with excitement, "Millions!"

Thank God, she's back. My real daughter has returned. All that happy energy and enthusiasm for life. That's the real Laura, not the cool dude who can't say her 't's.

There's just one piece of unfinished business, as the evening draws to a close. Hovering in a corner, as far as I know still waiting for her meeting with Laurie to occur, is the lovely Madeline, looking bored beyond belief. I walk straight to her, happy to be recognised at once.

"Hello, Iain. I said it with an 'i'."

"Thank you." She's smiling but tiredly. I'm annoyed Laurie hasn't found time to see her. I'll send him the second I've said my piece.

"Has he seen you yet?"

"No. It's okay. He's busy. It's been great for him. A really successful show."

"Look. I wanted to apologise, well, explain about earlier."

She's wondering, clearly at a loss.

"The comment about giving up smoking. Me telling you to stop."

"Oh that. It's fine. I'm sure you're right. It's the only bad habit I've still got."

"It was the reason, that's all. I didn't mean to sound bossy, like a teacher. I want you to be healthy. I want you to live a long, long life. That's why. Just that reason. I want you to go on."